T
MESSENGER

-

Jessica Gadziala

Cover image credit: Shutterstock .com/David Ryo

DEDICATION

To Crystalyn - for the last minute
Hail Mary when I needed it most.

-

-

Flashback - One week before -

"Augh," Jules growled, slamming the receiver back into the cradle, freeing her hands to rub at the headache forming in her temples, a sharp, insistent throb that she knew was going to make the rest of the work shift even more draining than usual. Because - she had learned from experience - the worst sound in the world when you had a migraine brewing was the scream of a phone that you just knew was begging for parts of you that you didn't have to give, and the bleep of the intercom followed by a male voice asking her to fetch something, making her realize just how loud the click of her own heels sounded on the hard floor.

Miller wasn't in the office.

She was the only one who *didn't* use the intercom.

My legs work just as well as yours do. That was what she had said when Jules had asked why she didn't ask her to go grab the file she needed.

There was a jingle and click, making her take a deep breath before opening her eyes, finding a bottle of Excedrin Migraine sitting before her on her desk.

She knew.

She knew without having to look up.

Because there was only one person in the entire office who would even notice that she had a migraine brewing - let alone bring her what she would need to tolerate it.

Kai.

"Take one," he demanded, using the slightly firm tone on her that he learned he needed to do from time to time. When she was being too stubborn for her own good.

She reached for the bottle, twisting off the cap, and throwing one into her mouth to chase down with her too-cold coffee - something she was so accustomed to that she barely even noticed it anymore.

She came a long way from the girl who always had to have Starbucks.

And always extra hot.

"Now, what's going on?" he asked, losing the edge in his voice as he hauled himself up on the other side of her desk, something he knew she hated, but did anyway.

"Not..."

"Don't," he cut her off, shaking his head, making his somewhat long, inky hair catch the light as his hand reached out to move the paperclips out of the brads compartment of her desk organizer.

"My dress," she admitted, feeling that all-too-familiar swirling discomfort in her stomach at speaking of her wedding in front of him.

"What's wrong with it?"

"I need to pick it up before five when the shop closes, or I won't be able to get it until Monday."

"And the wedding is Sunday," he supplied, knowing because he was, of course, invited. As was the whole office. Even Gunner. Who no more wanted to go than she wanted him to come, but he would. Because his girl would make him.

"And Quin wants me to sit in with his client at four-thirty to take notes."

"I'll grab it," he offered, automatically, knee-jerk, as she was convinced kindness always was to him, selflessness.

"No," she said automatically, emphatically, fighting back the stab of guilt inside.

He was the last person in the world she could ask to pick up her wedding dress.

She could call her mom.

Or one of her aunts.

Maybe even Miller if she was in town.

"Consider it done," he told her, jumping off her desk, giving her one of his sweet smiles, rushing off before she could deny him again.

She felt it then, replacing the guilt as he walked out the front door, a sensation not wholly unfamiliar around Kai.

An odd, tight feeling across her chest, something she never let herself analyze, finding herself oddly afraid of what she would find if she tried.

So she refused to.

And she went to take notes for her boss, finding her dress hanging in its pretty pearl-colored garment bag on the rack by the door, Kai gone for the evening.

It was really happening, she realized as she unzipped the bag slightly to see the dress.

She was really getting married.

And that dropping feeling in her belly?

Yeah, she was just choosing not to analyze that either.

ONE

Kai

She was getting married.

She was getting married to *another guy*.

And I couldn't get my tie tied as I stood in the mirror, looking at a face made almost unfamiliar with the new short crop of my hair that I had cut on a lark the night before, not sure where the impulse came from, just needing a change, just maybe hoping it would signal a new start.

Even if a new start was the last thing in the world I wanted.

Everything was changing.

Like a kid whose parents were splitting up, I was hung up on the little things, the way life would be different than it had before.

She'd belong to another man.

One who would do the errands she needed done, but couldn't find the extra hours in the day to do so herself.

One who would bring her coffee or lunch when he was passing by.

One who would rub that ache in her left shoulder from holding the phone between it and her ear, so her hands were free for other tasks.

I couldn't do those things anymore.

Maybe I never should have to begin with.

Maybe it was never my place.

And those were the things swirling around my head as I tried for the sixth time to get the tie to knot.

Maybe my mind was focused on those things because it knew it couldn't handle the other things.

Like how they would be buying a home together, decorating it, building a life in it, creating babies in it.

All her highs and lows, they belonged to *him* now.

For good.

In a permanent way.

In a way that came with rings, promises, and paperwork.

On a hiss, I walked away from the mirror, going into my kitchen, reaching into a cabinet to grab the whiskey - something I rarely had occasion to reach for.

But if there was ever a reason to drink, it was when the love of your goddamn life was marrying someone else.

I should have been happy for her.

It was a selfish kind of love to only want someone happy if they were happy with you.

I understood that.

I knew it was wrong to begrudge a woman her happily ever after simply because you couldn't star in it, couldn't be the one with the glass shoe, the one with the rose and the library, the one with the kiss that could break the spell.

Because she deserved all that.

More, even.

But I couldn't shake the feeling that her fiancé was the wrong man for the job. And I couldn't figure out if the feeling was a genuine one, or just my own jealousy talking.

Whatever it was, I didn't like him.

Hadn't liked him the day we met when he had shook my hand a little too hard, like he needed to exert his alpha-ness, when he hadn't looked at Jules when she spoke, when he teased her for liking flavor in her coffee, when he hadn't opened the door for her, let her reach for it herself.

He had just rubbed me the wrong way.

But Jules did think he was the right guy.

Enough to give him her hand.

Whether I thought he was worthy or not.

The whiskey burned its way down, a sensation I reveled in because it - for one short, glorious moment - took away from the crushing sensation in my chest, a feeling I had been dealing with for months, but had not seemed to be able to get used to.

Maybe I should have been counting my blessings that it was a short engagement.

Everything had been in hyper-drive since the two met. I had no idea whose choice that had been. It could have been either of them, to be honest.

Jules was the kind of person who, when she knew her mind, acted on it. With everything within her. So if she made up her mind about Gary, then, well, she would have charged ahead as soon as she saw a ring, throwing herself into the planning as she did with everything in her life. With determination. With tunnel vision.

That was Jules.

Driven. Confident. Hard-working.

Hell, I had no idea where she found the time to plan every single, minute detail of the event while working as hard as she did at the office. There before everyone else, leaving after most others.

She burned the candle at both ends just holding down her job.

I had no idea when she managed to squeeze in dress fittings, cake tasting, invitation creating.

And make no mistake - she did all of it.

If Jules had one flaw - and I wasn't sure you could even call it such - it was her utter inability - or unwillingness - to delegate.

So she was the one poring over fonts, over centerpieces, over music, over wine and food selections.

She likely hadn't slept in months.

I sighed as I looked at the time, realizing it was about as late as I could hope to leave without actually being late to the event.

Leaving my tie as it was - figuring I could get someone there to fix it for me - I grabbed my keys and headed out, an odd mix of crushed... and curious.

Curious because, well, I couldn't help it.

I wanted to see her vision for this day, what she chose, what she saw in her head when she thought of her wedding day.

Of course, a ridiculous little part of me really did hold out hope that I would find out because it would be *my* day too.

Hearts were fanciful things.

Mine was prone to way too much wishful thinking.

I pulled up to the venue, giving my keys to the valet who looked like he was suffering a bit in the heat.

I couldn't quite figure out what had possessed Jules to choose to be an August bride when she hated summer.

So much about this seemed odd to me.

But then again, it was odd to think that the woman I had loved damn near since the moment I met her was marrying someone else, so I was choosing not to over-analyze the strangeness I felt around me.

Like how the guest sign-in table was what one could only call hipster-rustic-chic with aged wood, up-cycled picture frames with images of the happy couple, mason jar candles, and a chalkboard.

Sure, the word 'chic' fit Jules, but the woman had never been a fan of anything rustic.

A compromise, maybe?

I stared down at the book where I was meant to spill my heart, give them my blessings, and my throat was in a vice grip.

Because if I poured out my heart, all that would be on the page would be *Marry me instead.*

With a grip firm enough to snap the pen, I wrote all I could.

Best wishes - Kai.

Because no matter what, that was true. I would never wish anything for her but the best.

"Do you need some help with that?" Sloane's voice called to me from my side, making me turn to find her in an ice-blue summer dress, making her hair and skin pop, standing beside Gunner who looked out of place in a suit, no matter how many times I had seen him in one before.

I would normally have smiled at the fact that his tie matched her dress perfectly, but my lips couldn't find the energy to curve up.

"With what?"

"Your tie," she explained, reaching out, twisting it into place with expert fingers. "What's in the box?" she asked, motioning to the white and gold wrapped present in my hand.

She had a registry.

I was supposed to buy off that.

I was supposed to get them something to start their lives off with.

Plates. Serving dishes. Nut bowls.

I couldn't bring myself to do it.

"Snowglobe," I told her, shrugging it off. Everyone knew Jules collected them.

I left out the details.

Like the fact that it was of the Kilkenny Castle.

Like it was from Ireland, the place she had always wanted to visit.

Like the piece itself was called Forever In My Heart - a fact that not a soul would ever learn. It could be my secret alone.

"Do you want to sit with us?" Sloane offered. "We got here early, so we got seats right behind her family."

"No, thanks," I told them, shaking my head, moving away down the path to the ceremony that would take place in front of the gazebo.

I didn't want to be in the front.

I wanted to be in the far back.

First to see her.

But with the worst view of the actual ceremony.

The chairs on either side were all wooden, but mismatched, something I would have sworn would drive Jules crazy. At the edge of the rows, two large whiskey barrels were set up, each with a frame on top with a blackboard framing that saying about how we're all family now, so sit wherever you want.

I went to the left, taking the end seat at the last aisle, seeing two rows of Jules' family up front, smiling, talking happily.

This was a joyful day for them, of course.

They wanted Jules to settle down, stop working so hard, allow a man to take care of her. As much as she would bristle at the idea, being someone who was very proud to take care of herself, though maybe she would take a break when she had kids.

And the office would be a different place without her around.

Hell, it would be a sad place for the three weeks she would be on her honeymoon.

Or maybe that was just me.

"Hey Kai," Gemma, Jules' younger sister said from my side, giving me a megawatt smile - her default one - that made her light blue eyes catch the light.

She looked a lot like her sister who looked a lot like their mother. The same red hair. The same porcelain skin. The same blue eyes. The same tall, lithe builds. The same freckles, even. But whereas Jules' were just a small fleck of them over the bridge of her nose, Gemma had them over her nose and across the tops of her cheeks. I thought it gave her a fairy look when I first met her, temping at the office after school when Jules needed an extra hand every now and again.

She was the light and airy to Jules' more regimented and firm. She flitted around the world, making everyone around her happier for her existence.

"Heya Gemma," I told her, managing to find a small smile for her. "Why aren't you getting ready?"

"Ready for what?"

"Aren't you the maid of honor?"

"Oh," she said, her face falling. And it was a damn shame for someone so joyful to look so sad. "There is no bridal party."

"What?" I asked, brows furrowing.

That made no sense.

Jules had a huge family and network of friends. She would have wanted some of them - especially her sister - up there with her on her big day.

"Gary doesn't really... have a lot of guests."

At that, my gaze moved around, recognizing faces - the guys from work, their partners or dates, the crew of her girlfriends with their plus ones, her family - both close and distant.

Actually, there wasn't a single face I didn't recognize.

"Sorry, Gemmy," I told her, knowing she would have wanted to be up there for her sister.

"It's okay. It's not about me."

"How is Jules?" I asked, unable to help myself.

"Beautiful," Gemma declared, beaming once again. "She looks like she's from a fairy tale."

I'd bet good money that those words weren't an exaggeration.

"Of course," I agreed, giving her dainty wrist a small squeeze. "Go get your seat, Gemmy. They should be starting soon."

"You're sure you don't want to come sit with us? Mom loves you."

"I'm good back here," I told her, lying.

There was nothing good about how I felt right then.

"You'll save a dance for me later?" she asked in all her adorable eighteen-year-old sweetness.

"You can have all of them," I promised her, watching as she floated off toward her family, leaning in to say something to her mother who looked over her shoulder at me, eyes almost sad before she shot me a smile that her daughters were lucky enough to inherit.

It was fifteen minutes later when people started checking their watches, their phones.

Because it was five minutes after the ceremony was supposed to start.

From his seat, Quin shot me a curious look.

Because if there was one thing we knew about Jules, it was that the girl was always on time.

Ten minutes after that, people started shifting uncomfortably in their seats.

Me included.

"Kai," Miller's voice said close to my ear, making me turn to find her leaning down from the aisle at me in the dark blue dress she'd chosen for the occasion.

"What's up?" I asked, keeping my voice low since she had as well.

"They're not here."

"Who's not here?"

"Jules and Gary."

I was not so good a man that I didn't feel a swell of hope. That maybe they changed their minds. That maybe she'd seen what I'd seen, got cold feet, ended things.

But Jules would have made sure someone handled things, let guests know.

She wouldn't just... disappear.

She wouldn't be that inconsiderate.

"She was here half an hour ago. Gemmy was with her."

"She was," Miller agreed. "She asked me to ask Gary something for her, and when I did, he was gone. I told her. And then went to grab her a drink, thinking he just got cold feet, but then when I got back, she was gone."

"No note?"

"And she's not answering her phone."

Again, not like her.

No matter what kind of chaos was going on.

"What are we supposed to do here?"

"I'll go look for her. You tell her mom. See if they can stall things until I get back to you."

"Kai," Miller said, shaking her head. "No."

"No, what?"

"No, I'm not going to make you go to track down Jules on her wedding day to another man."

"Don't worry about it," I assured her, jumping up. "Keep your cell close."

With that, I made my way out of the ceremony space, rushing out toward the valet who jumped up from where he'd been sitting on the curb, likely not expecting anyone to come for hours still.

I'd never been to Jules' place.

I knew where she lived since we all knew everyone else's addresses in case of emergencies, but I had never been there.

She lived in the nicer side of Navesink Bank, not quite the rich area, but right on the border of it, in a fifth-floor apartment.

I made my way down the hall with a welcoming creamy gold on the walls, gleaming dark wood floors, and elegant wall sconces.

Now *this*, this was Jules.

Elegant and understated.

Not rustic whiskey barrels and mismatched chairs.

I made my way to the end of the hall, 5B, finding the door opened slightly.

And Jules, well, she worked for Quin. She knew all about the uglier aspects of the world. I found it hard to believe she would just leave her apartment door open to anyone who might happen by.

"Jules?" I called, pushing the door open an inch, starting to worry when I heard nothing.

Deciding now was not the time to respect things like personal boundaries, I stepped inside a space that screamed Jules.

From the Sedona red hardwood floors, pristine and gleaming, to the white cabinets and white quartz countertops in the kitchen that immediately greeted to me. There were fresh flowers on the short L side of the counter too - white lilies. On the center of the island, a glass bowl was overflowing with fresh fruits - her favorite snack to keep the fridge stocked at work for her long shifts.

The living space was to the left of the kitchen was all her too. With a tufted cream couch and teal accent chairs surrounding an oversized white coffee table, and all wrapping around a large fireplace, above which she had a giant, ornate mirror. On the mantle, her prized collection of snowglobes. The one I got her in Russia right beside all the others.

No TV.

There were a few books on the coffee table - a mix of recent chart-toppers and true crime.

The whole space even smelled of her. Of the perfume that clung to her skin. Light and sweet, not a scent you would expect from her, making me wonder if there was a story behind it. There was always a story behind all her little bits. It made a black hole start in my chest at the idea that I wouldn't get to know them all.

"Jules?" I called again, turning the corner behind the living room to head down a hall lined with bulky white frames around pictures of her family.

There were three doors in all. Two beds and a bath, I imagined.

It was standing there that I finally heard something.

Mumbling.

Low, female mumbling.

Never knowing Jules to be a mumbler, I made my way toward the sound with brows drawn low, pushing open the door at the end of the hall, finding the master bedroom.

Again, all her.

The dove gray walls, the king-sized bed with a tufted white headboard, white comforter, white pillows, white nightstands and dresser. The lamps on either side of the bed were oversized, glass, with crystals dangling to catch the light.

There was a vanity on the free wall, something antique, making me wonder if it had belonged to her grandmother who had passed the winter before, just repainted white to match her taste. A silver tray sat atop, the only space in the entire apartment that I had seen so far that was cluttered. Littered with countless bits of makeup, brushes, and other various things I didn't recognize.

The mumbling was louder, coming from the sole door beside the dresser, the top of which was lined with candles and flowers.

Still... no TV.

But as I got closer, I saw a small dock hidden behind a white flower arrangement. Because Jules might not have watched TV, but she was a big music fan.

The closet door was open, revealing an oversized space lined with sturdy built-ins with carefully organized clothing, shoe, and handbag selections.

And then there she was.

The mumbler.

Jules.

Her back was to me, her body kneeling down in a back corner of the closet.

She was in her wedding dress.

What the hell was she doing in her wedding dress, digging around in her closet, talking to herself like a crazy person?

"Where is it? Where the fuck is it?"

My lips turned up without me even realizing. Because, while she was completely surrounded by men - and women - who cussed like sailors, I was pretty sure I had never heard her curse.

Unless an occasional 'hell' or 'damn' counted. Which they didn't.

She certainly never dropped f-bombs like a pro like she had just now, with the savagery that came with practice.

"Hey, Jules..." I tried again.

"Something. There has to be something."

Her voice had hitched.

I hadn't imagined that.

It had hitched.

Like she was crying.

Crying.

There was no stopping the little kick to my gut at the idea.

Because this woman could handle any untold amounts of pressure at work without so much as getting snippy with any of us or the clients. Save for maybe Gunner. But that was their own issue.

Nothing made her break her stride, made her lose her cool.

I certainly never saw the woman get teary-eyed, let alone cry.

If that bastard hurt her...

"Jules," I tried again, moving forward, pressing my hand down onto her shoulder.

She didn't start.

She didn't even seem to notice as she continued rifling through a box, throwing various items to the side, her perfectly manicured hands feeling the pockets of clothing items before tossing them.

Male clothing items.

Gary's clothing items.

"Jules, honey, I'm gonna need you to look at me," I demanded, kneeling down beside her, reaching to close my hand around her pale arm, giving it a small tug, forcing her to notice me through her little, well, mental breakdown.

That seemed to get through.

Her hands stilled while holding a pair of slacks, the fingers long, fine-boned, the nails perfectly manicured a light pink, her giant diamond gleaming on the fourth finger of her left hand. A finger that should have had another band with it by now.

A hard breath shuddered out of her body, her shoulders falling, her head turning.

Black mascara was smeared under her eyes, dried ribbons of it down her cheeks.

She'd been crying.

Not just a little bit, either.

Not judging by the way the mascara had slipped off her chin to drop onto the champagne color of her wedding dress.

I hadn't looked at it.

The night I had gone to pick it up.

Oddly, I wanted the surprise of it.

A luxury that was really meant for Gary, not me.

But I hadn't wanted to spoil it.

And here it was.

Spoiled by tears.

Before I could even see it in all its glory.

All I could see from her kneeled position was that the length skimmed the floor, tight up through the hip and stomach, floating outward near the thighs, and rouching around the bodice.

She'd gone understated with the jewelry, just wearing the tiny golden cross her grandmother had given her on her communion, as she almost always wore, and simple pearl studs clasped to her ears.

Her gorgeous hair was pulled back, as it pretty much always was. At work, usually a more severe look. Now, it was parted off-center, drawn to one side, and pulled into a knot right below and behind her ear.

Beautiful.

It would have been beautiful.

Were her eyes not completely freaking panic-stricken.

Not sad.

Not devastated as you would think if her groom ran off on her wedding day, not heart-broken as the tears would suggest.

Just freaked.

Worried.

Unsure.

I'd known this woman for years.

I had never seen her look unsure of herself before.

To see it now, that was a goddamned sin.

Especially on her wedding day, in her wedding dress, kneeling in her closet when she should have been sealing the deal with a kiss.

Her lips, lightly tinted with a pale rose lipstick, fell open, at a loss for what to say as she stared at me.

It took a long moment before words came out of her.

Words I never could have anticipated when it looked like her world was falling apart by the moment.

"You cut your hair."

It almost sounded like an accusation.

"Thought it was time for something new," I told her, shrugging it off.

Her brows drew down, analyzing this, and clearly deciding it made no sense whatsoever.

"You're supposed to be across town right now," I reminded her as though she could possibly forget such a thing.

"My family..." The words broke out of her, a shattered sound.

"Miller let them know that they need to hang tight until I got word back to them."

"You came," she mumbled, gaze suddenly dropping to her own lap.

"Of course I came. I'll always come if you need me to."

And she clearly needed me to.

Even if she wouldn't ask for my help.

Even if her pride would never allow for it.

"Jules..." I called when her gaze stayed fixed downward.

Her head shook, refusing eye-contact.

"Hey," I tried again, voice going softer as my hand reached out, gently snagging her chin, pulling her face up, waiting for a long moment before her lashes would flutter back upward, giving me a flash of that brilliant light blue that had caught me so off-guard the first time I saw her.

Before I saw the hair.

Before I saw the freckles.

Before I even saw her body.

It was those eyes.

Bright, smart, confident.

But right now, all I saw there was defeat.

Unable to stop it, my thumb moved out, stroking up her jaw a bit before I forced my hand to drop, reminding myself that this was hardly the time for that, that I was not her comfort person, no matter how many times I had attempted to establish myself as such.

"What's going on, Jules?"

-

Flashback - 1 month before -

The office was quiet.

It always was at night.

That was when Jules secretly enjoyed it the most.

She often thrived on the chaos. She was in her zone when the phones were ringing off the hook, when the intercom was barking orders at her, when files were being thrown on her desk, when she needed to make five coffees while trying to deal with hysterical new clients.

But there was something nice about when everyone filed out, when she was locked into the office by herself, cleaning up the waiting area, re-stocking the coffee station, reorganizing her desk, just getting things ready for the next day.

It was a habit she learned from her mom who learned it from her grandmother.

They never went to bed at night without spending twenty minutes cleaning up the counters and tables, loading up the dishwasher, running a quick vacuum if it was needed.

There was nothing like waking up to a neat environment, it made you feel like you were ahead of the day before it even began.

It was a habit she brought into the office.

Which was why she stayed back later than anyone else, even if the bulk of her work was done. It gave her the opportunity to hit the ground running in the morning when things were often chaotic while the men and Miller filed in, dealing with new or existing clients.

Music hummed to her through the speakers, a small luxury she only allowed late at night when she was alone. She always played music at her desk quietly, just loudly enough that it allowed her to keep her sanity when things got crazy.

But it was surrounding her now, a hug of sound to help her decompress after a crazy day.

She was leaning over her desk, wiping the surface with a cleaning wipe when she heard the code being punched into the lock.

She didn't bother to look up, knowing Gunner was working a job that might bring him back into the office.

The two hadn't gotten along since the day she started working there, always grating on each other's nerves, so there was no reason to look up, possibly initiate a conversation neither of them wanted to have.

But as soon as the door slammed, she heard a voice that was decidedly not Gunner's mumbling.

"Just an easy two-minute meeting," Kai's voice grumbled, making her head shoot up.

Mainly because Kai was not one prone to things like mumbling and grumbling.

Kai was all light and heart and a laid-back kind of charm that made him easy to be around, a good balance to all the overly strong personalities in the office.

She hadn't known he'd been out on a job. It must have been something Quin threw at him last minute after he had already left for the day.

But there was no mistaking it, he'd been on a case.
Because he had been roughed up.
His long hair was barely still wrapped in the bun it'd been in earlier, hanging loosely on the side of his head.
His eye was darkened, his lip split, blood splattering his white tee.
Rough.
She had never seen him look so rough before.
In fact, sometimes it was easy to forget that his particular niche in the business came with a certain degree of danger. More so, in some ways, than many of the others on the team.
Because Kai was the one who showed up and delivered news that was most often unfavorable to the person receiving it.
He was like a real-life version of the old saying about shooting messengers.
And, clearly, whatever news he had just delivered had not gone down the way Quin had suggested it might if it put the usually jovial Kai in a sour mood.
"Are you alright?" she heard herself ask without having been conscious of even thinking the words.
Kai's head shot up, almost like he hadn't expected her there. Even though the light was on, the music was playing, and, well, she was almost always there.
"Fine," he growled.
Growled.
And with nothing more, stalked down the hallway to his office, slamming the door a bit as he went.
She found her eyes watching the space he had vacated. A strange, undeniable tightening in her core had her stiffening, sure she was misinterpreting it, trying to convince herself it was hunger or cramps or a miserable case of stomach flu.
Not what she had a sneaking suspicion it actually was.
Not when she was engaged to someone else.
Not when she realized several months before that Kai was, well, over her.
Once and for all.

That that door was closed.

Slammed shut.

She'd swore she even heard steel bars clicking into place, locking her out.

Shutting off a possibility she had convinced herself she didn't want in the first place.

But this feeling, this one she was trying to deny, yeah, it was making her realize she hadn't proved it to herself.

Not completely.

Maybe in her head.

But not the other parts of her.

Damn.

TWO

Jules

There had to be something.

There was always something.

No matter how small.

Small things led to bigger things that led to figuring it all out. If you looked hard enough. If you were dedicated enough.

I knew this because I had eaten, slept, and breathed this world for years. Because I learned from the best of the best.

A team of fixers with various skills who took me in, trusted me, allowed me to learn the secrets of the trade, all the little ways dirt could be hidden, so I knew how to uncover it for myself should I need to.

And now I needed to.

So I *had* to find something.

Some breadcrumb.

Some speck of dust.

Some piece of paper.

Some freaking *reason.*

Yes, a reason would be most welcome.

Least logical, of course.

I had learned from Quin that the why was not all that important in the grand scheme of things.

But that was back when it didn't matter, when it was impersonal, when it was someone else's life being turned on its axis.

I suddenly had a lot more respect for the men and women in the office who held it together when their lives turned chaotic, sending them to Quin for help.

I mean, sure, a lot of them broke down. Raged. Cried. Shut completely off from the world and themselves.

But there were some stoic ones, the ones who listened to Quin as he detailed exactly how their lives were going to change, who didn't bemoan their fate, who simply accepted things as they came.

I never anticipated my life would turn on its head, of course. I was too careful. Too regimented.

But you couldn't help but have your mind wander sometimes. Lying in bed at night waiting for sleep to claim you, imagining yourself in odd, crazy situations you knew logically you would never land in, but pretend to navigate your way through it anyway, thought about what you would say or do, about how you would handle it. Somehow develop badass self-defense skills despite never having taken a class, spout an elegant diatribe despite the fact that you were the sort to choke on your own tongue and spit in tense situations.

I always saw myself as someone who would lift her chin, square her shoulders, and take the hit. Figuratively.

I wish reality lived up to my imaginings.

Because there was nothing noble about crying through your makeup on the floor of your closet in your wedding dress.

On your *wedding day*.

The day that was supposed to be the happiest of your life, full of joyful tears, kind words, kissing, dancing, cake eating. I was supposed to tell my mom to stop crying, but secretly adore the genuine joy of it. I was supposed to drink too much champagne, take beautiful pictures that would hang on my wall for decades, perfectly posed photos that my little girls would look up at with wonder and awe and hope much like my sister and I had with our parents' and grandparents' wedding day pictures.

The only tears I should have had were ones of genuine happiness.

Not these ugly ones.

These angry, bitter, confused, frustrated ones.

It all started out right, too.

I'd kicked Gary out the night before. As was tradition. You never spend the night before your wedding with your soon-to-be life partner. It was supposedly 'bad luck.'

I'd given him a hopeful kiss before shutting the door, going about two hours' worth of beauty primping with Gemma - face masks, hair masks, split-end trimming, exfoliating, lotioning, just getting everything as perfect as it could be.

Then I'd gone to bed early after drinking a ton of water, so I would wake up hydrated and not puffy.

My mom and sister came over early, bringing coffee and sweet breakfast treats - cranberry orange scones, banana crepes, cinnamon swirl muffins. We ate, talked, took it easy.

Then I started getting ready, showering, doing all the last minute things like shaving, tweezing my eyebrows, painting my nails.

My mom helped me arrange my hair, sticking in a small, delicate pearl clip she had worn on her own wedding day.

Borrowed.

I clasped on my cross from my grandmother.

Old.

I slipped on the pretty pearl earrings Gemma had gotten me.

New.

And then Miller had showed up with a Tiffany blue thong, giving me a smile and eyebrow wiggle.

And then I had my blue.

We made our way to the venue then where we had white wine while I did my makeup, then finally slipped into my dress.

I won't deny it.

As my family left to go find their seats, greet guests, I sat down in the room.

And I nearly sweat through my dress.

Nerves.

Just nerves.

Surely.

Just normal.

Everyone had nerves on their wedding day.

You were promising your future to someone, all your ups and downs, all your hopes and dreams.

That was a big deal.

If you weren't nervous, you likely weren't taking it seriously enough.

And me, well, I took it very seriously.

I looked at things all very logically.

Right down to choosing my partner.

I had a list.

I mean, I had lists for everything.

I had a list for acceptable nail color shades.

So of course I had a list of qualities I wanted in a partner. From the superficial - tall, fit but not too muscular, wore suits comfortably, had great hygiene - to the more serious. I wanted someone driven career-wise, someone who understood the demands of my job because their own was demanding as well. He had to be well-spoken, mature, a good driver, only a social drinker.

I even had a section for things I didn't want - manwhores, mama's boys, former or current drug users, gamblers, or binge drinkers, men who played video games, cursed too much, used potty humor, or, well, scratched himself when others could see.

I mean, really.

That one went without saying.

Like guys were the only ones who had itches in inappropriate places. That didn't mean you could scratch or readjust in front of other people.

But judging by the sheer number of men I saw doing such things in public situations, it *did* need to be said.

The list was long, a front and a back of a college-ruled piece of paper, an ongoing thing I had started - and edited on and off as things changed - when I was eighteen, understanding that the first step to *getting* what you want was *knowing* what you want.

I mean, after all, that was how I got the job I wanted, making the money I made, having the power I had.

I wrote it down.

Then refused to settle for anything less.

So why couldn't I do that with a partner?

Then there was Gary.

He checked almost every single box, only missing a few inconsequential ones about food preferences and family background.

That really didn't sound romantic, I guess.

And maybe it wasn't.

If I were perfectly honest about the whole situation, it wasn't exactly the whirlwind love story it looked like from the outside.

We seemed like we rushed into it, like we went from casually dating to mostly living together to engaged to almost married in such a short period of time.

What other explanation could there be except some unstoppable force of passion?

And, well, there was heat.

There *had* to be heat, y'know?

But it wasn't a wildfire of passion, love, that had us unable to spend another moment not joined in matrimony.

It was more like... I don't know... the right progression of things.

You dated to get to know someone, to see if you would work long-term.

Once you established that, you took steps *toward* that long-term situation.

That was what we had done.

Step by step until we were supposed to take those big ones. The ones down an aisle. The most important walk of your life.

Romeo and Juliet or Elizabeth and Mr. Darcy we were not, but that didn't mean it wasn't a good relationship, a great match, a couple to aspire to be.

And because so much thought had gone into the day, because I took it more seriously than I took anything - save for my work and personal finances - it made sense that I felt queasy and shaky and sweaty while I sat there waiting for it to be time.

"Do you need something?" Miller had asked, brows drawn down because, well, she knew something was up, that I was usually nothing other than completely composed. And I certainly looked anything but that right then.

So I gave her a little nothing question to ask Gary, just so I could have a moment completely alone to pull myself back together.

I never imagined - not in a million years - that she would come back with ashen skin, panic in her deep eyes, and tell me in her somewhat signature blunt fashion that she couldn't find Gary.

That he was gone.

His room empty.

His car picked up.

Gone gone.

I'd called him.

Of course I did.

Because I understood if he was feeling a bit like I was, if maybe he went for a drive, went to grab some of those gross 5-Hour caffeine drinks he liked so much to try to calm himself down before coming back, and going through with everything.

It wasn't until the fifteenth call - and the tenth unanswered text - that I started to freak out.

Miller went to check his room again in case he had come back.

And me, well, I left.

And as I yanked the skirt of my wedding dress up, so I could slide into my driver's seat, there was no mistaking the churning in my stomach.

Not just nerves anymore.

Something else.

Something more devious.

Something like a gut instinct.

Something that said things had just gone very wrong.

Not simply because he had gotten cold feet.

I could forgive that, move past it.

But because something inside of me said there was something very wrong.

About Gary.

I flew into my apartment building, calling out his name frantically, voice getting more and more hysterical by the moment.

Don't ask me what made me do it.

Turn into my guest room.

The room that acted as that as well as my office because I hated having electronics out where anyone could see them.

Butted up against the wall under a window that had a nice view of a park that was always packed on weekends with Little League games or families out for some fun, even lovers having picnics, or people walking their dogs, was my long, low, light pink writing desk - a silly, girly impulse purchase one night that I never regretted.

My computer was on top of it.

And, well, it was another situation where I was glad for my job.

Because the IT guy that Quin hired had told me how to turn my internal camera on my desktop or laptop into a security camera triggered by motion.

I had set it up because of a slight bit of paranoia about someone from work - since there were plenty of slimy characters in and out of the place - finding his way into my place. At least with the security camera, I would have a way of knowing that it happened if it ever did. And then I would have proof.

I usually only checked it if I was having a particularly bad bout of paranoia, when some client genuinely rubbed me the wrong way.

But then, gut clenched in a vice grip, determination making my heels sound like they would burst through the hardwood floor, I checked it for a whole new reason.

Because I never thought to look into Gary.

Not *that* way anyway.

And that, well, that was suddenly starting to feel like a giant, epic mistake.

One that could have horrible repercussions.

I moved toward the computer, sitting down in the chair, taking deep breath as I turned it on, and went in search of the saved camera feed.

And there was Gary.

In ten different files for ten different days, all time-coded when I would not have been home, when he really had no reason to be in my apartment seeing as he was supposed to be at work as well.

He looked good in all of them, too.

Of course he did.

He was one of those people who looked good with bedhead, who looked good when he was on the second day of the flu, who looked good doing tasks that no one would find someone looking good while doing - trimming their toenails, flossing their teeth.

He'd just been blessed genetically with unfairly flawless skin, great lips, green eyes, blonde hair that was somehow neither dirty nor white, but somewhere in the perfect middle, with a jaw meant for cutting glass, great brows, and a well-proportioned nose.

So his stupidly good-looking face was right there in a bunch of files. On my computer. Looking oddly determined.

My gaze moved downward to one in particular. One where his lovely green eyes were hidden behind black-rimmed glasses.

Glasses.

Gary didn't wear glasses.

But this Gary - computer Gary - Gary who wasn't supposed to be on my computer Gary - he wore glasses.

I sat there, heartbeat slamming against my ribs, making me queasy, moving through the videos, watching, listening to the click of the mouse, the tap of the keys, before the camera feed turned off, only being programmed to run for two minutes.

It was the final one when he finally spoke.

And the words sent a shiver down my spine.

Got you, bitch.

Why did I automatically think that *bitch* was me? I wasn't sure. But I knew. I knew like I knew I would get a headache if I wore my hair too tight that he was talking about me. About *getting* me.

And that video was dated just an hour before, still wearing the suit I had picked out for him for the ceremony, tie pulled loose.

He got me.

I have no idea what made me sure of it, what made my hands move to the search history, sure of what I would find, not even feeling a sinking feeling when it was confirmed.

My bank's website.

Taking a deep breath, I typed in my login information with numb fingers, and hit the enter button on a sharp exhale.

And it was gone.

Every last hard-earned penny.

Every penny that represented an early morning, a late night, an achy back, sore feet, headaches, sleepless nights, frazzled nerves.

Years.

Years of carefully saving for security, for my future.

All gone.

I felt the sting in my eyes even as I went to the transactions, sure there was no way he could get the money out. Not without me.

Maybe a part of me was naively hoping that there was simply some banking glitch, some screw up that would explain it all away. Maybe all the transactions were gone, were in some server somewhere, not lost, just momentarily misplaced.

But they were all there.

Right up to the last one.

The one that transferred every bit of my pennies to some unknown account somewhere.

I didn't even bother to sign out as I pushed away from the computer, tears starting to stream.

What was the point in signing out, being safe, when there was nothing left to take?

I tore through my apartment, looking for anything of his, finding nothing, infuriatingly nothing, even as my makeup smeared, my dress getting ruined.

And then I finally found myself in the closet, locating that one box he brought right at the beginning, loaded up with just enough stuff to get him through a long weekend. Before he began hanging things on the racks beside mine.

It was still there.

Full of seemingly random things. Clothes, grooming supplies, a few receipts, nothing to go on.

That was when I was aware I wasn't alone, that someone had snuck up on me.

Kai had snuck up on me.

Of course it was Kai.

Kai with his sweet smile and too-big heart.

Kai who was maybe the last person I wanted to see me like this.

A mess.

I mean, I never wanted to look like a mess in front of anyone.

But more so with Kai.

For obvious reasons.

Because - while it was a while ago - he used to put me on a pedestal; he used to think I was perfect.

That being said, he was there.

He was there, and I was losing it.

And I needed to purge some of it, spew it out onto someone else before it consumed me.

"He took it all," I told him, cringing when my voice hitched again.

"Honey, he took what?" he asked, voice doing that soft thing it did when I had a headache, or when I was barely able to keep my eyes open at work. That sweet voice that made my chest feel tight.

My eyes closed for a long moment before opening, watching those dark eyes of his, finding a bit of strength there. "He took all my money."

Kai's lips parted slightly as the words sank in, as he tried to find something to say. "How do you know that?"

"I have a security camera on my laptop. He was on it. Today. He said he got me. And my savings is gone."

"Can I go look?" he asked, making an odd, insecure part of me well up, thinking he just wanted to get away from my hysterical self.

I simply nodded, watching as he turned and left, moving through an apartment he'd never been in before like he knew all the secrets hidden within.

And I just sat there, listening to the hum of the air conditioning system running through a cycle, the air blowing into my back from the vent, making goosebumps prickle over my flesh, but I couldn't seem to think to get up, to move away, to grab clothes off the shelf, and get myself out of this lie of a dress.

So I sat there on my heels, legs going numb, much like the heart in my chest as Kai searched through my computer, seeing the sham of a man who told me he loved me, who had lied to my face, who had taken everything from me.

My security.

My future.

I wasn't sure how long I sat there, but when Kai came back, reaching down toward me to help me back onto my feet - a task that would have been nearly impossible with the long, silky material of my dress - pins and needles pricked with relentless attacks as my heel-clad feet met the floor once again.

"Shake some life back into them," Kai suggested, reading the situation, or - more likely - reading me like he always seemed able to do. All I could manage was to stomp my heels a few times, sucking in a breath when the pain intensified before going away. "Come on. Let's talk over coffee. Or a drink. I'm sure you could use one or the other."

Both.

I could use both.

But we walked back out of my closet, through my bedroom where my eyes landed on the bed, suddenly realizing I could never sleep there again. On that mattress. Where I had slept with him.

I wondered a little fleetingly if married couples felt the same way while going through a divorce - that neither wanted the bed, better just to put it in a trash heap. Or donate it. No one would want to sleep there again.

"Which one, Jules?" Kai asked when we made it to the kitchen, me in a bit of a daze, eyes darting around my home, seeing ghosts of Gary all around - sitting on the couch flicking through things on his phone, stoking the fire, in the kitchen making my coffee. Too strong. He always made it too strong. And only ever put a drop of caramel when I wanted three. Had told him so several times before.

"Coffee," I decided, pulling out a stool to the island, sitting down, watching Kai as he moved around my kitchen.

"How did you know..." I started, not being conscious of wanting to ask as I watched him find the coffee on the first try.

"You have it set up like you do at work," he answered the unfinished question as he slipped a pod into the machine, pushing one of my glass mugs beneath as he went back up into the cabinet for the caramel with one hand and into the fridge for the half-and-half with the other, putting a dab in, then three drops of the caramel.

A dab and three drops.

I had never even told him that.

Never told him that *several times* without him remembering.

"Thank you," I mumbled, hands closing around the mug, seeing my engagement ring catch the overhead light.

Sparkly.

So sparkly.

"Jules..." Kai's voice called as I reached to rip the ring off my finger, holding it up, then clawing at the settings with my nails, feeling them split, and not even caring, just needing to get the metal to loosen, so I could get the stone out. "What are you doing?" he asked when it finally gave, and I jumped up, going to get a glass, filling it with tap water, then setting it on the island, already knowing, knowing before I dropped the stone in.

But I dropped it anyway.

And it floated right under the surface of the water.

Fake.

He gave me a fake engagement ring.

Like he'd given me a fake relationship.

Like he'd given me a fake future.

"Diamonds sink," I heard my voice explain, looking up to see Kai's face, eyes understanding the situation, turning sad.

"Jules, you need to sit down," he suggested, holding an arm out toward my living room.

To a couch I had once sat on with my head on Gary's shoulder, telling him about the house I was planning to buy within the next two years, with at least half an acre backyard, so I could have a vegetable garden, with a ton of windows to let in the light, so I could have houseplants, with four bedrooms - one master, one for each of the kids I wanted to have, an extra, and then an office/gym hybrid, with an oversized kitchen to cook dinners in, with a front porch to sit and drink coffee on.

Suddenly, I didn't want that couch either.

I shook my head, taking my seat at the island again, taking a sip of my too-hot coffee, enjoying the burn, wondering if it could do anything for the ice slivers forming in my heart.

"I can see those gears turning," Kai commented. I could feel his eyes on the top of my bent head, likely waiting for my eye contact. "Why don't you shut them down for a few?"

"Shut them down? My savings is *gone*." There it was, the frantic hitch hinting at tears yet again.

"Yeah, honey. But it's not just that. You shared your life with this man. He betrayed you. He..." Kai paused, looking for the right words. "He hurt you, Jules. You need to process that. You're focused on the money. There is more than the money going on here."

"There's no fixing what he did to me," I shot back, tone resigned. "But if there is a way to get this money back, I need to do that. That is the one thing that can be done. So it has to be done. I don't need to... take to the bed and grieve. I need to... I don't know. Go to the bank. Or try to track Gary down. If that is even his name."

Ugh.

God.

Was that not his name?

Had I not known the name of the man whose body had been in my bed, whose hands had touched my skin? The idea made a wave of nausea wash over me, making me regret the sugar-filled breakfast I'd had earlier.

How could I not have known?

That I was being conned?

That I was just some mark, just a too-trusting woman easily fooled by a good-looking man?

Had I not been so damn focused on what boxes he checked off, maybe I could have noticed things being off, little things not adding up.

But, no.

I'd been too blinded by the picture-perfect facade of it all.

God.

When had I become so stupid?

Of any woman, I should have been able to see this from a mile away. Or, if nothing else, should have at least done a cursory look into him.

Not romantic, really.

But smart.

Safe.

"Augh," I growled, elbows meeting the cold quartz countertop as I brought up my hands to rest the sides of my head in.

"Talk to me, Jules," Kai pleaded, voice with a slight undercurrent of steel, asking, but demanding as well.

"I'm so stupid," I admitted, ignoring the way my pride took yet another hit. There would be nothing left of it after all this was done, I was sure.

"You're *not* stupid," Kai's voice shot back, firm, uncharacteristic enough to make my gaze move upward, finding him closer than he had been a moment before, right on the other side of the island. Seeing my gaze, he bent forward, resting his forearms on the surface, getting closer to me. "If this was him, if he did this to you, then he's to blame. Not you."

In my mind, there really was no *if* about it.

There was a buzzing in his chest pocket, making us both start slightly.

"Miller," he told me without even looking.

"Oh, God," I groaned, thinking of *that* whole situation.

A wedding venue full of friends and family.

Full of decor I hated, but had gone with because I knew Gary would like them.

I would have to tell my mom to tell our family and friends that the wedding was cancelled.

They would all think that Gary got cold feet, that I was some cliched bride-to-be left at the proverbial altar.

I'd be pitied.

Was there anything worse?

Hell, maybe I deserved pity.

I was certainly in a pitiful state.

In my wedding dress with a fake ring, smeared makeup, empty bank accounts, and a missing con artist of a fake fiancé.

"Jules," Kai's voice cut into my thoughts again. "Stop," he demanded, somehow knowing where my head was at that moment.

"I can't stop," I told him, feeling the sting in my eyes too late to stop the tears as they spilled over. Not sad, just angry, bitter purging. "My money is gone. All of it. I can't even get myself a cup of coffee!"

Okay.

Maybe that was an exaggeration.

I had cash in my purse.

We were planning on hitting the bank in the morning to get it changed over to rupiah for our honeymoon in Bali.

Five grand in cash.

That was something, at least.

I could keep gas in my car, food in my fridge until my next paycheck.

Christ.

Paycheck-to-paycheck.

I swore to myself that would never be my life. I had worked so hard never to have that happen. Personal financial freedom was important to me, was imbedded in me from a young age from everyone in my family. My parents - while liking the idea of me settling down some day to raise my family - they wanted to make sure that my decision to settle down was based on the right things, not because I wanted help paying my bills.

But I would have to deal with that now.

I was lucky, in a way.

Quin paid me well.

In a few months, I would have a little buffer in my account again.

But it would take years to get anywhere near what I'd had to begin with.

Years.

That bastard set me back years.

"So, I'll get you coffee," Kai declared, trying to keep things light.

But I couldn't find the muscle control - or the desire even - to smile.

"You know what I mean, Kai."

"I know what you mean," he agreed, nodding, voice getting what I called its 'work-edge' to it. Because Kai's normal voice was easy, laid-back, charming. But his work voice had a sharpness to it, a firm confidence. "You worked your butt off for that money, Jules. No one knows that better than me."

"I have to get it back," I decided, my own voice getting some of its spirit back.

"Okay," Kai agreed, no hesitation, straightening, reaching for the phone that had let out a short buzz. A text, maybe.

"No!" I all but shrieked, reaching across the island, closing my hand over his on his cell.

His gaze shot up, a look in his eyes that I couldn't quite interpret.

It seemed to take effort for him to find his next words. "No, what?"

"Don't tell Miller. Don't tell any of them. Please."

There was a desperate edge to my words, and I couldn't muster the desire to care about that.

"Jules..."

I knew what he wanted to say.

That if something had happened in my life, something criminal, then the combined knowledge and skills of Quin, Gunner, Finn, Miller, Lincoln, Ranger, and Smith would be invaluable. They would be able to lend a hand, make this a team effort, figure out who Gary really was, where he might be, track him down, get the money back.

"Kai," I started, voice thick. "They can't know."

"Why, honey? They all care about you. They would want to help."

"I... I wouldn't be able to face them again if they knew what an idiot I've been. Don't," I cut him off when he tried to object. "Don't say I'm not an idiot. I was. I rushed into this. I didn't think. I didn't... run a check on him." At that, Kai's lips curved upward, making my brows drawn low. "What?"

"Jules, maybe a couple dozen women in the whole world would think to run a background check on their potential partner."

"But *I* should have. *I* know better. Quin and everyone else would be thinking the same thing. You know they would. It's just... humiliating, Kai. I know you don't view it that way, but I do. I don't want them to know. Even if they would be helpful."

"Okay," he agreed, nodding. "I won't tell them."

"Thank you." The words came from somewhere deep. I felt like I was always thanking Kai, like he was always doing something good, kind, thoughtful, unexpected. This was just the newest in a long line of good deeds I had begun to know him for.

"But I am going to help you then."

"What? No."

The response was knee-jerk.

I couldn't ask that of him.

"You can try to fight me, Jules, but the end result will be the same. I'm not letting you deal with this on your own. You're stuck with me."

There it was again.

That tight-chest thing I got around him at times.

And, to be perfectly honest, the idea of not having to do it alone was appealing. Especially with my mood being so up and down. I needed someone level-headed, someone to keep their cool when I was losing mine.

Kai was good at calm.

"Okay," I agreed, nodding. "What am I..."

"Look," he cut me off, reaching to put his hand over top of mine. "I will handle Miller. And run to the office to do a quick check," he offered, meaning the background one I was supposed to run on him myself months before. "You need to get out of that dress. Maybe take a shower. Wash this all away. Then we will go check out his place together. Twenty minutes, tops," he assured me, knowing that giving him too much of a head start would mean he could be anywhere, maybe even out of reach before we could find him. "Okay?" he asked, needing confirmation.

He made it sound so easy.

So doable.

So much so that I had no choice but to believe him, to trust him.

"Okay."

-

Flashback - 6 months before -

She couldn't claim to hate being a hardass. She made her living having to be one, after all.

But there was no denying that Miller was very much hating every second of walking down the hall, and stopping in front of Kai's office.

Hell, it even took her a couple of moments - and slow, deep breaths - to be able to raise her hand to knock.

Because, well, it was one thing to be a bit blunt and in-your-face to some asshole.

It was another thing to do it to the sweetest guy you'd ever met.

She had a feeling it was going to feel like kicking a puppy.

"Come on in," Kai's voice called, calm, happy, completely oblivious to what was coming.

But it had to come, she reminded herself.

It would hurt.

But there was no avoiding that.

Because this was necessary.

To be honest, it had been necessary for a long time.

Everyone knew it.

Everyone saw it.

But no one would do it.

This office full of men, and she was the only one with balls enough to get it said already.

"Hey, Miller," Kai greeted, kicked back in his chair, legs off the corner of his messy desk, hands throwing an Earth-colored stress ball up in the air. "You need me for something?"

"We need to talk," she specified, closing and locking the door.

"Uh-oh. She's got her serious-voice on."

Miller liked Kai.

Loved, actually.

Maybe more than anyone else in the office.

Maybe it was because they had simply done so many jobs side-by-side, had been in the trenches with each other, forming bonds.

Or, well, maybe it was simply because the man was just... lovable.

If you needed one of his kidneys and half of his liver, he'd fucking give it. No questions.

That was just how he was.

And she had to be the one to tell him that he couldn't have what he wanted most.

"What's up, Miller?" he asked, putting down the ball, pulling his legs off the desk, leaning his arms on it, bringing him closer to her as she took the seat across from him.

Quin ragged on Kai about his office, being a man who liked things organized and classy.

But Kai thrived in chaos.

He had piles of files on his desk, research books nearly toppling off the dark wood cabinet lining the right wall. A wall he had bright neon thumbtacks sticking out of, holding up pictures that likely went with some of his files.

There was a backpack hanging off the hook on the back of the door, likely full of magazines, snacks, and changes of clothes. Wrinkled, knowing him.

He had music coming through his computer, and Miller reached across to shut it off.

"Enough," she said, the word coming out both forceful and pleading at the same time.

"Enough of what? My award-winning charm?" he asked with another of his smiles, the ones that lit up a room, making her feel all the worse for what was to come.

"Enough with Jules," she clarified, watching as Kai's brows drew together.

"What..."

"You know what I mean," she cut him off. "Everyone in this *office* knows what I mean."

"I haven't done anything inappropriate," he objected.

"Well, that's part of the problem, isn't it?" she asked, rolling her eyes as she reached up to run a hand through her long dark hair, settling it more to one side than the other.

"I'm sorry?"

"You choked, Kai," she explained shrugging a shoulder. "You saw something you wanted. And you choked. It was sweet at first, y'know? Who doesn't like watching a little crush blossom? Especially at work. But it stopped being sweet about a year and a half ago."

Kai's chest deflated as his head dropped slightly, looking at the surface of his desk.

He knew she was right.

He knew he had blown his shot.

"I can't help that I like her, Miller."

Like was a weak word.

Anyone who saw the way the man looked at her knew it leaned a lot more heavily toward love than like.

He looked at her like she was the sole reason he got out of bed in the morning.

Hell, maybe she was some days.

"I get that. I mean, I don't," she admitted as an afterthought. "I love how big your heart is, don't get me wrong, but I don't get how you can continue to love someone who doesn't love you back. At least not in the same way."

Because Jules did love Kai.

We all did.

He was the only person in the office who managed to make her smile on a rough day.

She hated anyone in her space, but never once told him to go away when he pulled up a chair to keep her company, to organize her clips and brads and pens - even though he had never organized his own.

She genuinely did care for him.

And maybe, just maybe, if he had found the courage to tell her how he felt instead of expecting her to piece it together herself, she might have been willing to let things get *inappropriate.*

"It doesn't matter if she doesn't feel the same," Kai said. And, what's more, he *meant* that. He didn't care that she didn't return his feelings, he still wanted to continue to treat her like she was the sun that everything in the world revolved around.

"Kai, she's minutes away from getting engaged. You know that. I know that. Everyone knows that. You've got to rein it in a little."

"He doesn't deserve her," Kai said, but there was a resignation in his voice. It was a damn shame, too, to hear it.

"I know."

Of course she knew.

She hated the weaselly little shit.

She didn't say that since Jules had her mind made up on the man after what seemed like their third date. And, well, who was she to say anything about relationships when she never managed to hold onto one?

Gunner called Gary fake.

Quin - usually one to mind his own business - went as far as to say he didn't like having the asshole in the building.

Jules was the darling of the office.

Our professional lives would fall apart without her. And she did everything without a complaint, without an attitude, even when one of the guys barked at her.

"But that is who she picked. We need to respect that. *You* need to respect that. Give her space. Let her man do the things her man is supposed to do."

The implication was there.

You are not her man.

"What am I supposed to do, Miller? Walk out of every room she walks into?"

"Treat her like you treat me," she suggested.

"Hey now. I treat you well," he objected, looking almost panic-stricken at the idea that he didn't.

"Well, yes. But you don't organize my desk. You don't warm my car up in the winter. You don't memorize my favorite lunch spots, and order only from there."

"Well, because you like fried and cheese drenched everything."

Miller smiled a bit at that, knowing he wasn't exactly a huge fan of Jules' preference for salads and fresh wraps all the time, but he happily ate them day in and day out since that was what she enjoyed.

"Just... take a step back, okay?" Miller asked. "For her, because I think it is going to make her feel weird if it keeps going on. But also for you, Kai. Because you can't be happy like this. And it is only going to get worse if she marries this guy. If they settle down, start the life you want with her. You need to move on."

"Yeah."

There was defeat and resignation in his tone.

Paired with the depth of sadness in his eyes, it pierced her. Made her feel like the lowest of lows. Made her second-guess coming in, speaking the words that had been stuck in her throat for months.

"I'm sorry, Kai," she told him, reaching across the desk to wrap an arm around his shoulders.

"You have nothing to be sorry about, Miller. You're right. I need to give her space."

And so he did.

THREE

Kai

That bastard.

There was nothing else able to penetrate my head as I moved toward Jules' front door, turning back at the last moment to watch the way she hunched over the island, letting out a shuddering breath that I could practically feel.

I forced myself into the hall, closing the door with a quiet click before reaching for my phone.

I had to take a few breaths, schooling the tension out of my voice, knowing Miller would pick up on it, read into it.

I wasn't going to break my promise to Jules. Even if the team would be an asset, would make this faster. If she wanted this just between the two of us, that was what it was going to be. And I would just have to step up my game.

I couldn't let her down.

We had to find the bastard.

And then I would hold him back while she beat the shit out of him.

"Christ, Kai. Could you take any longer? People are all assuming Gary got cold feet."

Cold feet.

More like a cold heart.

How the hell else could you explain his willingness to do something like that to Jules?

At least I could do her one small favor. Save her pride to her family and friends. Until she figured out how she wanted to handle it all herself.

"Jules called it off," I told Miller, the lie tripping off my tongue easily. I had needed to bend the truth more than a few times in my line of work. Not usually to co-workers, but with her not here to see me, I pulled it off.

"What? Why would she do that? Just minutes before the ceremony?"

"Turns out Gary was lying to her about some things. You know how Jules feels about that."

"Wow. So she just... cut him off? Just like that. I know Jules can run a bit cool, but that is ice cold. Well, at least he doesn't seem to have a big crowd here to be embarrassed for him. Where is Jules now?"

"Getting changed. Then catching a plane."

"She's still going on the honeymoon? Alone? Damn. She's my new hero. I bet she meets some hot Balinese man, and elopes on the beach."

"Yeah, that sounds like Jules," I drawled, rolling my eyes even as the familiar twinge of jealousy pierced my chest.

"Hey, you know what?" she asked, sounding pleased.

"What?"

"Maybe this means you get a second chance. But you have to nut-up this time."

"Believe me, that's the last thing on my mind right now."

"Hm."

"Hm, what?"

"Nothing. I just... I don't know. I figured you had just been putting on a show since we had that talk, that you didn't really move on. Just pretended to. I guess I was wrong."

She wasn't wrong.

She couldn't have been more right.

I had simply played a part since that night with Miller in my office.

I created a wide berth around Jules. I stopped organizing her desk stuff. I stopped hanging with her when I could have been in my own office. Since I couldn't just suddenly stop ordering from her favorite lunch places, I just started to go out right before like I had work to do, sitting down at the local sub shop all by myself like a loser instead.

I stopped talking about her.

I attempted to look like I noticed her less.

I played a part.

Apparently, convincingly enough.

"Jules wanted to know if there was any way someone could tell everyone to go ahead and have a nice meal on her. Maybe have Gunner spread the news. He likes being the bearer of bad news."

"Yeah, no worries. Will we be seeing you at the party?"

"I'm gonna give Jules a ride to the airport. But if I get back in time..."

"Sounds good. I'll save you some not-wedding cake."

"Thanks, Miller."

With that, I made my way to the office, throwing myself into research on the guy who broke Jules' heart - even if she was too focused on the money to realize it yet.

Gary Truman.

Thirty-two.

And, well, to his conman credit, just enough came up.

Just enough to convince any girl who searched his name that he was legit. And unmarried.

He had all the right social media accounts - Facebook, Instagram, a Twitter that he never posted on.

The right stuff with some pictures, some shared posts.

Not a lot, but passable.

Women accepted that most guys didn't update as often as they did, didn't do selfies, didn't add in all the work and life information.

Nothing about this Gary Truman would set up red flags unless you knew to look for them.

Because his oldest post was about two and a half years before. Likely around the time he met Jules. He'd uploaded, shared, and posted a lot those first two weeks, giving the appearance of a longer period of time if someone wasn't investigating enough to look at the dates.

And outside of social media, there was nothing. No old defunct LinkedIn pages; no links to old blogs or newspaper articles about how he hit the home run in a game in high school.

In fact, the only other posts about Gary Truman, aged thirty-two, belonged to someone in jail for armed robbery.

He was a ghost in a day and age when it was impossible to be a ghost.

I took a picture off his account, uploading it to a friend who had done some work for me in the past, grabbed my laptop, stuffed it into my backpack, and headed back to my car, grabbing salads on the way - hers with romaine, spinach, carrots, cucumbers, almonds, and honey mustard dressing, mine with iceberg, croutons, and ranch because salads were, well, tasteless and pointless without some bread and fat.

I got there about half an hour after I left, hoping she'd taken the time to maybe cry it out in the shower in private, but hadn't fallen into some kind of depression over the whole thing.

The sooner we got to work on this, the better the chances of finding Gary before the money was all gone.

I let myself back in, closing the door quietly.

"Jules?" I called, putting the salads down on the island beside her half-drank, now cold coffee. "I'm back," I added when I got no response, waiting for her, not wanting to go in search of her only to find her in a weak moment she might not want me to share.

I could hear movement a moment later, footsteps coming closer. Not heels, as was her usual, but I figured maybe she just hadn't slipped them on yet.

I couldn't have expected sneakers.

Or, well, any other part of the Jules that came around the bend of the kitchen, and into my line of sight.

Because Jules, well, Jules liked her image. She put time and thought into her outfits, her hair, her makeup, her jewelry selection. There was never a day when she showed up to work after too-little sleep with a look that clearly said 'screw it.'

She always had on work attire - dresses or slacks with blouses or blazers.

Even when she was called in at two a.m. when there was an emergency client, she somehow managed to slip into a dress, pull her hair back, put on heels, and fix her makeup, and still be there in under twenty minutes.

That was just how she was.

Or so I thought.

Had I not been so distracted by her on her knees in her wedding dress, I might have noticed that her closet did boast things that others might consider daily outfits, but Jules would likely call leisure wear.

Because, apparently, it was there.

I knew that because Jules was wearing it.

Light wash jean capris - neither tight nor loose, just skimming the gentle curves of her body, the cuff falling just below her knee, exposing a few inches of her lower leg and ankle before you found pure white - so white she either never wore them before, or was obsessive about bleaching them - low sneakers.

For a shirt, she had on a simple v-neck white tee that, like her pants, framed her body without hugging it the way her usual clothes were known to do.

She had on her cross, but nothing else. Nothing at her ears or wrists. Or, well, fingers. Since her fake engagement ring was floating in a glass on the kitchen counter.

Perhaps the most shocking, though, wasn't the clothes at all.

But what was above her neck.

Her hair, normally pulled back for convenience during her long work shifts, was left loose around her shoulders, the gleaming red waves framing a face made younger and more vulnerable without any mascara to darken her naturally light lashes, or filler in her brows, or liner on her water line, or color to her lips.

This wasn't Jules the executive assistant slash office manager slash personal assistant slash zoo keeper that she was when we always got to see her.

This was simply Jules.

And, amazingly enough, because I didn't think such a thing was possible, she was even more beautiful than usual.

"You got me a salad?" she asked, brows drawing together.

"You keep next to nothing in your fridge," I informed her, something new I had learned about her while making her coffee.

"I would claim it was because I was planning to leave for vacation, so I had emptied out. But I honestly don't keep much more than that in there on a regular basis."

"You're always at work," I said, understanding. My fridge was usually only full of takeout containers, condiments, and drinks.

"Exactly," she agreed, moving past me toward the kitchen, taking a drink of her cold coffee. "Maybe we should put it in the fridge," she suggested, reaching into the bag to pull out the containers, going into mine to pick the croutons out, placing them in a baggie before putting the salads themselves into the fridge. "I think it would be smart to get to Gary's place sooner rather than later. It's a long shot, but maybe we would catch him even. Before he skips town."

Not wanting to crush her hopes, I said nothing even though I knew there was no way he had taken the money then stuck around. Not when she was expecting him at an altar. Knowing she would come looking for him. If I knew anything about this - and I did - he had likely already hit the road. Not even stopping back at his apartment for whatever he had left behind.

"Alright," I agreed. "Let's go check it out."

"I've never been in your car before," she commented, tone a little hollow as we rode the elevator down.

"I've never been in yours either."

"Is it like your office?" she asked, choosing the words carefully.

"You mean a wreck?"

"That's what I meant," she agreed, giving me a small smile. It didn't come close to meeting her eyes.

"See for yourself," I invited as we walked up next to my tan Jeep, something I had chosen because it was roomy if I needed to catch a nap while on the road.

A glamorous life it was not, but I had always been able to sleep anywhere.

I bleeped the locks, and Jules went for her door, but not quite before my hand got there first, making her jump back.

She'd gotten too used to that fake fiancé of hers not opening things for her.

"Well, this is surprising," she decided, looking around inside before pulling herself up.

When on a long job, my car was every bit as hectic as my office. But once a job was over, it got cleared out, hit the wash for an exterior and interior detailing.

It was less because I was obsessive about it and more because old food wrappers brought bugs. And, while I could sleep a lot of ways, with things crawling on me was a hard no.

"Point me in a direction," I demanded as I turned the car over, stifling the inappropriate surging of happiness inside at seeing her in my car. Such a small thing, but also something like a milestone as well.

Jules, for me, had invaded one part of my life in a physical way.

Work.

That was it.

She had never been in my car, my place, had never come out to eat with me, for drinks, movies, nothing. She was the only person in the office I hadn't spent time with outside of work. And, of course, the one I wanted to with most.

That being said, I didn't like the circumstances. I didn't like that she sort of had to be in my car, that she was here because she needed my help, not because she actually wanted to be.

She steered me straight out of Navesink Bank, twenty minutes south to Eastontown to a large, winding complex of red brick apartment buildings of simple up or down units, not full floors. The grounds were bright green even during a crippling heat wave and subsequent drought. A set of little girls were riding baby bikes down one of the many paths as their mother watered her window boxes.

It was straight out of a movie.

My closest thing to a next door neighbor were the opossums that hung out in the woods behind my place.

"Nice place," I said because, well, it was.

"Yeah," she agreed, but it was clear she was seeing it through a different lens than I was, probably over-analyzing every interaction she and Gary had shared at this location.

"It's like a labyrinth in here," I mumbled, having somehow made a wrong turn, ending up in yet another section of buildings.

"Take the next left. And park. We have to walk around to the front," she explained, already reaching to un-click her belt. "Top floor," she told me, reaching for her set of keys, producing one with a dark blue rubber cover around it, differentiating it from the white one for her place, the black one for work, and - if I had to guess - green for her mom and pink for her sister - their favorite colors.

"Oh, heya there, Jules," a woman's voice called, making us both turn to finding her standing in the screen cutout of her door. "You making sure he got everything?"

"Hey, Jean. Got what?"

"The rest of his things," Jean specified, giving the two of us a smile, making her wrinkled face go warm and grandmotherly. "He was moving most of it out earlier. I'm sorry to see him go, but so happy for you two. The wedding is soon, right?" she went on, oblivious to the tension overtaking Jules' body. "Who is this?"

"Yes, soon," Jules composed herself enough to say. "And this is Kai. My..."

"Stylist," I interjected. "We are going for her last fitting after we make sure Gary got all his things. He said something about thinking he left a box in his closet."

"Okay. I won't keep you. I remember how hectic things were around my big day to Luis. And that was many years ago, you know," she went on, giving me a knowing look. "I bet things are even more demanding now. Send me pictures, will you?"

"Sure thing, Jean." Jules made the fake promise with genuine pain in her eyes. Not for her, it didn't seem. But for Jean. For her grandmotherly enthusiasm for her happily ever after. The one that would not take place.

With that, Jules stuck the key in the lock, and moved inside to the small landing, barely big enough to turn around in, making my body almost press into hers before she took off up the staircase, footsteps muffled by the pretty hideous brown carpeting covering the steps.

I moved into a somewhat cramped space - at least in comparison to my own and Jules'. A living room was to the left, melting into a dining space that appeared to curve into a kitchen. To the right, you could see the white tile of a bathroom, then doors at the end of the hall. One open, one closed.

"Jules," I hissed under my breath, closing my hand around her upper arm, trying to pull her to a stop as she went to charge off toward the rooms. "He could be here," I told her, urging her to realize that a cornered man was a dangerous one.

"Good. I won't have to travel far to whip his ass," she told me, yanking her arm away, and charging down the hall, turning into the open door with reckless abandon.

I was right at her six, moving into what was the master bedroom. Not empty, but bare.

The king-sized bed was still there, held by the ugly black metal frame with attached headboard. There were sheets on the bed, but no comforter or pillows.

Two medium-wood nightstands flanked the sides, each with a matching lamp, but nothing else.

I'd bet all the drawers were empty.

As was the dresser that Jules was searching through a bit frantically, pulling one completely out, dropping it carelessly on the brown carpet that seemed to cover all the floors in the space save for the bathroom and, I imagined, the kitchen.

Finding nothing, she went into the closet, seeing nothing but wire and plastic hangers, something that seemed to make her growl before she turned back to me, a look of hopelessness in her eyes.

"What about the spare room?"

"He always said it was where he stored all his extra boxes."

"You've never been in there?" I asked, surprised. Who had entire rooms that you had never at least seen?

"No," she said, shoulders falling a bit, seeming to finally see the oddness of that. Especially after dating for well over a year, closing in on two.

"Alright, let's check it out," I offered, moving into the hall, letting her go before me, throwing open the door, and fumbling around on the wall to find the switch to the darkened room.

I had a feeling that as soon as the bright light flicked on, she regretted finding the switch in the first place.

Because it was one thing to know you had been tricked by a conman.

It was a complete other to see it all mapped out in front of you in stark, undeniable detail.

Not only had she been conned, this had been a long game.

He hadn't just met her, gotten to know she made good money, that she had a lot stashed away, and *then* decided to use that.

No.

From the looks of things, he had clocked her a good long while before they had ever actually officially met, that he had watched her, studied her.

Hell, he had seen her in jeans and a tee years before I had - someone who spent every long workday with her for years.

Jules moved a few feet in, walking over toward a wall, giving me her profile, her hair tucked behind her ear, showing me her parted lips, her wide eyes.

Because what she was looking back at was herself.

Going to work, coming home much later, going to the gym, getting takeout, having brunch with her mom, going to the movies with her sister.

There was a picture of her window shopping at a pet store.

One of her getting out of her car, her skirt hitched up much higher than she would have allowed anyone else to see.

Another with her sitting in her car at work, hands clutching the wheel, head resting at the very top of it.

Just tired it seemed at first.

But there was another snap a moment later of her looking up, makeup running.

I forced my eyes away from the endless pictures, a part of me wanting to look, to see all the parts of her life. The other part of me, though, knew that this was not how she would want me to see her, when she wasn't aware, when she wouldn't have wanted to be seen - in weak moments, in compromising moments.

I moved toward a different wall, finding handwritten pages, the chicken scratch making it actual investigative work to figure out what was written there.

The first page had basic facts. Full name, address, work, known hangouts.

The next had a list of, well, all of us. Along with scribbled notes.

I snorted when I saw a note next to Gunner's name that said *Bad blood. Why?*

My stomach knotted as I scanned down to my name, knowing that if he noticed the animosity between Jules and Gunner, he no doubt picked up on the situation with me and her.

Kai. In love with her. She's either oblivious or uninterested. The poor sap.

It was better than I expected.

My head turned over my shoulder, seeing Jules still simply scanning the seemingly endless photos of her, trying to, I imagine, piece it all together as well.

I turned back to the paperwork, figuring it would give me a lot more than any of the pictures would.

The next sheet I reached for was more in-depth information on Jules.

Height. Weight. Shoe size. Food preferences. Cup size. And, right there at the bottom, a different list. One I didn't quite get until I read a few of the lines.

Fantasies.

The bastard wrote down a list of the things she liked - or wanted to try - in bed.

Unable to help it, my hand curled inward from where I was holding it, crumpling up the words into a tight ball, crushing it in my palm, the anger a rather foreign, uncomfortable thing as it worked its way through my body, getting my veins heated, my skin crawling.

I swallowed back the acidic taste to my saliva, forcing myself to go to the next piece of paper, just finding basic little life notes, little tidbits about herself she had given him, things he wanted to appear to remember. So he could come off like the doting, perfect boyfriend.

I mean... how far was he willing to take this?

If he hadn't gotten into her bank account this morning, would he have fully committed? Married her? Gotten his name on her accounts, so the money was his as well?

Then leave her?

Hell, leave her possibly pregnant? To raise a baby on her own?

Jules was a careful person, a woman all about timelines. She would have made sure there were no oopsies before the wedding. But she also wanted to be a mother. And likely before she got too much older. I would bet that she would have ditched contraceptives, and let nature take its course pretty soon after the wedding.

I moved to the small square folding table with a matching chair set up like a desk against one wall, finding a mass of paperwork that made me suddenly feel I needed to get my things in order on my own desk.

I pulled out the chair, sitting down, knowing this was going to take a bit with the sheer number of documents there.

Pieces of Jules' mail

An old bank statement showing the hefty savings she had meticulously accumulated having worked for Quin since he opened. Every damn bit of it was hard-earned too.

And he saw it as an easy way to set himself up for a couple years.

There was another sheet of paper in his chicken scratch, a bunch of random words and number combinations.

Except none of them were random.

Her mother's maiden name.

Her sister's birthday.

The name of their childhood golden retriever.

Her zip code.

From the looks of things, he'd been trying to figure out her passcode for her account for a long while, jotting down every bit of information thrown at him.

I couldn't help but wonder what actually did it, what was right, what parts of her past she used to protect her present.

And why today?

Of all days, why and how had he figured it out on what was supposed to be their wedding day? Had she said something to him? Or had he found something when he had gone back to the apartment that he had never noticed before?

Burning questions, all.

Finished, I pushed out the chair, moving to stand, turning to check on Jules, see if she was managing to process the information better than she had been a moment before.

Seeming to sense the motion, she slowly turned from where she was holding a picture of Gemma, her head thrown back, laughing, everything about her radiating light and love as she so often did.

"It was never real," she concluded, tone hollow, lacking any emotion at all, just a dead recount of the situation as though it didn't involve her. And certainly not her heart. "What's that?" she asked, jerking her chin toward my hand, one I hadn't realized was still clutching that one piece of paper. The one I knew she didn't want to see. The one I knew would shatter her calm.

"Nothing," I objected, moving to take a step to the side as she advanced me.

"It's not nothing. If it was nothing, you wouldn't be trying to protect me from it," she shot back, knowing me maybe a bit too well.

"Jules, this stuff he wrote down... it's not important."

"It's important to me," she specified, brow raising, getting a bit of her spirit back. The kind that said she would stop at nothing to get the paper in my hand, to read what I so badly didn't want her to. "Give me the paper, Kai," she demanded, moving in right in front of me, hand going outward, fingers curling impatiently. "Fine," she grumbled when I didn't hand it over. Her hand closed over mine, fingers wiggling between, snagging the piece of paper, pulling it out of my closed fist.

I leaned back against the wall, the air exhaling so hard out of me it almost sounded like a sigh as I watched Jules carefully unroll the paper, try to flatten it out so the awful handwriting was more easily seen.

It took a minute.

As it had with me.

Just going over the basic things like her size that, while invasive, wasn't anything to be freaked out about.

I could see it the moment she realized what the other list was.

Her lips parted.

Her eyes widened.

Her breathing simply stopped.

"Oh, my God," she whimpered, seeming to lose whatever strength she had that had kept her on her feet.

She slowly sank down, knees hitting the ground.

Both hands were still holding the paper, pulled so tightly that it looked about ready to rip down the center.

A fracture started in my heart at the complete and absolute horror on her face.

Because if there was one thing that should be sacrosanct, it was the intimate parts of you, the things meant only to be shared between partners. Because you would never give that to a person if you didn't think you could trust them with it, that they would value it, that they would respect it enough to keep it private.

And here it all was, written on paper for anyone to see. For him to analyze. To possibly use against her. Use to manipulate her.

"Hey," I started as I lowered down in front of her, not sure I even had the right words, but knowing I needed to try to find them. For her. For her sanity. To get that horrific look off her face. My hand reached for the paper, pulling it away, surprised when her fingers allowed it, crumpling the page up again, dropping it, and reaching to snag her chin, forcing her face up, giving it a second before her eyes found mine. "He's a conman. This is what conmen do. They study you. They find information on you."

"He *wrote it down*," she hissed, trying to take a deep breath.

"Yeah, Jules. But, I think, for his eyes only. Nothing here implies anyone other than him was involved."

"And my eyes. And *your* eyes." Her voice did that hitching thing again, but her eyes were completely dry.

"I stopped reading," I told her, watching as her eyes closed hard. "No, look at me," I demanded, giving her chin a little squeeze. "As soon as I realized what it was, I stopped reading. Your secrets are yours to keep, Jules. And I would never betray you like that."

Either simply knowing me, or hearing the sincerity in my tone - or both - she gave me a short nod. "I know that," she agreed, letting out a breath that made her body tremble with its intensity.

"What's going on in there?" I asked when she just continued to sit there, looking off to her side, but not seeming to see anything at all.

"I don't even know," she admitted, and I knew it was another sucker punch to her pride to even say such a thing, for a woman so sure of herself to feel so utterly lost. "What are you thinking?"

"I'm thinking there's nothing here to go on. He likely took his electronics. He's meticulous in his research, so I think he would be smart enough to take anything pointing to his plans. I think we need more to go on."

"He had a job," she suggested.

"But did he really?" I asked. "He fabricated a whole life..."

"No, he had a job," she insisted. "In a building. I've been there. I surprised him with lunch or dinner when I could get away for an hour."

That made sense, really.

This was a long con.

Don Juan jobs often were.

It took a while to gain a woman's trust.

Longer to get access to her finances.

If he didn't have enough of a savings from a previous job, he would need to support himself through the research and implementation process.

"What'd he do?"

To that, she let out a humorless snort.

"Accounting," she supplied, reaching up to rake a frustrated hand through her hair.

"Road trip?" I asked, trying to keep my tone lighter, trying to keep her from going too deep in a hole while there was still so much work to do.

"Kai..." she said, shaking her head.

"What?" I asked, brows drawing together, not entirely sure what that tone of voice was, pretty certain I had never heard it before from her.

Her head shook again. "I can't ask..."

"You're not asking. I'm offering," I cut her off, tone a bit final, not wanting her to think there was any doubt or hesitation for me.

"Kai, it's my concern, not yours."

"It concerns you, Jules, so it concerns me too."

I didn't care that maybe that was saying too much, showing my hand, proving that all these months I had just been playing a part, that my feelings were now as they always had been.

I watched, waiting to see the recognition, but all she gave me was a slow exhale, closing her eyes like she was attempting to find some patience or strength - or combination of the two.

"What happens if we find nothing at his office either?"

"Jules, if there is one thing I have learned from working with Quin - and everyone else - it is that there is always something. No one is good enough to erase everything."

"Except Finn," Jules interjected.

"Except Finn," I agreed. "But I very much doubt that Gary is anywhere near as good as Finn. There will be something somewhere to go on."

"And then what?"

"Then we track the lead."

"It could take a while."

"Yeah, it could," I agreed.

"You need to work. I'm, ha, I'm on my honeymoon for three weeks. No one will notice me gone. But you... you need to be there."

"I need to be on this case," I countered, shrugging. "I will feed Miller a story. She will buy it."

Of course she would.

Because she never would have figured me for a liar.

I felt a stab of guilt at having to do it, but if someday it all came out, Miller would understand.

"And what if Quin needs you?"

"Jules, honey, let me worry about me, okay?"

"I'm going to worry too since I am what is getting in the way of your work."

"Listen, what is going on with you is more important than Quin maybe getting pissed with me, okay? So stop. This is my priority right now. *You're* my priority right now. So, let's stop talking about it, and get working on it. Yeah?" I asked, getting to my feet, reaching down to offer her my hand.

She looked up at it for a long moment, her brows drawn together over her light eyes.

Just when I was sure she was going to refuse it, was going to get to her feet herself, her hand slid into mine, tentatively at first, then curling in as mine did, allowing me to carefully pull her up.

"Yeah," she agreed, giving me a nod even as her shoulders squared, her chin lifted, her spine went to steel.

And that was the Jules I knew.

But, I realized, that was not - as I had thought - the whole picture, the whole woman.

Maybe some would feel like a dream was shattering to realize that the woman they had loved was only a part of who she really was.

But all I could feel as we left the apartment was excitement. Even pleasure. That there was more to know. That there were parts of her that I would get to know that others would not.

Selfish, maybe.

But true nonetheless.

Flashback - 10 months before -

"Ladies," Kai's voice broke into the quiet moment Miller and Jules were enjoying in the sitting room on the second floor.

Miller had been crashing there, being on-call for a job, and figuring it would be easier to stay close in case she was needed.

Jules had been cleaning out and restocking the fridge as she did a few times a week - always keeping the place prepped in case of emergency clients coming in, needing a place to stay.

Miller had come out, convincing Jules to get off her heel-clad feet for a few moments, both of them sitting on the couch talking about her upcoming case.

"How did you know we would be here?" Miller asked, seeing the cardboard carrying tray of coffee. And, well, his hot chocolate. Since that was all he drank.

"Quin said you were crashing," he supplied, handing Miller her coffee. "And Jules always restocks on Tuesday nights," he added, giving Jules that *look* he always gave her. His usual puppy-dog look, but mixed with longing and devotion. She reached for her coffee, giving him her usual pleased, but somewhat oblivious look right back.

"You wanna sit and shirk responsibilities with us?" Miller suggested, waving a hand toward the chair.

Kai looked over at it, a mix of tempted and resigned to his fate. One that would take him clear across the country to piss off a rather large cocaine smuggler. You know, just another day at the office for him.

"I got a job. But you ladies have fun. And make sure Gunner or Finn walk her out later," he added, talking to Miller about Jules. "She's too stubborn for her own good sometimes," he added, moving off to the door, leaving as quickly as he had appeared, but creating something new in the air around them, a new dynamic, something that Miller felt the need to comment on.

"You can't tell me you haven't thought about it."

"Thought about what?" Jules asked, taking a sniff of her caramel coffee before tasting it. It would be perfect. Because it always was. This was Kai they were talking about here. He always got your order right. That was just how he was.

"About Kai."

"What about him?"

"Oh, come on," Miller said, rolling her eyes. "You had to have thought about giving him a try."

"And why would I do that?"

"You are a young, vibrant woman in an office full of Grade-A dudes, that's why."

"This is work," Jules insisted, as Miller figured she might. All this time, and she had never seen her so much as eye-bang any of the guys. And they were all eye-bangable. Even if you didn't actually want to go there. For work or, well, personality reasons.

"Oh, I'm sorry. Is it no longer work-appropriate to have a functioning vagina? What do you do, unscrew it before you come in every morning? Come on."

"I'm seeing someone."

Ugh.

Yes.

Gary.

Who no one - save for her - liked.

The pretty boy with a good resumè. And a shitty personality.

I guess there was no accounting for taste.

Who was she to judge?

She hadn't had an actual relationship in... well, she wasn't even sure.

"So what? You haven't always been with him. Tell me you haven't considered Kai. Especially with how into you he is."

To that, her body jerked back, but Miller had a feeling it wasn't necessarily surprise. Just shock. That someone else had noticed? Or had the lack of decency to bring it up?

Miller had never been accused of being completely tactful.

Call it being the only girl in an all-boys club. She picked up on their completely tone-deafness to subtlety a long ass time ago.

"He's never said anything to that effect," Jules insisted, back ramrod straight.

"Right. And you are dead, dumb, and blind to boot."

"Miller..."

"Don't 'Miller' me like I am being ridiculous. You're the one who has had that man trailing after you like he's in a goddamn rom-com since the day you started here. And you are going to try to act like you don't know?" Miller asked, head bobbing to the side a bit, pure attitude. "He's cute," she insisted. "Tell me you at least see that."

"He's cute," Jules confirmed, as if such a thing needed confirmation. Saying Kai wasn't cute would be like saying Gunner wasn't hot, regardless of her personal feelings about him.

"And sweet."

"And sweet," Jules agreed.

"And funny, interesting, talented, well-mannered..."

"Yes, all those things too."

"Then what's the problem?"

"There's no problem," Jules said, shaking her head. "I just... work is important to me. I would never mess that up."

"So you can't ring the devil's doorbell to the idea of Kai in your *head* because it might mess up work? Doll, of all these mens' varied skills, mind-reading is not one," Miller informed her with a smirk.

"The devil's doorbell?" Jules latched onto, lips twitching.

"Mhmm. And you know what they say..."

"No, what do they say?"

"If you keep ringing it, eventually he's gonna *come*."

To that, she got a full on laugh, a light, musical sound, one you didn't often hear from Jules.

Except, of course, when Kai was getting it out of her.

She let the subject go, knowing that if she pried too hard, Jules would lock down tight, and she'd never get anything out of her again.

Besides, she had gotten what she had wanted.

She got her to admit that Kai was cute and interesting. And worthy of attention.

If Miller knew her - and she thought she did - she suspected that the only reason Jules never gave Kai serious consideration - the work ethic thing aside - was because he didn't check all the boxes she had in her head somewhere.

Jules was all about her boxes.

Hell, even after all this time, Miller still caught her actually checking off a daily to-do list before going home at night.

Kai was clearly missing a few of her boxes.

It was a damn shame that she was too stubborn to realize how much fun could be had with a guy who seemed completely wrong for you on paper, but was oh so right in real life.

FOUR

Jules

I like Miley Cyrus.

There.

It's out there.

And not the cool, edgy, naked on a wrecking ball, licking various objects with a short haircut Miley Cyrus.

I mean cowboy-booted, All-American girl up on a truck bed singing *Party in the USA* Miley.

I maybe even had a dance to go with it.

Okay, fine.

I totally had a dance to go with it.

And I sang it in my hairbrush too many times to mention.

And the reason I was thinking this in the car on the way to my fake fiancé's work, you might be wondering?

Because of the man sitting beside me.

See, he didn't know about my deep, dark Miley guilty pleasure.

He didn't know I binge ate Ritz crackers in my car when I was stressed.

Or that I sometimes taped two of my toes together to keep my feet from hurting during long work days in heels.

Or that I sometimes had a slight obsession with my extraction tool, making my face all red and splotchy for half a day while it recovered.

He didn't know all that stuff.

The silly stuff.

The ugly stuff.

He saw one very small part of the picture from a distance. Not up close where you could see all the brushstrokes, all the little mistakes, all the smudges.

I knew what everyone thought, what they even said when they thought I couldn't hear.

That Kai was in love with me.

I wasn't blind.

I had seen his crush-like behavior since I first started working for Quin.

But that was what it was.

A crush.

Puppy love.

You couldn't love someone until you got to know all about them. And he didn't know all about me. He knew just the surface.

That being said, I was only human. My body reacted to things that my mind didn't get a chance to mull over.

So when he got soft and sweet, when he said the exact right things at the exact right times, it impacted me. It sent a shiver through my belly. It made that chest-tightening thing happen.

And today, today he had been full of the right words, the right looks, the right touches.

More right than anyone else could have been.

He was good at that.

Knowing what I needed to hear.

He was good at it all.

My mom was obsessed with a book about love languages, swearing it was the sole thing that helped revamp her marriage when it - inevitably, it seemed - started to get a bit stale after a couple decades. And I had sat and listened to her go on and on about how my dad showed love through physical touch and giving gifts and that she gave it through words of affirmation and physical touch. And that the reason they went stagnant was because they didn't 'speak the same language.' So once they learned to speak it, everything changed.

Because I had heard so much about it, I had this knee-jerk ability to see it in everyone, even if I wasn't sure I bought into it.

And Kai?

Kai showed love in all the ways. Affirmations, touch, time, gifts, and service.

It was so much.

So incredibly much.

Maybe even too much.

Even if I truly believed he loved me for me - not some image he had of me in his head - I wasn't sure I could accept that much love. I wasn't sure I had it within me to hold onto it all.

"Jules?" Kai's voice called, snapping me out of my wandering thoughts, making me realize the car was stopped, the engine just idling. "You want me to go alone?" he asked, misreading the moment, my absent-ness.

"No," I objected immediately, voice a little off. "They know me. I can get in without it raising too many eyebrows."

"It's a Sunday, honey," he reminded me. "No one will be here except maybe some security guards."

Right.

What was wrong with me that I hadn't realized that myself?

I felt like my brain was in this thick, toxic fog, like nothing could break through.

I hated not being on my game.

I hated feeling like I was behind, frantically trying to catch up.

That wasn't the image I wanted to project.

I worked so hard never to come off as someone unprepared or low to pick things up.

It had been a long day.

And it was barely the afternoon.

I was just drained - physically, emotionally, and, let's face it... financially.

I would feel better once we had some answers, once I knew the situation wasn't completely hopeless.

"How are you going to get in then?" I heard myself ask, watching as what could only be called a sly smile pulled at his lips, a look that said *Come on now, Jules*. "Oh, right," I said, nodding.

So, this was how I would become a felon.

What a wild day.

If you had told me twenty-four hours ago that everything I knew myself to be - careful, safe, smart, and law-abiding, would be completely ripped away from me, I would have had a good laugh. Likely a much-needed one. But also a completely disbelieving one.

But there I was, following Kai to a side entrance, watching him jimmy open a lock, leading us easily up a stairwell to the floor I told him Gary worked on.

"What about the cameras?" I heard my worried voice ask when we got to the door to the floor.

"This isn't some big operation. They would likely only watch them if there was something wrong. Since we won't be triggering anything or taking anything, there would be no reason to check them."

I suddenly felt foolish for the idea in my head of some guy sitting in the basement surrounded by half a dozen security cameras, one hand poised over the phone, ready to call the cops, and have us hauled in for breaking and entering.

That was a situation even Quin might not be able to fix.

I guess - as much as I did know - there was still a lot to learn.

Hopefully, though, not firsthand.

I was a lot of things.

A adrenaline junkie was not one of them.

And, I was convinced, there had to be a part of you that was drawn to that to be able to live the lifestyle Quin and his team did. Even people like Finn and Kai who you would never normally think that of. They were drawn to this not only because Finn had a skill for cleaning and Kai had a innate ability to talk his way into and out of any situation.

They lived their lives constantly flirting with danger, with threats from bad people and the 'good guys' in equal turns.

A hand closed around my wrist, gentle but insistent, tugging me forward, yet again making me realize how in my own little world I was as he pulled me into a hallway, holding up a hand to me, silently asking me where we were going.

I had no idea what was happening until my hand moved on its own, until it slid up, finding his palm, his fingers, curling in on instinct, on impulse. Under mine, his hand twitched, almost like he was going to pull away before his hand curled into mine, fingers lacing between, gripping tighter.

And there it was again.

The chest thing.

I took a deep breath, trying to move past it, as I turned away, pulling him with me down the hall toward Gary's office, dropping his hand as soon as we stepped inside, feeling the odd need to shake off the sensation there, like a tingling, a current of electrical shocks over the surface of my palm.

Kai moved past me, head ducked, hand opening and closing a few times as he went around Gary's desk, immediately getting to work on his computer.

Left feeling useless - one of the most hated sensations I was familiar with - I walked around his space, mildly annoyed when it smelled like him, looking for things maybe I had missed before, so caught up in my own dreams and ambitions for us as a couple that I was blind to warning signs.

There were no pictures.

But, for me, that wasn't unusual.

No one at the office had personal pictures on their desks or walls.

There was a suit jacket on a hook behind the door. I went to it, feeling around in the pockets as Kai clicked around on the keyboard.

I found a receipt for gas, another for the coffee he had brought me one afternoon. Without the caramel he knew I wanted. There were a couple of quarters. And a lighter.

Lighter.

My Gary hadn't smoked.

It would have been a deal-breaker for me.

But just like Computer Gary wore glasses, I guess Office Gary smoked.

Just one more falsehood, one more reason to beat myself down a bit.

I mean, how could I have believed him when he said he smelled like cigarettes because he took his break outside with people in the office who smoked? How naive could I be?

"Not as smart as he thought he was," Kai mumbled, drawing my attention, making me spin to find him scrolling with one hand while writing with the other, a talent I absolutely did not possess, and definitely envied a bit.

"You found something?"

"Any chance you guys considered Connecticut for a honeymoon destination?" he asked, smiling about the raised-brow look I sent him. Who went to Connecticut for their honeymoon? "Then I think we have something. Give me one more... yep," he declared, nodding. "He was looking at a new townhouse development being built. I guess he has his sights set on the Nutmeg State."

"Nutmeg State," I repeated, lips twitching. "You're making that up."

"Nope. It's not the official one, but it is widely used," he declared, jotting down an address before powering down the computer. "So... road trip?"

Was there really a choice?

I needed to know.

Kai would never let me do it on my own.

And, quite frankly, with my head all over the place, it was reassuring to have someone around who could keep theirs on right.

"Stop back for salads and a bag?" he suggested when I just stood there, processing.

"Ah, yeah. Don't you need to..."

"Got some clothes in my backpack," he declared. Because, well, of course he did. Everyone in the office had a bag packed. In case of last minute trips out of town.

"How far is it?" I asked once we were safely back in the car, no embarrassing mugshots of fingerprinting in our futures, it seemed.

"About two and a half hours. Not too bad. We could be there well before dark."

With that, we went back to my place.

Kai repacked the salads while I threw some things into a bag, just in case we ended up needing to stay overnight.

It was only when we were on the road again, this time for an extended ride, that Kai's hand went to fetch something out of his glove box, producing a red iPod, plugging it in, then toggling through with deft fingers since he never once took his eyes off the road.

You could have knocked me over with a feather when a very familiar voice came booming out of the speakers a moment later.

My gaze went to Kai's profile, scrutinizing it for a long moment as Miley started singing about a *Hoedown Throwdown*.

I figured it a fluke as I sat there, staring out the window.

But when Miley transitioned into Britney and then Britney into Nikki, I found myself turning, watching him for a long moment until he hit a light, turning to me. "What's up?"

"This is my playlist." It came out like an accusation. Maybe it was. Because he had my playlist. How did he have my personal playlist? *Why?*

"Yeah," he said simply, nodding.

"Why do you have my playlist? How?"

"I follow you."

"I'm sorry?" I heard myself ask, tone a bit sharp.

"On Spotify," he specified. "You make the best playlists."

"Really?" I asked, suspicion plain in my voice. "So you're a big Miley fan, huh?"

To that, he snorted. "No. But I figured your Come On, Get Happy playlist was needed right about now. If I had my choice, we'd be listening to Billy Joel Soothes the Soul."

"You've memorized my playlists?"

"Only a handful."

Since I had at least three dozen, that was not that many. But still... odd. Surprising. And, to be perfectly, one-hundred-percent honest... almost a bit scary.

Not because I thought it was creepy, that Kai was some kind of stalker.

But because of what it meant.

It meant that he *did* see more than I realized.

It meant he saw some of the silly parts of me that next to no one got to see.

And he didn't seem to view me any differently because of them.

"Want something different?"

I reached for the iPod he handed me, scrolling through playlists I had poured over, trying to make each one set a mood, evoke a feeling.

What I really felt the need for in my soul was Sounds of Sadness. But I didn't want that to overtake me, let the bad feelings out, where someone else might be able to see it.

So I picked *Drift Away*, something meant for relaxing at home with some wine, just unwinding down after a long day.

"This one is my favorite," Kai declared, surprising me, always having figured him for an upbeat music kind of guy.

I guess I didn't know him as well as I had thought.

I wasn't sure how I felt about that.

And on a day when there were too many things to feel about, I chose not to feel at all.

It was a survival technique.

I wasn't sure I could handle it all if I let it take over me.

So I took it all, smushed it together, and locked it away. To be dealt with later. When I was alone. When no one would be around to see the breakdown. When no one would watch me need to meticulously sweep up the wreckage.

Because I wasn't capable of letting someone see - or especially help me clean up - my mess.

"So this is what my money is buying him," I murmured when we turned into the neighborhood with one fully finished row of townhouses - show models - and about a dozen half-built ones.

"Not if we can help it, Jules," Kai consoled, the optimism maybe somehow grating on my nerves. Because, sometimes, you just wanted to hear someone say *You know what? You're right. This sucks*. Then again, I was in the midst of some existential crisis. I wasn't thinking like I might normally. Because normal me would be plotting, planning, making lists, breaking down a bigger, seemingly impossible problem into smaller, easier to handle pieces. Certainly not sitting in the passenger seat just watching the world pass by me.

I didn't know who this me was, but I couldn't seem to shake her.

"I think this is the office," Kai said, pulling up to a trailer with a trio of cars to the side, and a sign that said Open on the door.

"What's the plan?" I heard myself ask.

"We look for who is in charge. Then ask him about Gary."

I didn't question him, didn't demand more details. Like who we would say we were. Why we would say we were looking for Gary.

I just climbed out of the Jeep, followed Kai in, and let him do the talking.

Again, not like me.

I liked to be in charge.

I liked knowing that my fate was all in my hands.

Maybe I just didn't have the energy.

Maybe I simply trusted Kai.

But whatever the reason, I stood by at Kai's side as he spoke to the woman - named Abby - who was around my age, sitting at the desk with long coffin nails in a bright purple color that I couldn't seem to look away from.

And I said nothing.

As we were informed that we had just missed the manager, Ron, and that he wouldn't be back until the following day.

Kai said something with that smile of his that had the girl going from professional friendly to flirtatious, giving me another glimpse of how he was good at his job.

"We'll come back tomorrow," I interjected, not even caring that I was cutting Kai's sentence off, my voice a little sharp. "Are you ready to go?" I asked, making Kai's brows draw together, trying to read my reaction.

I didn't think he would have much luck.

Since I didn't understand it myself.

I certainly didn't know what made me reach for his hand again. But I did it. And started pulling him with me toward the door.

"We'll see you tomorrow," I called to the girl at the desk before pulling Kai outside, dragging him with me back to his Jeep.

"Jules," Kai called, reaching out with his suddenly free hand as I reached for the handle, pressing it into the door, holding it closed, forcing me to turn back to him. "Take a breath," he demanded, surprising me, making me realize I had barely been doing so for several long moments. He waited, watching me suck in a deep breath, then release it slowly. "Okay. Now, what is going on?"

"What do you mean?"

"You're... not acting like yourself."

"You barely know me," I declared, lips spilling the lie like venom, wanting it out of me and onto him, no matter how unfair that was.

"Okay," he said, nodding. "Do you want to come back here tomorrow?"

"It's the only lead we have."

"Alright," he agreed, something in his tone that I was sure I hadn't heard there before, something that was akin to frustration. But that seemed unlikely. The only time I had ever seen him frustrated was that one night he came into the office roughed up. "Do you want to head back to Navesink Bank, and drive up here tomorrow, or get rooms?"

There would go a few hundred I really could use to save.

But it was stupid to drive two and a half hours back to Navesink Bank.

Besides, I wasn't sure I was ready to go back to my apartment, to face all the falsehoods I would find within those walls.

I just didn't have it in me.

As much as that bruised my ego to admit even just to myself.

"It's probably smart to stay around here," I told Kai. "You want me to look..." I started, so used to doing their research for everyone at the office that I automatically reached for my phone.

"I got it," he told me, opening the door, letting me in while he reached for his own cell. "Only one in the area," he declared, climbing into his seat, tossing the phone into the cupholder.

And with nothing else, he drove us out of the half-built development and to the hotel.

Saying nothing.

I would never accuse Kai of being annoyingly chatty, but he usually had something to say, some way of keeping a conversation going. Even in awkward and tense situations. Which this was more and more feeling like, to be perfectly honest.

Or maybe that was just me.

I certainly felt awkward and tense.

And while tense might have been an old friend of mine, having never really been someone able to completely relax, awkward was an entirely new sensation.

"You're quiet," I commented, unable to take it anymore, wanting my old Kai back, the one who would have been making comments about the town, about the music, telling jokes. Something. Anything.

"Just thinking," he came back with, not helping the situation at all.

Because now I couldn't seem to hold myself back from demanding what it was he was thinking about.

"About what?"

"Strategies. Plans. That kind of thing."

"Well, I am a strategies and plans kind of girl."

"Usually, yes. But today, I think you are a sit in the passenger seat and get lost in your own thoughts kind of girl."

He wasn't wrong.

But that was exactly the problem.

I didn't want to be lost in my own thoughts.

Just as those words were starting to work their way up my throat, over my tongue, we were pulling to the parking lot of a white stucco five-floor hotel with an overhang for valet.

Valet.

My gaze went to Kai's profile as he drove us under that overhang, wondering if this truly was the only hotel in the area... or if it was the only one he thought I would be willing to stay in. Because there had to be somewhere less expensive, one of those long, low motels off the highway where you might catch bed bugs or an STD from simply walking into it.

But before I could ask if there was anywhere else, he was hopping out, rushing around the hood to beat the valet to my door, pulling it open for me.

Gary hadn't been much of a door opener.

And, to be honest, it was one of my biggest pet peeves about him. It didn't even cross his mind to do it when my hands were full, or when we were all dressed up, and heading to a fancy restaurant.

Maybe it shouldn't have bothered me. Of all women. Since I prided myself so much on being independent, on taking care of myself in every way possible. So of course I could open my own door.

I guess it was simply that it had nothing to do with sexism or feminism or anything like that. It was just basic good manners. And that had always been one of my requirements.

But since he was good about most other things, I let it slide. Even if it irked me.

Kai fetched our bags, leading us into the hotel with still nothing to say.

The lobby was as spacious as you'd expect with how giant the place was, all creams and champagnes and the occasional hint of a rose gold.

I was too busy admiring the enormous glass chandelier hanging over the center of the space - and maybe wondering how the hell one cleaned such a thing, let alone changed the lightbulbs - to notice what Kai was saying to the pretty brunette at the check-in.

That was until I heard three words.

"Only one room..."

My attention snapped to her, finding her focus on Kai, and his on me.

"The next hotel is half an hour away," he told me, shrugging, leaving it up to me. "It's only a king," he added, not two queens or fulls as one might expect.

Thirty minutes wasn't far, not really.

And I wasn't even the one doing the driving.

But I felt drained.

Like I wouldn't be able to keep my eyes open for the walk to the elevator, let alone have to get back in the hot car, drive to a new place, then see if they had any openings at all.

"We'll take it," I told the girl, reaching for my wallet, only to see Kai beat me to it. "Kai... no..."

"What? It's a business expense, right?" he asked, giving me a mischievous little smile, knowing I was the one who handled the company credit cards, and that Quin just blindly signed off on them.

It wasn't until she had swiped it and handed it back to him that I realized he hadn't handed her a company card, one I knew to be gold since they all were, but a platinum one that must have been his own.

I should have fought him on it.

But I couldn't muster the energy.

I'd pay him back.

When all this was done, I'd figure out what the room cost, and pay him back. Even if I had to discreetly sneak it into his paycheck to keep him from knowing about it because I knew he would never take it from me.

"Coming?" Kai asked, head dipped to the side, holding up two room keys, waiting for me to show any sign of life at all.

"Yeah," I agreed, letting him lead me down the hall, to an elevator, then up to the fourth floor, down another hall, then finally to our door.

He let us into the hotel room, only the third one I had ever been in my life, and by far the nicest. Not that that should have been a surprise given how gorgeous the outside, lobby, and even the hallways were.

But this felt like, well, coming home.

Everything from the pristine - and unexpected - gray-wash hardwood floors, to the white nightstands and dresser, to the slightly shimmery champagne-colored drapes that skirted the ground, suited the style I liked most.

Clean.

Classy.

Understated.

My eyes roamed over to the bed, large enough for two, surely, but somehow seeming small, but with a beige tufted headboard, beige sheets, and pure white comforter.

I found reassurance in that.

Having a bit of a *thing* about things being in order and clean, the idea of a stark white comforter said that the thing needed to be washed - and often - to keep it that clean-looking.

I turned to find Kai watching me, and found myself wanting to ask if *this* was why he picked the room, because he saw the room pictures online, and knew I would feel at home here.

Well, at home without all the ugly memories attached to all the items scattered around.

I was suddenly very strangely pleased by the fact that Gary hated my snow globes, that those were still mine and mine alone, that his touch and voice hadn't tainted those for me as well.

At least that was something.

I could get new furniture, new clothes, but there was nothing I could do about the snow globes, about the meaning and attachment behind them.

So I was almost foolishly thankful that he hated them.

"How about I go find us some dinner?" Kai suggested as he put our bags down on the dresser beside the TV. "Wraps?" he asked, expecting an automatic yes. Because, well, salads, wraps, fruit, and oatmeal were pretty much ninety-eight-percent of my diet. I'd been raised to eat healthy, had kept the habit as an adult because it was what I was used to, and because it kept me in shape without having to kill myself at the gym.

I wasn't - luckily - an emotional eater, having never learned the behavior in my youth.

But just this once, yeah, I wanted to eat my feelings.

"Actually... do you think there are any pizza places nearby?"

"Pizza?" His voice and look on his face matched. Surprise. Confusion.

"Do you like pizza?"

"Everyone likes pizza," he shot back, face softening. "What kind do you want?"

"Mushroom and onion."

"Alright. Mushroom and onion it is. I'll be back in like... half an hour."

He went to move past me, opening the door before the words escaped me finally.

"Kai..."

"Yeah?" he asked, turning back as I faced him as well.

"Thank you," I told him, voice a bit thick.

"For pizza? No thanks nec..."

"No," I cut him off. "Not just for the pizza. For everything."

His head ducked to the side, ear nearly touching his shoulder, eyes soft. "Don't mention it, Jules."

With that, he was gone, leaving me with the tight-chest thing.

Trying to think of anything but that - or the fact that my partner for the past almost two years was a liar and a con - I moved further into the room, finding a small tufted beige chair beside the dresser, sitting down, looking out the window at the slowly darkening day.

Not thinking.

I decided not to think as Kai got pizza, as he came back with it, as he sectioned it off onto plates he'd had the foresight to ask for, as we ate in silence while he flicked restlessly through the TV, trying to figure out the stations, eventually settling on an old *Golden Girls* rerun.

He shifted somewhat uncomfortably in his seat on the edge of the bed, seeming restless with the awkward silence, but willing to allow me it if that was what I needed. "Hey Jules?" he asked as I decided my stomach couldn't fit another drop of grease.

"Yeah?"

"Have you talked to your family?"

My family.

God.

How had they all managed to slip my mind?

"Even just a text," he told me as I hopped up to dig through my purse to find my phone. "Just tell them you will fill them in tomorrow. Today has been crazy enough; I'm not sure you can take anymore."

My pride wanted me to object to that, to insist that I could handle more, I could handle anything that came my way. But, quite frankly, it simply wasn't true. And Kai would know it was a lie.

"Yeah," I agreed, shooting off a text to my mom and sister telling them I would explain everything after I got some sleep, not to worry about me. "I'm gonna take a bath," I declared, digging in my purse to find a small plastic squirt bottle.

"What the hell is that?" Kai asked, brows drawn low.

"Bleach and water."

"You keep bleach and water in your purse? For what?"

"For situations like this," I suggested, rolling my eyes a bit.

"Do I want to know what other random items live in that?" he asked, jerking his chin to my slightly oversized bag. But it was okay. They were still in vogue. I had no idea what I would do if those mini wallet purse things became the *thing* again.

"Let's just say, if the world ended tomorrow, I could live out of it for a solid ten months. Give or take."

"I believe it," Kai said as I moved into the bathroom, taking a deep breath, reminding myself I needed to keep taking them as I scrubbed the deep soaking tub, as I stopped the drain, filled it with steaming water, dropped salts and bombs in, as I slowly stripped out of my clothes, feeling oddly dirty despite the fact that I had bathed twice already that day.

I wasn't sure I would ever stop feeling like there was a film covering my skin, put there by hands that didn't love me like I thought they did.

I sank down in the water, feeling it lap up to my chin, a shiver moving through me despite the overly hot water because a new, startling thought broke through the fog of my brain.

Gary had this *thing*. This *preference*. This *fetish,* in a way.

He only liked to have sex from behind.

He only ever wanted to screw me when he couldn't see my face.

Christ.

How the hell could I have just looked over that for so long? Accepted that even though it wasn't something I liked, it stole the intimacy I so badly craved?

Why had I made so many excuses for him over the course of our relationship?

When had I become so accommodating, so willing to settle for things I most certainly did not want? Or even like remotely?

He fucked me from behind because he didn't want to see the face of his mark while he used her in the most despicable way possible.

Used.

That was absolutely what I felt.

Maybe I had felt that way each time he touched me.

Maybe *that* explained why I hadn't known the sensation of an orgasm in so long I was pretty sure I forgot what one felt like.

Maybe it wasn't stress, exhaustion, a position I hated. Maybe it wasn't those things. Maybe it was because a part of me knew something was off, but the other part of me had been working so hard to suppress that knowledge. Maybe in suppressing that, I'd suppressed my own pleasure as well.

My head slammed back against the porcelain hard enough to rattle my teeth.

I was supposed to be angry with him.

That should have been my dominant thought.

But all that could penetrate was about me.

Anger at *myself.*

For missing the signs.

For becoming someone in that relationship that I didn't even recognize.

Someone weak, compliant, someone willing to give so much of herself that she lost pieces - hell, chunks - along the way.

What the hell would I fill those spaces with?

Self-loathing?

Were those going to be the new pieces of me?

It would be so easy for that to happen.

Effortless, really.

So many women had it happen, without realizing, without even truly being a part of the process.

I'd seen so many women - friends, family members, clients at work - who became shadows of their former selves after something happened to them, something they took no part of, but shouldered the blame and guilt and shame of it all regardless.

They didn't see it happening.

But I could.

I could see it, feel it, and I owed it to myself to stop it, to fill those spaces with something else, something that would improve my life, not destroy it.

What I could fill myself up with, that was still up in the air.

More work, most likely.

Some books about the tricks of conmen, probably.

Some relentless hours at the gym trying to purge these feelings inside that were demanding to come out in the most offensive way I could think of.

Tears.

The ones I blinked back relentlessly, pinning my eyes closed, pressing my palms to the lids, refusing to let any more of them fall.

Better to let them out in sweat.

Salt water was salt water.

I was convinced they were interchangeable.

Or at least I would make them so.

Because I damn sure wasn't going to cry about it.

About *him*.

I didn't use this phrase often but it seemed appropriate.

Fuck him.

Fuck him seven ways to Sunday.

He had gotten my body, my time, my hopes, my plans, my *money*.

He wasn't getting anything else from me.

The water turned cold before I finally climbed out, wrapping myself in a fluffy white towel that was long enough to almost skim my knees as I stood in front of the mirror, washing my face, brushing my teeth, going through the motions.

When life is falling apart, angel, take care of the things you can, my grandmother used to tell me when some minor - or major - crisis would rock our family, leaving most of us feeling powerless. *Wash your face, sweep your floors, make your bed even if all you are going to do is crawl right back into it in an hour. Create order in the chaos.*

That, well, that I could do.

I took care, slathering on the lotion I kept in my bag, brushing my hair free of tangles, slipping into the silk blush-colored shorts I had packed, only pausing when my hands pulled out the matching camisole.

I never had to give much thought to my pajamas before, having lived in a room with my sister, then alone in adulthood, never having to think about things like bras and cool, unforgiving of nipples material.

But I was thinking about my pajamas now.

With a single bed in the other room.

And Kai to share it with.

I was thinking about how my shorts hitched up a bit in the back, creating a sexy cheeky thing if I didn't pay attention. And that the bodice of my shirt scalloped down a bit to show a swell of breast. That the air was pumping in the space. There would be no way to prevent my nipples pitching under the silk top.

Bare arms, bare legs, a hint of belly.

But I only had one other outfit to wear.

For the next day.

A dress.

I couldn't wear a dress to bed.

And I had a moral opposition to wearing my dirty day clothes again after bathing.

I took another breath, hauling the camisole over my head, sliding it into place, deciding I would just roll onto my side facing away, make sure the covers were pulled up high.

With that, I flicked off the light, moving into the bedroom finding Kai had darkened the room as well, only leaving a light on dim over near the door.

He was already in the bed, in a simple white tee, a little loose around his slim body. I had this odd longing to see his inky hair tickling the collar. I never thought I would get attached to a colleague's hair.

The bed - large enough for three people really, seemed oddly cramped as I rounded the unoccupied side, pulling back the covers, climbing in, settling on my side like I told myself I would, seeing some lights through the pulled blinds of the windows.

It was a long couple of minutes of nothing save for the occasional door clicking in the hall, the quiet ding of the elevator, the muffled sounds of a TV in another room.

I hated hearing the noise of a television at night, but I suddenly wished Kai had flicked it on, just to make things less awkward.

But then he finally did break the silence.

"Hey Jules?"

I took a breath, feeling it fill my lungs to burning, knowing his soft voice often came with things I didn't always want to hear.

"Yeah?"

"It's okay to feel about it. I know you've been thinking about it. But you need to feel it too."

My body turned, curling on the side facing him, finding his gaze on me already.

"I'm afraid if I start feeling about it, I might never stop."

"So what?"

"So... no one wants that," I told him, feeling sure of it down to my marrow.

No one wanted messy me.

Everyone wanted cool, calm, collected, in-charge Jules, one that could handle whatever you threw at her without so much as breaking her stride.

They didn't want me falling apart.

None of them.

"I do," Kai insisted.

"No... you do..."

His hand moved out so fast I barely noticed the motion before I felt my chin snagged between two of his fingers, shocking me enough to make me lose my sentence.

"A man you were supposed to spend the rest of your life with, who you thought loved you, who you shared every part of your life with, saw you as nothing more than a mark, stole everything you have worked yourself to the bone for over the past several years, and then left you on your wedding day."

Somehow, hearing it, hearing it from someone who knew all the ugly bits, knew how deep the betrayal went, it made it something. It made it bigger, more real. Took it out of shallow 2D, put it into three dimensions full of bright, Technicolor detail.

It broke down the defenses, put gaping holes in the wall I was trying to hide it all behind.

"Jules, sweetheart, you gotta purge it. If you don't, it's gonna eat you alive."

That was it.

My defenses were stripped ruthlessly away.

The tears flooded and poured before I could even stop them.

A choked whimper burst out of me unbidden.

It was hardly a moment before I felt hands reach out to me, pull me close.

Kai rolled onto his back, pulling me securely to his chest.

One of his arms went around my hips, holding me close.

His other hand went to my hair, gently sifting through the damp strands as I soaked through his shirt, as my body racked with the intensity of the feelings he claimed he wanted me to purge.

I bet it looked a lot like heartbreak.

What he didn't know was he held me through it all was it was anger, frustration, confusion, shame, embarrassment, fear.

There was not even a drop of heartbreak.

Because the deepest, darkest, ugliest secret I would never share with anyone was the fact that I had been ready to marry a man I hadn't been in love with.

Not even a little bit.

-

Flashback - 18 months before -

He wasn't a workaholic by nature.

In fact, his job didn't even demand it.

He was simply meant to step in when a suave tongue and his particular type of charm was needed. To deliver news no one wanted to hear. To land metaphorical blows. Occasionally actual ones. Or receiving them. That happened less than you'd think given that his presence usually meant that everything you gave a damn about was going to hell.

He'd also pitch in on everyone else's cases if they needed a hand.

But he wasn't - in any way shape or form - married to his job.

So why was he suddenly at the office three hours past when he wrapped up his file on his most recent case?

Yeah, that was the question.

And the answer?

Jules.

The answer was always Jules these days.

Why was he happy to crawl into work at the crack of dawn?

Jules.

Why was he happy to be heading stateside again after a job when he was normally a fan of traveling?

Jules.

Kai reached up, pulling his hair loose, having noticed a few weeks ago that she was oddly fascinated with it, had found her watching it, found her fingers curling into themselves like she was trying to hold back from touching it.

There were a lot of things he could chalk up to wishful thinking when it came to the redhead who single-handedly kept the office from catching fire most days.

This was not one of those things.

He knew it.

He'd seen it often enough to be certain.

She was fascinated with his hair.

So he had - naturally, since he didn't have a whole lot of other cards to play - played that one. Always remembering to free the strands from the tie he usually pulled it back with if he was going to be in close proximity to her.

At this time of night, you would normally find Jules at her desk, typing up the handwritten notes everyone threw at her - barely anything more than chicken scratch.

If it was just half an hour later, it would be too late.

Because then she would be moving restlessly around the office, wiping surfaces, straightening magazines, loading up the coffee bar, her heels clicking relentlessly as she did her final nightly rituals.

Jules was a creature of habit.

And she got snippy if he got in the way of her cleaning process, having a system that she didn't like getting interrupted. Not even by help.

So if he missed her between her note dictation and shoulder-roll, he wouldn't get to spend any time with her at all.

Perhaps it was pathetic of him.

To watch her.

To search for windows.

To leap through them when they opened.

Hell, he even felt embarrassed about it himself at times.

But what were you expected to do?

When you found that person?

That one who came into your life just like any other person, suddenly one day, unexpectedly, innocently even.

But turned your entire life on its ear.

He couldn't even tell you why.

She'd been beautiful, sure, but his life afforded him the luxury of seeing countless beautiful women in an untold number of countries.

Beautiful was as common as not-beautiful.

But it was something else.

It was something that made him stop breathing, finding the air hard to inhale because it was suddenly thick with something he didn't have a name for, something that made everything slow down, made a tingle work its way up his spine.

And he knew.

He knew like he knew the sun would rise the next day, like he knew he would have jet lag after a trip to Australia.

He knew.

She was it.

The one.

It was something he hadn't planned on, had hardly been a participant in.

It happened.

He'd been along for the ride.

And what a ride.

So he didn't care that he looked weak and pathetic, that he seemed like some lovesick puppy.

You did whatever it took to spend some time with the woman who you knew you were meant to be with.

Even if she was clueless about the whole thing.

So he stopped at the coffee station, making her a cup while he straightened up a bit before she could see him and yell at him about it, and he made his way toward her desk, finding her sitting there, spine set to steel as it always was. He'd never seen her so much as slouch a day in this office. Her long, delicate fingers topped with perfectly manicured light pink nails tapping relentlessly at her keyboard, eyes pinned to the piece of paper with Lincoln's messy handwriting scrolled across it, at an angle instead of on the actual lines, as he oddly did.

He moved forward, placing the coffee down beside the one she had been nursing for an hour, stone cold no doubt. Pulling a chair over from the sitting area, he reached across to tidy her desk organizer, to tap the papers back inside their file folders, to toss curled up sticky notes into the small bin under her desk.

"I would have gotten to that," Jules said, voice soft. It didn't sound like one, but he knew it was. A thank you. Sometimes with Jules, you had to read between the lines.

"Yep. But now you don't have to," he offered, turning to find her already watching him. He flicked his head to clear a strand from his eye, seeing her eyes watch the motion as his hair moved backward.

Worried about being caught, her gaze flew to his, eyes a bit wider than usual.

Her eye-contact game was generally strong.

With everyone else.

With him, though, it had this tendency to skitter, to flutter, to find other places to land.

But right then, it held.

And her lips parted.

And he could have sworn there was something in her gaze, something unmistakable, something heated.

Something that hinted at the idea that she felt it too, whatever it was between them.

And a hint, well, he could work with a hint.

He pulled in a breath as his hand went to the back of her chair, as his fingers curled in, pulling it slightly, making the wheels bring her closer, her thigh brushing his.

His other hand went on the desk, fingers itching to grab her hand, but wanting to take it slow, knowing this was delicate.

When her eyes didn't break away, seek another target, the lids only getting heavier, he eased his way closer, heart hammering under his ribcage with the anticipation, with the rightness of the moment.

"That mother*fucker*," Gunner's voice yelled from the front door, somehow punching in the code without them hearing, so lost in their moment, making both of them jolt, flying backward, the moment gone, the chance lost.

There were no words to describe the sinking in his gut at that.

And the sneaking, niggling suspicion that he wouldn't get another try.

"I am going to rip his fucking cock off," he added, storming past the desk toward his office.

Kai took a deep breath, trying to find a voice that didn't sound so tortured.

"Fenway?" he asked, looking back at Jules, whose eyes held for the barest of seconds before flitting away.

"Fenway," she agreed with a nod.

Time would tell he was right.

He didn't get a chance again.

She started dating someone right after.

FIVE

Kai

She had cried.

Relentlessly.

Soaking through my shirt, her slight body racking forcefully.

It tapered off after a while, sniffling replacing the quiet sobs.

But she stayed.

She stayed there on my chest, her knee pressing into my thigh, her hand on my shoulder. Curled into a fist at first, then curled into my shirt after.

She stayed there as her hair went dry between my sifting fingers, as my shirt dried under her cheek. As she finally drifted off to sleep.

It felt like I had waited a lifetime to have her just like she was then, on my chest, resting peacefully.

It never occurred to me to specify that I wanted her there because that was where she wanted to be, because she found joy there.

Not because she was hurt, broken, because she needed someone to tell her it was okay, that they would hold her together as she fell apart.

Regardless, I got something I had wanted for a long time.

To hold her.

Even if I had to do so while she cried over another man.

One thing off the bucket list.

She rolled away sometime in the pre-dawn hours, curling up on her side beside me, her backside wiggling against me as she settled, making me need to take a few, deep breaths, reminding myself that I was a good guy, not the kind who saw women in the grips of personal crises as an opportunity.

Sometimes it sucked being the good guy.

Sometimes you got blue balls and a black hole in your chest.

I passed back out, waking up alone with the light streaming through the opened blinds, making me let out a loud grumble, never having been the get up and get going kind of person, preferring to hit snooze a few times, to give my body the opportunity to wake up slowly.

Jules, I figured, was not of the same mind.

I could hear noises from behind the closed bathroom door, the sliding of something across the counter, the clicking open and closed of something. Products, makeup, something. Then the distinct sound of her heels on the tile.

The softer, less guarded, aching Jules was gone. Hidden behind the work Jules.

Maybe I should have felt disappointed. But as much as I liked the unguarded Jules, I liked work Jules just as much. I didn't feel the need to pick and choose which parts of her I preferred. I liked the whole package.

Pulling myself up in bed, I waited as she went through her routine, noticing a low hum of her music likely coming from her cell. Not Miley. Not anything upbeat like I imagine she used to pump herself up every morning in preparation for her long days. It sounded low and crooning. Like country. Which was yet another piece to the Jules puzzle. I never would have figured her for a country music fan.

"Oh, you're up," she declared, stopping short at seeing me sitting there waiting for her.

She chose to pack a simple work dress I had seen her in a few times before, tight but not clingy, in a deep eggplant purple color. I knew without seeing it that it had an exposed silver zipper from the hem all the way up her back and between her shoulder blades. The bodice was cut high - as they almost always were with her work clothes - going straight across her chest right under her clavicles. Her feet were in a pair of nude heels, casual by her standard with only about a three-inch heel. Her hair was pulled back as it so often was, something that should have drawn attention to swollen eyelids thanks to all that crying. But she must have been up long enough to use cold compresses to bring that down. Her eyes were as bright as ever.

"How long have *you* been up?"

"I get up around five-thirty most days."

"Christ," I grumbled at the very idea. "Why?"

"Normally, I might workout, then clean up, make breakfast, shower, get ready. Get coffee. Get to the office. There isn't enough time for all of that if I got up later."

"You have a full day before most of us even wake up. You know, life wouldn't explode if you decided to give yourself some slack, Jules. But," I went on when she tried to interrupt me, "you might *implode* if you don't ease up on yourself a bit."

"Thirty," she said on an exhale.

"Sorry?"

"The plan is to slow down when I turn thirty. When I was supposed to be married, settled in a home, then maybe becoming a mom."

"*Planning* to relax kind of defeats the purpose. And, honey, that is years away still."

"Bill Gates said he didn't take a single day off in his twenties."

She had a planner that said *Hustle hard in your twenties so you can relax in your thirties*.

"What do you do on Sundays?" I asked, knowing she had most of the day off unless there was a big case. She would stop in the office in the morning, but generally only stayed a few hours at most.

"I have brunch with my mom and sister. Then I run errands, get my dry cleaning, deep clean my apartment..."

"Your apartment is immaculate. What could require something called 'deep cleaning?'"

To that, she shook her head as though I was clueless. "Scrubbing the fridge, the oven..."

"But you are never home to cook."

To that, there was simply a look of almost... helplessness.

Like she couldn't help it.

Like she needed to deep clean it even if she didn't use the oven at all.

No wonder she and Finn had always seemed to get on well even though she hadn't forged deep bonds with anyone at the office. When he was going through one of his *spells* or whatever the PC way of describing his tendency to get completely OCD, and clean until his fingers bled every few weeks. She was the only one capable of calming him down when he came into the office to scrub the heating ducts, the bathroom until the bleach smell would make you light-headed, your office without your permission.

In fact, if she was out running an errand for someone, Quin would actually call her back to rein in Finn.

Because she understood him.

Because she had a bit of a compulsion to clean things herself.

"Do you ever just sit around and relax?"

"I read before bed or while dinner is cooking, or waiting for delivery."

"Why don't you have a TV in your apartment?" I asked, unable to help myself. Who didn't have a TV? Even just to watch the news?

"We weren't allowed to have electronics in our bedrooms growing up. Mom thought they made you dumb if you spent too much time in front of screens. And it is too easy to lose hours or whole days with screens. If I really need to watch something, I will go on my computer or laptop. But I usually just don't have the time anyway. Plus, they're ugly," she added, giving me a little smile. "Do you want anything from the buffet?" she asked, going to grab her key card.

"Grab me whatever," I said, climbing out of the bed. "I'll get done while you're gone."

She clearly wanted to get moving. I didn't want to get a frustrated Jules on my ass.

With that, she ran off while I showered, coming back with fruit bowls, granola bars, coffee for her, orange juice for me, and, oddly, a side of bacon. At my questioning look, she shrugged. "I didn't know if the fruit and granola would be enough for you." We ate in mostly silence before she turned to me, bursting out, "What are we going to do, Kai?"

"About what?"

"About Gary. If we track him down. What do we do? I don't think he is just going to politely hand over my money. Not after all the work he's put into this."

"Tell you what. You worry about the diatribe you are going to throw at him. Let me worry about the rest. Okay?"

I knew it wasn't an easy request, that to women like Jules, asking them to just trust you implicitly was just about asking too much.

So I wasn't exactly expecting it when she watched me for a long moment only to nod.

"Okay."

With that, we headed back out to the construction site, finding the boss, Ron, was in as predicted.

"What can I do for you, dollface?"

I resisted the urge to snap at him. Jules resisted the urge to curl her lip. But just barely. We both understood what was at stake here. Her whole savings. Her future the way she wanted it. That meant it all.

Neither of us would risk that.

"Yes, actually. You've been working with my fiancé," she declared, not so much as a hitch in her voice at the word. "About the building of our house," she added, reaching for her phone, producing a screensaver she hadn't changed yet - her and the jackass on the pier, her hair whipping back, both of them smiling, his arm tight into her hipbone.

"Oh, right. Of course," Ron said, not losing the skeezy way he was eyeing Jules. "Matthew. He never mentioned a fiancée."

"Oh, you know Matt. Kind of off in his own world. Anyway. I have a suspicion he did not go with the floors and counters I told him to pick. Would you mind showing me?" she asked, laying on the sweet pretty thick, something only me - who knew her best - knew was utterly fake.

"Do ya want me to just show you the book? Or would you like to go see it in person?"

"Oh, it would be great to see it in person. If you have a few minutes to spare for me."

"Darling, we can take as long as you need," he offered as the secretary typed off something on her cell. "Do we want to bring your..."

"Personal assistant," I supplied. "I'd rather stay here and catch up on some emails."

"We won't be long," Jules promised, just barely stiffening as his hand found her lower back to lead her out the door.

"Ugh, men," Abby declared, flinging her phone into her purse. "You put the lid on the honeypot, and they start threatening to go elsewhere."

"If he uses cheating as a threat, maybe he isn't someone who deserves your honeypot," I suggested, watching as she nodded.

"Damn straight. I'm gonna grab a coffee.You want one?" she asked, waving toward the open door to her boss's office where a Keurig machine was set up.

"Got any hot chocolate pods?"

"Hm," she mused, thinking on it for a long moment. "Maybe. I think we picked some up in case anyone brought their kids. I'll go dig around."

"I appreciate it."

She had barely crossed into the other room before I was up at her computer, doing a quick search for 'Matthew.'

I found a number, took a quick picture of it, and rushed to get back to my seat before she knew anything was amiss.

"You lucked out," she told me, handing me a styrofoam cup steaming and filled almost to the brim with hot chocolate.

"Thank you," I told her,taking the drink, and waiting. Waiting. Waiting.

"Can I say something?"

"Sure," I agreed, glad for something to do other than listen to the clock tick, wondering what that sleazy fuck was saying to Jules, if he was putting his hand on her again.

"I don't know if you have a close bond with your boss or not..."

"We're pretty close," I offered, hoping it would give her the push she needed to say whatever it was she was contemplating.

"It's just... that fiancé of hers..."

"What about him?"

"Well, there's no nice way to say it. But... he's a sneak."

"A sneak?"

"He was sniffing around. Caught him going through some files once when he thought he was alone in the office. And, well, he hit on me." She shifted a bit uncomfortably. "I know sometimes women don't want to hear those things from other women. But maybe she will believe it if it comes from you. If I was her, I would want to know."

"I will see if I have any sway. I appreciate it. I never liked the guy either, but figured I was just being paranoid."

"I just *knew* he wasn't being straight with me," Jules' voice declared as the door swung open. "He picked the subway tile!" she told me, making her voice sound exasperated, but amused even as her eyes looked close to rolling at the way Ron moved in close enough to her to brush her butt with his hip as he moved past.

"Well, no worries. We caught it, darling. I will make a note about the changes. We'll keep it our little secret. You two can have that talk in private."

"I really appreciate it. You've been so helpful. I've given him my number to keep me updated in case Matthew comes back and makes any other changes that I may not have agreed to."

"Good idea. Better to have the argument now than have to live with subway tile for the next fifty years."

"Exactly," Jules agreed. "You about ready? I have that meeting in an hour."

"Yep. All set, I agreed, giving Abby a smile. "Thank you," I told her, waving the cup, but letting my voice fall heavy.

Most people would have kept their mouth shut, let the weird feelings regarding the situation just fester, build into a small sliver of guilt that would nag them at random times. She didn't do that. She said something. The world needed more people like that.

"Ugh," Jules growled as soon as she got in her seat, digging a bit frantically in her purse until she produced a small green bottle of hand sanitizer. "I need enough of this to bathe in," she declared, squirting it into her hands, then rubbing the glob all the way up her arms before working it in between her fingers and palms."Do they make hand sanitizer for your brain?"

"What'd he do, Jules?" I asked, stomach turning over at the potentials.

"No need to put your 'I will murder him' voice on, Kai," she told me, shooting me a small smirk. "He was just your garden variety sleazeball. Tried what he thought he could get away with. Made some gross comments about newlyweds breaking in their home. Nothing too crazy."

My stomach eased up as I handed her my phone. "I got his number. And the secretary said he was a creep and manwhore. She wanted me to see if I could convince you of that before you went through with the marriage."

"Everyone saw it but me," Jules grumbled, looking out her side window before seeming to shake off the dark mood. "So what now?"

"Now I have the number traced. If he makes a call, it will ping on the closest cell tower. Then we can find him."

"If he makes a call."

"He'll make a call."

"But who knows when, right?"

Unfortunately, she was right. The waiting for people to surface part of the job was the longest and most frustrating. Maybe he would make a call while driving, ping off a tower towns or counties away from where he was actually setting up camp. You never really knew.

"Tell you what... we already missed check-out for today. We can hang here one more night, see if he pings, we are close, can track it down. Hopefully track him down. If not, we will head back and wait. This isn't a matter of if, Jules, just when. We're going to find him."

"Okay," she agreed, giving me a curt nod as we turned down the street toward the hotel.

"Jules?"

"Yeah?" she asked as we made it back into the room.

"You need to call your mom," I reminded her, watching as she moved around in a sort of detached numbness.

Angry, upset, even purposeful Jules, I could handle that. This? This cold, detached, automaton? This was bothering me. Worrying me.

Because it would be too easy.

To let this part of her become all of her.

And that would be a goddamn tragedy.

Her mom and sister would be good for her, shake her up, make it hard - if not impossible - to keep up the facade. Even if she didn't give them the real story, she would have to give them enough of it to convince them, to get their indignation up, to force them to get some anger or disappointment, or something, anything out of her.

"Oh, right," she said, nodding, reaching for her phone, looking down at the screensaver for a long moment, face completely blank, before pressing her finger to the home button to unlock it, then scrolling through her contacts. "I'm just going to take a walk around the parking lot," she told me, already moving toward the door, not wanting to share this part of her life with me, something I had no right to be hurt by, but found myself being nonetheless.

So I took a page from her book.

I got to work.

I was only thirty minutes into it when my cell started screaming from its place on the nightstand.

I didn't need to look.

I knew it was Miller.

"Hey, Miller."

"You missed a hell of a party," she declared, voice rough like it always got when she had too much to drink. Jules' dad had sprung for an open bar. "Lincoln tried to run game on two of Jules' cousins. Who both had his number. And long story short, he ended up pants around his ankles tied to a tree in the woods being courted by a curious fox. While Finn cleared plates like part of the wait staff. And - miracle of all miracles, if you ask me - Sloane got Gunner to dance with her. *Slow* dance with her."

"And you had too many glasses of tequila?"

"Too many glasses of tequila? I had no plans of ending up bare-ass naked on a dance floor which we both know would be of high likelihood if I had too much tequila. Smith and I had scotch. Ranger even showed up for a bit, shifting uncomfortably in his seat like the mountain man shut-in he is. He hadn't gotten the news about the wedding being off. So what kept you? I thought you were going to try to make it."

"I got a call. From Bellamy," I improvised.

"Oh," she exhaled, sounding suddenly serious. "Is he reconsidering Quin's offer?" she asked, knowing how doggedly Quin had pursued Bellamy who was just as dedicated to dodging an offer that would fund the entire economy of a country while he bounced around the world like some boxcar hobo.

"You know Bellamy. I need to tread carefully with this. I don't have any answers yet. I might be away for a few days though. You know how this goes."

"I haven't seen Bellamy in years, but I vaguely remember waking up in three countries in as many days because of him."

"I don't want to get Quin's hopes up, though."

"Right. Yeah. I will just say you went to hang out with Ranger. No one will be any wiser."

Since it was damn near impossible to get in touch with him. Most of the time, if you wanted him for a job, you simply had to park in the Pine Barrens then take the hours-long trek to his little ranch to tell him.

"That's a good plan."

"You'll keep in touch? Let me know how it goes?"

"Of course."

"Don't look away from your drink. Lincoln swears he put something in his beer last time they hung out. Ended up in Vegas with a mini pig and no memory of the previous twelve hours."

I chuckled at that, totally seeing it as possible. "Well, can we really blame Bellamy for that? This is Lincoln we're talking about here."

"This is true. Alright. Well, you two have fun. I am going to curl up under a cold compress and moan for the next few hours from all the fun I had last night."

"Bananas and ginger, Miller," I reminded her, having practically needed to force them down her throat after a job in Russia where she was plied with enough vodka to send a man three times her size to the hospital with alcohol poisoning.

"Yeah yeah yeah. I keep them on hand now. Don't end up in a hotel in Vegas. But if you do, I get to keep the mini pig."

"I'll do my best," I agreed. "See you in a few."

I had barely hung up when I heard the bleep of the keycard in the door.

A different Jules walked in than walked out. It wasn't one that I wanted to see, but it was better than the other one.

This Jules was red in the cheeks, was stiff in the shoulders, had her chin jutted up so high that it looked painful.

"How'd it go?"

To that, she exhaled hard, walking over to the window, kicking out of her heels, going up and down on her tiptoes several times to stretch out the aches.

"They're worried about me. They told me how they both - both mom *and* Gemma - didn't like Gary. Gemma likes everyone. She thinks Gunner is *charming*. Gunner. Charming. And..." she trailed off, closing her eyes.

"And what?" I prompted, sensing she needed the push.

"He hit on Gemma!" she exploded, throwing an arm out toward the window, face crushed.

"What?" I snapped, more than just surprised. Pissed. Gemma, who was like a little sister to everyone in the office, who - while she was technically of-age - was way too young, too sweet, too innocent to be hit on by some giant sleaze like Gary.

"At work one night," she went on, turning to stare out the window. "Right under my damn nose. Cornered her at the coffee station, pressed her back against the wall, said something about how convenient all the empty offices were for a quickie."

If I thought I was mad before, it was nothing compared to the way my blood was boiling then.

It didn't take a genius to know how Gemma must have felt right then, trapped by her sister's boyfriend, too sweet to want to ruffle feathers by pitching a fit, feeling lost at what she was supposed to do, how she was supposed to act.

"He made it so my sister didn't feel safe telling me about how he had been inappropriate with her..."

"Hey," I said, voice softer than I felt right then, moving up behind her. "You can't blame yourself for that. You didn't know."

"I should have known."

"How? By becoming a psychic? She didn't tell you, Jules."

"She never should have thought that my feelings for some guy were stronger than my love for her. That was my screw up."

"That's not fair. Your sister knows you love her more than anything. But you know Gemma. She doesn't like to rock the boat or upset anyone. And she knew if she told you, you'd have dumped Gary, and she didn't want to be responsible for that. This isn't on you. Stop taking things onto your shoulders that don't belong there. Pretty soon, you won't be able to carry it all."

"I feel like I am drowning in all of this," she admitted, voice low, losing the rod that was usually implanted in her spine, her shoulders just barely brushing back against my chest. "Just when I start to surface, one more thing comes around to push me back under the water."

The crying in bed episode aside, I didn't know the protocol, didn't know what indulgences she would allow, what she would deem appropriate.

But, unlike all the nights over all the months over the years I had known her, I just plain didn't care.

Taking a steadying breath, half-expecting rejection, I lowered my chin down on her shoulder, feeling her stiffen immediately, then slowly start to relax, actually leaning back into my body in the process. There wasn't even a hesitation before my arm went around her, giving her body a squeeze.

"I'm not gonna let you drown, Jules."

"That's not your job," she told me, but her voice didn't hold that sharp edge to it like it might if we were in a different place at a different time.

"I don't look after you out of obligation. I do it because I want to."

Arm around her lower belly, I could feel the slow, deep breath she took, holding it for a long second before exhaling in a way that made her body shake slightly.

"Why do you like me, Kai?" she asked, making me almost shock back at the words, at the bluntness of them from someone who had always put blinders on and tiptoed around the issue.

"What?"

"Why do you like me? When I haven't done anything to encourage it. When I haven't lead you on in any way."

I paused for a second, unprepared for this, this talk I had been dreading, the one she had seemed so glad to avoid ever having.

What was there to say but the truth?

"I don't like you because you like me, honey. I don't want you because you might want me back. I just like you because you're you."

There was a pause, the room quiet, but my heart was slamming so hard in my ears that it was all I would have heard even if a war was raging outside our door.

It felt like an eternity that we stood there, bodies touching, minds racing.

Her voice was low, barely audible, when she finally broke the silence.

"You don't want me to want you?"

Her head had turned as she started speaking, her gaze finding mine over her shoulder. And I could have sworn I saw things there, things I had only gotten traces of before.

Vulnerability.

And, dare I even think it, desire.

There were no words for the electrical current that moved through my system, it vibrated at the tips of my fingers, my toes, my scalp, a surreal, overwhelming sensation I had never known could actually exist.

"I wouldn't be presumptuous enough even to hope for it, Jules, but of course I would want you to want me."

Her air shuddered out of her again, her lips pressing together then parting as her eyes found mine again.

"Maybe I..."

I didn't need more than that.

I wasn't going to blow my shot for a second time.

My free hand lifted, sliding up her jaw, lifting her chin slightly, hesitating only to see if there was a hint of rejection before pressing my lips down to hers.

A tremble coursed through her body at the contact, making my fingers crush into the flesh of her hip, using it to turn her to face me fully, looping around her back instead, hauling her tightly against me as my head slanted, as my lips pressed harder, feeling hers beneath gain boldness, become demanding.

Her hands, once balled at her sides, rose, both of them looping around my neck, pressing her body more tightly to mine.

A low, throaty moan rose from deep in her chest, vibrating against my lips, ripping every bit of self-control I had left away as I moved forward, walking her back, pressing her up against the wall.

Her gasp gave me an invitation for my tongue to move inside, stroking over hers as desire became a fire through my system.

Jules's hands moved down my back, sinking into my ass, dragging me tighter to her body, my cock pressing hard at the juncture of her thighs. Her body shuddered at the contact, a sensation I had dreamed of for months, for years.

It wasn't until her hands released my ass to snake up under my shirt, her fingers teasing over my skin that a thought was able to pierce through the veil of bliss that was a long-wanted dream coming true.

She was hurting.

And *she was trying not to hurt.*

It was no coincidence that this happened when she had gotten off the phone with her family, learning yet more bad news about her ex.

She wanted to forget for a moment, to get lost in something that felt good.

And while I was fine with being someone that felt good to her, I didn't want to be the regret afterward, the realization that she had acted on impulse instead of actual desire.

Summoning a self-control I didn't know I could possess when it would mean giving up everything I had ever wanted, my lips pulled from hers, my forehead pressing against hers as I struggled to even out my breathing.

"Kia, please," Jules' voice whimpers, hands raking down the skin of my back, sending another jolt of need through my system.

"I'm trying to be the good guy here, Jules," I told her, my voice rough even to my own ears.

Her lips found my neck, her warm breath moving over the skin. "Just this once, don't be the good guy." I was considering it for a split second before she finished the thought. "Be someone else."

My eyes slammed shut as my air rushed out of me much like a sigh because, well, that was what it was.

Because she was just solidifying the sneaking, niggling suspicion that had made me pull away in the first place.

This wasn't about me.

This was about her.

About her pain.

Her disappointment.

Her need to escape.

She would have found that with any man.

It had nothing to do with me.

And my pride could take a lot.

It had taken hit after hit after hit since the first time I met Jules.

But it couldn't take this.

I couldn't let myself be nothing more than catharsis for her when this... this was going to mean a lot to me. It was going to mean everything to me.

And I knew, like I knew the sun would rise in the morning that she would never look at me the same after, once she had gotten a chance to think it through, to analyze it with a clear mind. She would never let me near her again. Partly because she thought it was being kind, not leading me on. And maybe even in part because she was resentful that I took advantage of a weak moment.

Better to deal with her disappointment now than deal with her anger for years to come.

"Unfortunately, Jules, I can't be someone else. I'm just me. And I can't take advantage of the fact that you're acting on hard feelings."

Against me, her body stiffened.

Her hands moved away from my skin, sliding out of my shirt touching only the material of it as her body pulled backward. She took the couple centimeters behind her body and the wall to make sure our foreheads were no longer touching.

"Okay."

Her voice was ice.

Frigid.

A sound I had only heard once or twice before when she and Gunner were going at it.

Pure disdain.

Toward *me*.

The realization was a punch to my gut even as she slid away from me, rolling her neck.

"Jules..." I tried, voice soft as I attempted to grab her wrist.

She yanked almost violently away.

"It's fine."

"Clearly, it's not," I countered.

"I'm a grown woman, Kai. If I say something is fine, it's fine. Let it go."

"Where are you going?" I asked as she grabbed her purse.

"I'm getting coffee," she declared, storming out before I could stop her.

I didn't realize it at the time, but I should have followed her.

Because she never came back.

-

Flashback - 24 months before -

She wasn't blind.

People could accuse her - and often did - of being a lot of things. Stubborn. Detached. Ambitious. But no one would ever accuse her of being unobservant.

She saw everything.

She saw the heavy lids on Smith's eyes, indicating another night of restlessness, nightmares horrific enough to keep him from even trying to sleep.

She saw Finn's bloody fingernails, the way the pads of his fingertips were pruned even after getting to work, suggesting he'd been awake for hours with his hands in bleachy water, scrubbing things that were already clean enough.

She saw the wrinkled mess of Lincoln's shirt, knowing that he had likely crashed on the couch at work instead of at home because he and whichever girl he was dating at the time were on the outs.

She saw the way Miller stiffened when someone mentioned foreign concepts to this crew like family. And love.

She saw everything inside the office that had become like a second home to her.

She wasn't blind.

To it.

To him.

To the way he was overly attentive, the way he noticed things most didn't.

Without her even having to explain them, he seemed to get her moods, the triggers for them, how to help her overcome them.

If she hadn't noticed those things after working with him for as long as she had, you'd have to call her dumb.

She'd noticed.

But she'd also noticed him coming in with bags of foil-wrapped burritos for him and Miller, with cardboard carriers full of coffee from She's Bean Around despite not drinking coffee himself. She'd noticed him picking up mail at the PO box for Quin, picking up Lincoln when he needed a designated driver, grocery shopping for Ranger to bring him things that he could not get from the land in the Barrens where he lived.

Kai, she had concluded a long time ago, was just *that* kind of guy. Kind. Selfless. Attentive. Able to predict what others might want or need.

It would have been weird if he did all those things for others and did nothing at all for her.

"Come on, cut out of here early," Miller demanded, leaning on the edge of her desk. "It's been a long ass week. I don't think any of us have been able to leave this place for more than an hour or two at a time. I am suffocating on the testosterone. You must be too. Let's head out, get some drinks, talk about girl things." She paused there, looking off over Jules' shoulder, brows drawn together. "What are girls things again? I vaguely remember things like nail polish and waxing horror stories."

"I have a mountain of work to do," Jules told her, waving a hand at the files that needed scanning, the loose leaf paper that needed transcribing.

"You always have a mountain of paperwork to do. Besides, it will still be there for you in the morning if you go out for a drink with me now."

"Miller... I..."

She fumbled for the words, to explain the borderline compulsive need she had to prove herself, to deserve everything she had gotten, everything Quin had offered to her.

She'd been green as could be when she walked into the office and all but insisted on the job.

He had given it to her.

Then he had paid her handsomely.

So handsomely, in fact, that people had things to say about it. About how normal secretaries and personal assistants didn't get paid half or even a third of what she was paid, about how there was no way she got the salary she got simply because she came in early and stayed late.

The implication had always been there.

You're clearly sleeping with your boss.

It was insulting, obviously. Even if Quin was great looking and successful. She never would sleep her way to the top of anything.

She would never sleep around at work, period.

It never worked out.

And, without fail, if things went down in flames - as they invariably were sure to do - it was always the lowest man - or, let's face it, woman - on the totem pole who paid for it, who found herself out on her ass for it, without a good reference, without a solid way to get another well-paying job.

She wouldn't risk that.

Even the rumors of it.

Not for anything.

So she kept everyone at a distance.

She worked herself into exhaustion to feel like she'd earned every penny of her income.

Cutting out early was out of the question.

Even if she had been pulling nearly eighteen-hour days all week like everyone else.

Leaving things to be dealt with in the morning was inexcusable unless she was sick.

"I appreciate the offer, but I am going to catch up. I don't want anything else to pile up on top of this mountain."

"Fiiiine. Suit yourself, workaholic. I hear lack of fun ages you, though. Worry lines and all that."

"I've invested in a good eye cream," Jules informed her, smile pulling at her lips. "See, there was some girl talk."

"I guess it will have to do. Maybe Lincoln will go with me. Even if I know he will ditch me for some short skirt at the bar."

"Lincoln headed out already. I think only Kai is left."

"Psh, I'd have better luck convincing a preacher to go out and get trashed with me. Alright. Solo date it is. But if I end up dead in a ditch because I had no one out with me, I expect you to feel guilty as hell."

"It's a deal," Jules agreed, lips twitching as Miller made her way out the door, locking her back in.

An hour later, she was finally finishing up the transcriptions of the ridiculously bad handwriting of none other than Gunner, who she had a sneaking suspicion just wrote so badly to vex her.

She'd just lifted her head from where it had been tucked down near her chest to see her screen, feeling a blindingly sharp pain shoot from between her shoulder blades and up the back of her neck, making an audible hiss escape her as she automatically reached back toward it, trying to ease the scissor-sharp sensation that simply kept rolling instead of easing.

"Got a knot?" Kai's voice asked, soft like it so often was, making her gaze shoot to where he was moving out of the hallway of offices, head dipped to the side as he approached.

"I think someone snuck up and stabbed me in the back," she told him dramatically, smile a little wobbly even as he started to move behind her.

"May I?" he asked, pressing his fingers to her hand that was doing absolutely nothing.

Since her useless hands could do nothing and the pain was starting to make her wonder if maybe she should go and get a scan or something, she figured there was nothing to lose, and moved her hand away, curling both of them into each other on her lap as Kai's hands came down on her shoulders, one staying as an anchor on the side not bothering her, the other searching, searching, intent on a destination she knew nothing about until he found it, making her whole body lurch, trying to get away from the pressure.

"This is gonna hurt, honey, before it gets better."

The words were laced with apology, enough that she almost forgave him as he doubled down on the pressure, sinking fingers into the sore spot, working them in a circle that made pricks of pain shoot off in half a dozen directions, making her hands clasp each other until the skin went white.

But then, slowly, as promised, the pain eased, the pressure became less of a punishment... and became something more.

Something good.

Something that made her breathing deepen, but somehow become more erratic, as his second hand started moving too, sinking in, finding all the sore bits and working them out with deftness, without her having to say a thing about them in the first place.

Soon, the relief deepened, heated, became something else entirely, building in such a way - slowly, gently - that she couldn't see the signs pointing to what they were until a stab of something that was decidedly not pain shot between her thighs, making her breath catch, her heart stutter into overdrive, her breasts get heavy, nipples hardening, lips parting on a silent moan.

A tremble moved through her, and she wasn't sure if it was just internally, or if Kai could feel it as well.

If he did, he made no show of responding to it as his fingers kept working their magic, making a forbidden thought course through her brain.

What else could he do with those fingers?

The shock of that made her stiffen, trying to steady herself with a deep breath. "That's so much better, thanks," she told him, hoping her breath didn't come out as airy as it felt, and stifling a surge of primal disappointment when his hands moved to her shoulders, gave a small squeeze, then dropped away completely.

"Glad I could help," he told her, meaning it, because he always meant what he said. He was one of those people, the ones who were impeccable with their words. And even pure enough to be so with the motivation behind them.

Unless he was on a job, she supposed.

"Are you heading out?"

"Not until you do," he declared, moving off toward the hall as she just sat there, chaos pulsing between her thighs under her desk. "I'm gonna walk you out," he added, leaving before she could object.

Alone, she sucked in a deep breath, looking for composure, forcing her legs to hold her weight as she stood, hands gripping the edge of her desk as she realized there was no stopping the sensation inside, that she couldn't think straight.

Cold water.

She just needed a little cold water.

On that thought, she let herself into the bathroom, locking the door, moistening a paper towel with icy water, placing it at the back of her neck, body shuddering at the contact, but finding no relief from the pressure in her lower stomach, the insistent aching in her core.

Unable to think of anything else, convinced she wouldn't be able to without some relief, her hand found the hem of her skirt, sliding the tight material up until her hand could slip between her thighs.

Her fingers met the wet material of her panties - proof of her aching desire - pressing down into her clit.

By the third circle of the swollen bud, she felt the orgasm rip through her body, making her teeth nip into her lip to keep from crying out, her hitched breath loud enough as it was against the hollow tiled room. Her hand slammed down on the cold, unbending porcelain of the sink as the waves crashed and crashed, threatening to pull her under completely, to refuse to let her surface before she finally managed to pull in a gasping breath, pulling herself back onto solid ground.

She wasn't sure how long she stood there, trying to bring calm back to her frazzled nerve endings.

But when her eyes met her reflection, she saw it there still.

Desire.

Hell, need.

Raw.

Undiluted.

In its purest form.

For Kai.

No.

She shook her head at herself as if to shake the thought free.

No.

It wasn't Kai.

Not really.

It was the touch, the good feelings.

It had been so long since she'd been touched.

Her body had simply reacted, had done what it was designed to do when flooded with feel-good sensations.

It was a response.

Like a knee jerk.

Like a sneeze.

Just a body working as it should when faced with the right stimuli.

That was it.

At least that was what she stood there and convinced herself of for the next fifteen minutes.

And that was what she told herself every time the memory of that night flashed across her mind in rare, quiet moments. In bed. In the shower.

It wasn't Kai.

It couldn't be Kai.

SIX

Jules

I paced the snack area of the lobby for ten minutes, knowing I looked like a lunatic doing so in my bare feet, but allowing myself not to care. Just this once.

There were other things on my mind for a change than how other people might perceive me.

Kai.

Kai was on my mind.

More specifically, making out with Kai was on my mind.

I didn't plan on it.

I'd gone into that room in my sour mood because there was simply nowhere else for me to go. Had I brought my car with me, I'd have gone for a drive, music blaring, trying to shake the anger and guilt and disgust before someone else had to deal with me.

But I didn't have that luxury.

And I didn't want to spend any more time in the lobby area with the employees watching me like I was some kind of lunatic while I talked to my mom and sister in occasionally hushed, then manically loud tones.

"Just... forget about him, Julie-Bean," my mother had told me as we were saying our goodbyes. "Lay on that beach, get some much-needed vitamin D, drink, read, look at half-naked men. And don't think about him."

Don't think about him.

I was sure she was out of her mind as I made my way back to the room.

I mean how could I forget about him when my little sister - the sister I was supposed to protect, the sister who was supposed to look up to me - had been cornered and made uncomfortable by the man I had chosen to marry? And then that situation had forced a wall of a lie between us.

How could I forget him?

But then I had gone back in the room, had started unloading on poor Kai yet again.

And he moved behind me.

He put an arm around me.

He rested his head on my shoulder.

He just kept giving, giving, giving.

Like his well was bottomless.

And I had given him, well, nothing.

The question had burst from me without thought, something I had apparently needed to ask for a long time, but had never let myself do so.

And his answer had done something to me, had thawed the ice I felt building inside, little bits that had been there for years, for decades, but also the glaciers that had formed since the morning of my wedding.

He melted me.

And, suddenly, something that had never been an option, something that I wouldn't even allow myself to think about seemed oddly possible. Seemed almost necessary.

The need overcame me in an instant.

And the second his lips pressed to mine, I knew that I had never wanted anything more, had never needed someone so much.

It overwhelmed me completely, my body nothing but overly sensitive nerve endings just begging for touch.

And all I wanted was more.

Everything.

And then he had stopped it, refused to bend.

Maybe it wasn't fair, maybe it was selfish of me, but all I felt as I walked out of that room was complete and utter rejection.

It was a somewhat new sensation for me.

I had never been someone to initiate anything, so I had never needed to learn how to cope with what it felt like to be turned down.

It was an ugly thing, a gray cloud that worked its way through my system, choking out anything with any light until everything within me felt dark.

I felt the embarrassing sting of tears in my eyes as I finished off the last of my vending machine coffee, tossing the cup, and making my way toward the exit of the building, intent on getting some fresh air while also saving myself the humiliation of crying in public if that proved unavoidable.

Fresh air proved to be a pipe dream as I took a step outside, the humidity assaulting me immediately, making my skin feel sticky within seconds, causing a little trickle of sweat to move down between my shoulder blades as I took a few steps to the side to get away from the valet area.

How the hell was I ever going to go back up there and face him again?

He'd want to talk about it, too.

He was that kind of person.

Not like me, the kind who just pushed, pushed, pushed things down, dealt with the side effects in private.

I hated *those* conversations.

The ones involving feelings, hopes, fears, disappointments.

I had this humiliating tendency to get choked up when I talked about important things.

I'd just as soon avoid that happening in front of anyone.

Especially someone who I would have to face professionally every day until, well, I didn't even know.

But I would have no choice but to go up there and face him.

Whether I was ready for that or not.

Or so I thought.

The blow came out of nowhere, the pain at shattering thing for the barest of seconds before I felt nothing at all.

Because the world went black.

-

Consciousness was a mere suggestion at first, a sliver of light in a world of darkness. But it felt far away, like it would take too much energy, too much effort to drag myself toward it. So I swam in that nothingness for a while, grumbling at the light that seemed to shine a bit brighter with each passing moment.

A low, pained sound escaped me as I made my way toward it, feeling as though it took every store of energy in my body to do so.

And as soon as I got there, launched myself into the brightness, my world was full of pain.

It was nothing short of a crippling migraine , the likes of which I had never experienced before - and I was experienced in the awfulness of migraines - immediately overtaking my whole head.

It started as a piercing at the back right of my skull, but wrapped its painful grip all the way around, making it pound behind my eyes, in my temples, made an aching tightness overtake my neck and jaw.

It hurt everywhere at once, making it impossible to do anything but experience it, fight back the wave of familiar nausea.

My knee-jerk reaction was to raise my hands to cradle my forehead, the pressure the only thing that could stave off the worst of the pain.

But as I tried to do so, I felt the pull preventing movement.

A pull.

And a burn.

I didn't have to have experience with it before to know the sensation.

Rope.

Around my wrists.

Pain momentarily forgotten, my eyes flew open, finding myself in mostly darkness.

But there were things I could see thanks to a small window letting in a slit of moonlight.

A bathroom.

I was tied up in a bathroom, my wrists bound under a floating sink. I could feel the cold, unyielding underside of the sink against my temple, my neck cocked awkwardly to the side to accommodate it.

"Ow," I whimpered, trying to think past the screaming inside my skull, the aching in my shoulders, the crick in my neck.

Kidnapped.

Someone kidnapped me.

The hysteria bubbled up, rampant as a wildfire hellbent on destroying a forest.

I took a deep breath, banking it down, forcing myself to focus, to think, to be objective.

A surefire way to ensure your own demise was to panic in a life-or-death situation.

And a kidnapping, even if you had no idea the motive, was always life-or-death.

Because even if their intent from the get-go wasn't murder, it would be the inevitable outcome. I'd see a face, hear a voice, notice distinguishing characteristics.

Any young guy wet-dreaming about crime in his bedroom at night knew from a few *Cold Case* episodes that witnesses could be their undoing.

And semen.

Semen was usually their undoing as well.

But I couldn't let my mind go there.

Not then.

Not even if that was the logical worry to have.

Rape.

Because why else would men take women off the street?

But I couldn't get so hung up on the terror of that that I couldn't think straight, couldn't stay in the moment.

The moment where I was alone in a bathroom.

Who knew how long I had.

Minutes.

Hours.

But it was time.

Time to think.

Time to plan.

Time to try to escape.

My fingers curled upward at my bindings, looking for the knot, the edge to try to grab, pull, work the restraint free.

If I could get the rope off, I could haul myself out that window.

It was small, all bathroom windows were. But I was slight. I could shimmy myself through.

I could get myself out of it.

To what? I had no idea.

The ground?

Nothing but open air?

Hell, I might be willing to jump, take my chances at shattered bones - or even death - than the fate that might befall me at someone else's hands.

There were things worse than death.

Working at Quin's for as long as I had, reading the true crime I had an insatiable appetite for, I understood that. Viscerally.

I'd rather end up with every bone in my body broken by my own choice than be held down and gang-raped by men who got off on pain and power.

I would make that choice if I had to.

"Ugh," I growled after what felt like ten long minutes of trying to find the edge to the rope with no luck.

My arms arched further up, making me suddenly thankful to Gemma who dragged me to yoga any chance she could get, making me able to twist my body in interesting ways. It was something that proved completely useless most of the time, but just this once, just this once it could help save my life.

Once I got out of here, I was going to treat myself and Gemma to a year of twice-weekly yoga sessions. And I wouldn't back out just because of work.

My wrists turned, letting my hands reach around for what I was attached to, feeling a rush of victory when I felt something other than what I had been expecting - and dreading - a metal pipe, but instead some sort of curved metal tube thing that, while not exactly pliant, could absolutely break. Likely from where it had to be connected to the actual pipes, probably held there by a washer and some glue. If I could just get my arms up a bit further, I would try to work the washer free.

But even as the thought - and subsequent relief - formed, I heard it.

Footsteps.

Slow, steady, like they had all the time in the world, like having girls tied up in the bathroom was no cause for concern, and certainly not for a quickened pace.

Dread worked its way up my thought at the possibility that that was the case. That this was no cause for alarm because this was the norm. That maybe I was at the hands of some psycho serial rapist murderer.

Granted, I hadn't heard of any, and I was pretty up on current events. But this wasn't New Jersey. This was Connecticut. Different state, different crimes, different psychopaths behind them.

Who knew what kind of crazy resided in the *Still Revolutionary!* state.

I had a feeling I was about to find out though.

Panic gripped my system, compressing my rib cage, crushing my heart and lungs, everything that made breathing and life possible as my arms pulled frantically against the binding,my body scooting forward, giving me more leverage as I yanked until my arms screamed, until my shoulders threatened to break, feeling uselessness and hopelessness overwhelm me as I felt no budging at all.

There was a hand on the knob.

A turning.

More light streaming into the room.

On a choked sound I knew I would berate myself for if I lived through this ordeal, I gave it one last desperate yank.

And flew forward a foot as the tube gave, as freezing water started spurting everywhere, covering me, soaking through the material of my dress before I could even wipe the water out of my face enough to see who had moved into the room.

I didn't need to see, though, as things would turn out.

Because I could hear just fine.

"You always were a lot more trouble than you were worth."

Gary.

I shouldn't have felt shock, a punch to the gut sensation I really had no right to feel.

Because, of course it was Gary.

I mean, sure, a lot of crime was random.

A lot of women taken were taken merely because they were at the wrong place at the wrong time while being the wrong gender.

It came down to that a lot of the time.

But in my case, this was the most logical outcome.

I had been actively seeking out a man who had clearly been a skilled conman, intent on stealing back the money he took from me after a long job that had him playing my boyfriend. And fiancé.

It would have been naive to think he would just... let me do that.

But, in my mind, it wasn't just me.

It was Kai and me.

And if we ran into some serious trouble, it would be me and Kai and Quin and Gunner and Miller and Smith and Finn and Lincoln and Ranger.

So I wasn't alone.

I wasn't working alone.

And because of my backup, I had felt stupidly invincible in the whole endeavor.

And maybe, just maybe, there was a naive little part of me that didn't think Gary was capable of kidnapping me, of... what? Killing me?

But that *was* naive.

Because this man had lied to my face almost every single day for years. He had used my body. He had stolen my trust. He had ripped away my security.

He was capable of many things I never would have been able to reconcile against the man I thought I had been sharing my life with.

Had I been thinking clearly instead of fighting through the pain racking my system, instead of trying to escape, maybe I would have come to this very logical conclusion.

That of course if I was being kidnapped, it would be by the man I was trying to track down.

"This is a stupid move, Gary. If that is even your name."

"Of course it's not. Just like it wasn't true that I hated TV and loved healthy eating."

He looked different.

It took me a long time to decide if that was just because the rose-colored glasses were off, was because all I could see when I looked at him were eyes that looked into mine while he lied to me, hands that touched my sister, a body that had used mine.

All that was surely a factor that somehow made me not realize before that his eyes were just slightly too wide set. Which they had to be to accommodate the broadness of his nose - not obnoxiously so, but enough that it couldn't truly be called classical, Roman, but that wasn't all of it.

He looked different because he was different.

The face he kept shaved had a couple days' worth of stubble. His eyes were a deep brown color. I had no idea if the color I had always known was the fake color, or if this was. His hair was darker. And his clothes were no longer what I was used to - the uniform he had used to fool me, based on my personal preferences. No. He looked like some wannabe surfer dude in wine red board shorts and an ill-fitting white tee, the V of the neck pulled wide from over wearing it. You could see chest hair. Some medallion - cheap and golden - was nestled there as well. It was something I had never seen before, but something that looked worn, soft from age around the edges, whatever pattern had been pressed into the surface rubbed nearly invisible.

I didn't know a damn thing about this man standing before me.

And he knew damn near everything about me.

That was a humbling sensation, one that chafed, one that overwhelmed me completely, made me oblivious to the way the water continued to soak through me, made my thoughts too slow to realize I should have been using the time to try to work the rope off my hands now that they weren't tied to another object.

But all I did was watch as he went so far as to turn his back on me to bend down and shut off the water to the sink, soaking through his white tee in the process.

It wasn't until he turned again, face full of disgust - a feeling he was not entitled to because that was *mine* goddamnit, that I could feel my thoughts coming back, that I started working at my hands, finding the rope slipped without burning thanks to the frigid water.

"You could have walked away from this," I told him, angling my chin up, feeling my teeth ache from how tight my jaw was clenched. "If you just gave the money back. They'd have let you go. Move on to con some other poor woman who was too blind to see you for what you truly are. But now? Now, that won't be an option."

"They?" he asked, sneering. "I believe you mean *he*. That poor sap who has been mooning over you for years, and has no idea how fucking dull you are. Think his interest would fade in a flash if he had to sit around and watch you speed clean your already clean apartment every single night of the week."

It shouldn't have hurt.

After everything else, there shouldn't have been anything left that he could use against me to wound me.

But that was the terrible beauty of this, wasn't it? He knew me well enough to know exactly what to say to pry my rib cage open and beat my already bruised heart.

The pain was a sharp and throbbing thing, stealing my usually quick wit, preventing me from finding anything to say to hurt him back.

"What'd you do? Bat your wet eyelashes at him, and he swore he would move Heaven and Earth to get your money back?" He asked, again making it impossible to say anything. But this time, because there was nothing *to* say. That was - whether I had purposely batted or not - exactly what had happened. "Didn't anyone ever tell you it was cruel to lead a man around by his dick?"

To that, I felt myself snort even as the cold started piercing in through my layers of skin, sinking into bone-level, making me wonder if I could ever feel warm again, cursing myself for the shivers that racked my system. "Who are you to lecture me on being cruel?" I asked, eyes shooting daggers at him. I refused to say the words, but he knew them regardless. *After you slept with me, kept a record of all my intimate secrets?*

"I'd say 'Nothing personal,' but that'd be bullshit. It was personal. And, personally speaking, you are a dead fucking fish in bed."

It should have been rage I felt.

He, after all, had no right to even mention the sex that had been nothing but a job to him.

But rage wasn't what I felt.

It was hurt.

And, incredibly, guilt.

Because there had been niggling thoughts in my head right along those lines. Because I hadn't been able to orgasm. Because I knew he knew fireworks hadn't gone off for me. And I had felt this overwhelming sensation of brokenness, of ineptness, like I wasn't woman enough, like I wasn't good enough if my body wouldn't work like it was supposed to, how I wanted it to.

I forced back the hurt, and shot back at him with pure bitterness instead.

"Maybe if you hadn't insisted on fucking me from behind like a dog all the time, I could have mustered up some enthusiasm for you. And, while we're on the topic, my clit is about half an inch higher than where you thought it was."

If he wanted to go low, I could go lower.

And I knew I had landed a good blow when his eyes slitted low, his back tensed. "Never heard any complaints."

"Because I was too busy praying for it to be over."

The next moment would prove to me what a great actor he had been all the time I had known him. Because I had never seen even a hint of violence in him before.

But as we sat in the flooded bathroom, his hand shot out, closing around my throat, fingers sinking in at the sides, cutting off my protests, my air, then dragging me onto my feet by my neck, pulling me off my soles entirely, dangling like a rag doll, like a convict in the gallows.

"Careful," he growled in my face, voice vehement enough to make the words spit onto my skin. "You're not in fucking charge here, Jules," he added, slamming me back against the wall hard enough for my teeth to crack together, for another wave of pain to overtake my skull.

This time, a wave of nausea accompanied it, making me wonder how I could throw up when I couldn't even breathe. My lips were tingling. My head getting fuzzy.

Just when I thought oblivion - both welcome and horrifying - would overtake me, his grip loosened then slid backward, sinking into my hair, yanking viciously, hard enough that I couldn't keep in the whimper, not even to save my pride.

"Yeah, bet that is hard for a control freak like you. But this is my world now. I'm in fucking charge here."

"What's your endgame then?" I asked, fighting back the tears the crippling pain in my scalp was causing. "You know Kai is going to figure things out eventually."

"Yeah, that puppy is the least of my concerns."

That *puppy* walked into heavily guarded compounds, told men toting semi-automatic weapons that, sorry, but they can't have back their wives, children, key witnesses in their murder trials.

That *puppy* stared down men and women far more ferocious than this man before me.

That *puppy* cared about me, would go to *war* for me.

That *puppy* still snarled when you rattled his chain.

I felt a sick, sordid, gruesome need to see him when he broke off said chain, when he lunged at my ex, as he ripped out his throat with his teeth.

"That puppy is part of a pack," I reminded him instead, not letting him know how big a threat I thought Kai could be, not wanting to put Kai in danger until he knew to be on the lookout for it. "They could rip you apart and not leave a trace."

"Luckily, that won't be a problem," he declared.

I didn't know his exact intention until it was too late, until I felt myself jerked forward off the wall, then slammed face-first into the jamb of the door.

But by then, I was unconscious again.

I woke up faster the next time. My subconscious must have been aware of the danger this time, cognizant of the fact that this could very well be a life or death situation, and I really needed to be awake to try to handle it.

Soaking wet still, I knew I couldn't have been out for too long.

The wetness was compounded by something else as I became aware of cinder block walls and dirt floors. I could feel the grit of it down my legs, arms, the side of the face that was resting against it.

Dirty.

I hated, hated being dirty.

I felt the immediate swell of panic, the need to shower.

I tried pushing it down, knowing it was useless to hope for things I clearly could not have, but there proved to be no way to stop myself from shooting upward, ignoring the whirling of my brain, trying to slough the dirt off, only managing to make it rub against my skin, gritty and uncomfortable.

I wiped my hands against a small patch up my side where the material wasn't filthy, deep breathing, trying to think, to focus, to search for an exit.

There were windows, the kind you found in basements, a foot or so long, maybe eight inches wide, enough to let in light, but not to drag myself through. Even if I could get myself up that high.

My eyes drifted over the exposed beams of the ceiling, following them down the unfinished walls, before I finally saw the staircase - wooden, steep.

I pushed myself up, forcing my body to hold my weight, to ignore the pain in my skull, scalp, and face.

That could be dealt with later.

I was halfway to the stairs when I realized I couldn't just... climb them and walk to freedom.

Not-Gary wouldn't have gone through the trouble of kidnapping me if he planned to just run off like he could have if he hadn't taken me.

He would be there.

Waiting.

All-too happy to hurt me some more.

With words.

With blows.

At this point, I didn't know which was worse.

I took myself to the dark corners, finding empty buckets, one half-full can of paint, some rope, and - blessedly - a pile of rebar.

My hands both reached down, taking one into each hand, always preferring to be over prepared than under.

Armed, I made my way back to the stairs.

I had no idea how well I could defend myself, if I had the skills necessary. But there was one thing I *did* know. I had the will. To fight my way out. To beat the man I had shared a life with to get away. To kill him if it was necessary.

It wasn't until my foot hit the somewhat slippery to my wet and dirty feet stair that I thought to look up.

To look up and see what lay ahead of me.

Only to feel a crushing sort of disappointment to find something in the way.

A piece of wood.

Thick.

An old door, maybe?

Laid over the whole opening that could have led to the upper floor.

Pride completely abandoned under my bubbling hysteria, I flew up the stairs, dropping the rebar, slamming at the wood with useless fingers, powerless palms, feeling splinters slide under the skin, yelling, screaming.

It wasn't until I heard him that I stopped.

He was chuckling.

At me.

And that was about all I could take.

My pride, pounded unrecognizable, but still fighting, forced me back down the stairs, grabbing my rebar weapons, sinking down the wall. Once my butt landed down, my pride finally gave one last, gasping breath. A death exhale.

My hands rose up to my face as the tears started, fast, uncontrollable.

And I did all I could do.

I prayed Kai could come and save me.

-

Flashback - 28 months before -

"Does he always growl at you?" Gemma asked, standing at her desk spritzing the roots of her orchid with water.

"Gunner?" Jules asked, distractedly trying to sort through the mess of paperwork he had dropped on her desk. From what she could tell, there were five different ones all shuffled together. He did it to screw with her. He always did. Ever since that *conversation* a bit after she started working there.

"Yes, Gunner," Gemma agreed, and Jules could feel her gaze on the top of her head but didn't look up.

"Ah, yeah. He always growls at me."

"Why?"

"Because he doesn't like me."

"That's ridiculous. Everyone likes you."

"No, Gemmy, everyone likes *you*. I often have a tendency to rub people the wrong way. And he rubs almost everyone the wrong way."

"So... there's been a lot of... rubbing?"

"Gemmy!" Jules half-gasped, half-scolded, finally looking up at her sister.

"Don't look so outraged. I know all about rubbing. And all kinds of other things."

"Oh, my God. Stop. Last month you were still wearing pigtails and jellies."

"Please," Gemma said, rolling her eyes. "I'm not a kid anymore, Jules."

"You're my kid sister. And you are forbidden to do any kind of *rubbing* or anything else that you know all about."

"So you did. Rub," she specified, a dog with a bone on the matter.

"Oh, gross. No."

"Gross? He's gorgeous."

"He's a brute."

"Right. And you can only date people straight up and down. In suits. With impressive resumes and plans for his future."

"You make me sound like a snob."

"No. No," Gemma said more firmly, upset that anyone would think she was being nasty. "It's just... how can you know that that kind of guy is the right kind of guy for you?"

"If someone checks all your boxes, you know they have the same plans for their lives."

"Plans. Goals. How very un-romantic. What if there's a guy. And he doesn't wear a suit. And he doesn't pay into a 401k. Say he grows blueberries, raises baby goats. Say he is always in plaid and jeans and smells a bit like hay. He doesn't check any of your boxes. But he *loves* you. I mean he really loves you, Jules. Thinks you are the reason the sun wakes up every morning? What if the man who can love you best doesn't check a single one of your boxes?" she asked as Kai's office door closed, the shuffle of his sneaker-clad feet moving down the hall until he burst into the doorway, giving Gemma the soft smile everyone was known to do before shooting one in her direction as well.

She looked back at her sister, having to shake her head a bit to brush away some weird fog hanging over it.

"Then I guess he isn't the right guy."

SEVEN

Kai

I knew she needed some space, needed to think things through, but it had been almost an hour.

I was starting to get worried.

I battled with myself for another twenty minutes before I finally grabbed my keycard, cell, and keys in case she maybe took a walk.

It was another thirty minutes later, after searching the lobby, the grounds, doing a quick sweep of the close area she could have walked to that the panic started to grip me.

This was Jules.

She was smart.

Careful.

She wouldn't have taken off somewhere.

Even if she was angry with me, she would have texted at least.

But there was nothing.

I wasn't feeling like myself as I tore back into the hotel, going past the front desk and down a side hall meant for employees only.

And I wasn't acting like myself when my hand just started slamming on the door of the security room.

Impatient.

Frustrated.

Crazy situations, those were my job. I lived on that adrenaline. I thrived on chaos. I prided myself on being able to keep my calm even in unpredictable, dangerous interactions. I could talk my way into whatever I wanted, or out of whatever I didn't want. Without the other person realizing they were the ones giving up things. At least until it was too late anyway.

But I couldn't muster the calm, the cool I would need to schmooze my way into what I wanted this time.

This was Jules we were talking about here.

To hell with charm.

I'd knock the man out and take what I wanted if he didn't cooperate.

The door pulled open, revealing a guy around middle age with thinning blond hair, brown eyes, and a ruddy red rash across his cheeks.

I could talk you up for an hour, get you to show me the security footage without a hint of resistance. But I don't have the time," I told him, watching as he stiffened up, knowing what I was asking was against the rules. "Do you have daughters?"

"Three," he confirmed, chest puffing up slightly. It was a crapshoot going that route. I took a chance thanks to the ring on his finger and the Grandpa mug on his desk.

"How would you like it if one was missing, and some guy behind the cameras won't let you get a peek, so you could see if something happened to her?"

"You look young to be a father."

"The woman I love is missing," I admitted, the emotion leaking into the words, and I couldn't have cared less about that.

Let him hear how raw I felt.

Let him know how panicked I was, how my heart was a frantic base beat in my chest.

"If anyone asks, I'll say you forced your way in," he warned me.

I didn't care.

"I'd happily take the jail time if she was safe," I told him, shrugging as he moved inside, letting me follow, closing the door.

"What's your girl look like?"

I didn't correct him.

I didn't tell him she wasn't my girl.

Because, quite frankly, she was.

She was my girl.

Even if I wasn't her man.

"Thin. Red hair pulled up. In a purple dress and flat feet."

"Flat feet? You two have a fight?" he asked a bit absently as he moved out his chair to sit down.

"Yes. She was getting some air. About... an hour ago. I already searched the common areas, outside, took a drive to see if she was walking or getting coffee somewhere. There's nothing. And the cops won't hear me out until she's been missing for a while longer."

"And any idiot who watches crime shows knows it is usually too late then."

"Exactly," I agreed, moving in behind him to watch over his shoulder as he rewound the footage, catching Jules coming out of our room.

If I wasn't completely mistaken, she didn't look frustrated or angry or shut down.

She almost looked... hurt.

My heart, still speeding, took a hit at the very idea that I had done that. Hurt her. The last thing I would ever want to do.

"Getting in the elevator..." he narrated, skipping from screen to screen, pointing her out like I wasn't as diligent as he was in finding her. "Into the lobby. Getting coffee..."

If I wasn't mistaken - and I wasn't because I was watching her more intently than I ever had before - she reached up to rub at her eye.

To swat a tear, maybe?

Damn if that didn't knock my air out.

"And here she seems to notice everyone looking at her in all her barefoot glory," he went on, pointing to Jules walking outside to get some air.

It wasn't long.

Just after she moved away from the valet, getting almost out of eyesight of the camera.

She couldn't see it, the shadow, being that it was behind her.

But we could see it.

I could hear the guard suck in his breath at the same time I did.

My body braced for it as though it was going to happen to me instead of Jules.

I'd much rather it was me.

But wishful thinking wouldn't change the reality. The reality where Jules had a piece of metal piping slamming down on the back of her head, surely sending pain shooting off for the split second before she crumpled down to the hard ground. There was no sound on the video, but I could swear I heard her land. Hard.

Then the shadow wasn't a shadow anymore. It was a man.

I knew.

I knew before I had any reason to know.

Even though it could have been anyone.

I knew it was him.

Then he was moving into the camera feed like some damn amateur, looking a little different, but mostly the same, leaning down, dragging up Jules's body like it was nothing more than a sack of grain, something he need not take care with. And I guess, why would he start now? After all the damage he had already done.

"Son of a bitch," the guard hissed, already reaching for the phone as he scanned one last time, catching the corner of a car as it pulled away. Not much. But enough for a make and partial license plate. I could work with that.

"Do me a favor?" I half-asked, half-demanded.

"What's that?"

"Don't tell the cops about me until they come here to see the tapes."

"Want to get some time to rough him up yourself. I understand."

"Thank you."

"Go get your girl," he called as I was running out the door, already scanning through my contacts, bringing my phone up to my ear. "I have a make and plates. Give me information," I demanded as soon as I heard a voice.

It was curt and unlike me.

But that was how this business was at times.

There would be no hard feelings. If there were, I'd soothe them over.

Right now, it didn't matter.

Jules mattered.

Only ever Jules.

I had no idea what his plan was. This Gary who was not Gary. And not Matthew. This man who was nothing but a face and some decent acting skills. This man who was no one.

I should have been spending more time looking, trying to find someone who matched his identity. To know what I was up against.

Was he just a conman?

Just a Don Juan, seducing and stealing from rich women? It was an old con, one that didn't have as much footing in these days, these days when most women were skilled internet private detectives about all the men in their lives. But it still happened. And he was young and attractive. He could set up a nice life for himself that way.

Or was it worse than that?

Did he have a different kind of criminal past?

Assault?

Rape?

My stomach knotted tighter at the idea, at the possibilities.

Of what she could be going through.

Because the only reason to take her was to silence her.

And to silence her, well, he knew Jules.

He'd have to kill her.

He'd have to know, surely, that it wouldn't stand.

We'd never let him get away with it.

Me, Quin, Lincoln, Smith, Miller, Ranger, Finn, even Gunner.

Not one of us would stand for it.

If he hurt her.

If he took her away from me.

There wasn't a corner in this world, not a cave her could burrow into, not a rock he could climb under where I wouldn't find him, drag him out, and make him pay.

Slowly.

Painfully.

Bloodily.

I was a good man.

I was careful with my words, careful more with my fists.

But that didn't mean I couldn't use them, that I didn't know how to use them.

I'd never had the happiest of upbringings. My house wasn't filled with love and light. It was full of exhaustion and expectations, parents who worked themselves nearly to death and wanted me to excel in everything I ever did to ensure a better future for me. My happiness was not a factor.

The only relief I had found was in the bi-weekly martial arts classes with my grandfather.

He taught me control.

He gave me an outlet for the frustration I had.

He showed me that violence was the last possible resort.

He told me that men - real men, good men - did not swing first.

But for Jules, I'd be happy not to be a good man.

I'd be happy to take every skill I had ever learned and use it to make her asshole of an ex suffer for any fear or pain he put her through.

But my plan was to get there first.

Before he could do any real damage.

Bumps and bruises and fear - those I could deal with. I could patch up. I could soothe over. I could teach her how to trust men - and herself - again.

She would be okay.

I would make sure of it.

But I had to get there first.

Because if he just wanted her dead, he could have shot her. Right there in the hotel parking lot. Fled. Left the pieces for others to pick up.

He didn't want to do that.

He wanted to be careful.

He wanted to make sure he was long gone before anyone got a whiff of him on the air.

I had time.

Not a lot.

But some.

If I could keep my mind focused, I could find him. I could find her. Get her out of there. Bring everyone else in to deal with the aftermath. Whatever that may be.

My phone rang in the cupholder, making me reach for it with fingers so desperate it slipped through, making me veer off the road with a screech of tires, trying to find it on the floor at my feet.

"Yeah? Tell me you have something."

"Same name. Matthew. He's got all the papers for it. That costs a lot. He must be good at what he does. But all the papers lead to some half-built housing complex..."

I was barely even listening as I threw the car back into drive, as I peeled out onto the highway.

Of course.

Of course that was where he would take her.

It was empty still, abandoned. No one lived there yet, not even in the finished units.

The staff would have left at five like all builders did, then the office workers not long after that.

It would be safe.

Quiet.

No one would be there to see him at all, let alone report it.

No one was anywhere within miles.

No one would hear her scream.

The darkness was the most obvious thing, there being no streetlights, no lamps lighting the driveways or front porches. Not yet.

Darkness everywhere.

I cut my own headlights, knowing a surefire way to be seen was to let those shine around in an area that was meant to be desolate.

I prayed my engine wasn't loud enough to be heard.

I thanked God that Ron had the good sense to have the main road paved even before all the houses were done.

There were so many units.

The ones without walls were written off immediately.

If, by chance, the local cops did patrol this area, he needed to make sure he wouldn't be seen.

So the mostly or fully finished units were the only options.

It could have been any of them.

It would have been smart to be any others.

With no trail leading back.

Not even a fake trail.

But I knew.

I knew which one it was.

I knew it was the one he had wanted to shack up in after leaving Jules penniless.

I knew it was that one because he would want her to pay there, for taking that away from him.

Stealing his little vacation after his *hard work.*

I didn't pull up.

I parked a while away, hidden behind one of the partially built houses. I took off on foot, heart hammering as I closed in on the house. His house. Technically, her house. Since it was her money that was paying for it

Honestly, if he hadn't banked on me, his plan was pretty solid. He could kill her and bury her in the basements of one of the half-finished houses. By the time anyone found her body - if ever - he would have been long gone, likely conning some other woman out of her money.

He knew what he was doing.

He had likely done this before.

Taken a life.

He was being too calm, too collected about it.

Most new killers were impulsive, planned the clean-up after the deed was done.

I came up on the back of the house, seeing a hurricane light on in what was the kitchen, the subway tile looking even more stark thanks to the bright LED bulb.

I saw no one at first from my spot perched right below the window. But shifting to the other side, I finally saw him.

Not-Gary.

Standing beside the island, digging through a black duffel bag, naked down to the waist of his board shorts. His hair looked damp as well.

I stifled a surge of panic that maybe I was too late, maybe he had killed her and showered already.

It would do no good to jump to conclusions.

I moved away from the window, feeling a pit in my stomach at losing sight of him for the couple seconds it took me to get to the steps leading up to the door at the side of the kitchen.

I slowed there, going up careful not to make a sound, wondering a bit fleetingly if he had been careless enough to leave the door unlocked. If he thought he was safe out here in this vacant neighborhood, he might have. For the sake of convenience.

Hell, as if to prove my point, there was a wheelbarrow with the name of the contractors hired to build the houses propped up beside the stairs. This house was done except for a few finishing decor touches. There was no reason for there to be a wheelbarrow there anymore.

If he was carrying a body out, he wouldn't want to fiddle with a lock.

That worked in my favor.

By the time he heard the door opening, I would be through it, and halfway across the room toward him.

So long as he didn't have a gun that could stop me first, I had no doubt that I could take him.

From that angle, I could see him from the side, watching as he started pulling items out of his bag, placing them on the island.

And it was right then I knew without a shadow of a doubt.

This man was a killer.

An experienced killer.

Because he was pulling out very specific items.

Gloves. The long kind that would go up to the elbows. Like butchers wore.

A long-sleeve shirt.

Long pants.

Cheap sneakers.

A hat.

The outfit he would kill her in, then burn or bury, get rid of somehow, someway. Items he likely got at a big box store with cash. Impossible to trace even if they were somehow found.

They would ensure that none of him would transfer onto her.

My skin went cold at what came out next.

A simple, but thick, plastic bag.

See, the way someone killed someone said a lot about them

Guns, they were impersonal. That was why pros used them. It was a quick, efficient way to take a life that involved as much - or as little - contact between you and your victim as you wanted.

Knives could be personal or not. Pros used them sometimes too. They were quiet. The death could be quick if you knew where to sink the blade in. They could also be weapons of passion. In cases of overkill, it was always a knife.

But a bag, that took someone with ice in their veins.

It took a long time to suffocate someone.

Movies made it look fast.

A plot device because the reality was grim and uncomfortable.

It took a good six to ten minutes to suffocate someone to death.

The movies showed the first forty-five seconds of it. While the blood started to flood with carbon dioxide, forcing it to panic, thrash, fight.

But in the movies, that was where it all ended.

In reality, it took about two minutes for the body to slip into unconsciousness, but the body could still thrash. And then from there, you had to stand there holding the bag for another four to six minutes.

You would literally be standing there holding a bag over someone's head for ten minutes.

Ten minutes.

Thinking the whole time because this was not a crime of passion, an impulsive, angry decision. He'd just be standing there, taking Jules' life while he, what, thought about what he was going to have to drink afterward?

He was going to calmly, coldly, determinedly steal Jules' life from her.

Steal her from me.

Not on my fucking watch.

Before I could think more on it, my hand went to the knob, turning it without even thinking to, and charging inside.

Not-Gary's head snapped in my direction. But even as the surprise registered, I was plowing into him, body wedged low, shoulder taking him in the gut, knocking him back onto his back on the unyielding tile floor.

From there, there were no thoughts.

Just actions.

Blows.

Taking some.

Giving more.

Until I became aware of the open bleeding of my knuckles, the pain in my fingers, the fact that I was just bashing in a face attached to an unconscious body.

Not wanting to take any chances, I dug through his bag, finding rope, taking a moment to truss him up like a pig, finding - predictably at this point - duct tape in the bag as well, putting some over his mouth.

I would worry about him later.

I had to worry about Jules now.

Grabbing the hurricane lantern, I moved through the house, checking the rooms one by one, finding nothing but a mess in the first-floor bathroom, the tubing pulled out of the wall, water pooled on the floor.

I almost missed it in my rush to locate her.

But as I turned to head out the door, the light caught the red.

Blood.

Jules' blood.

My stomach tensed as I tore through the upstairs, panic welling up more and more by the minute.

Nothing.

There was nothing upstairs.

Nothing downstairs.

I stopped mid-stride as I went to double-check the main floor rooms again.

The basement.

She had to be in the basement.

I opened closet doors, looking for the stairs, finding nothing.

Until I was back in the kitchen, pulling open what appeared to be a pantry. Oddly, the floor leading to it was a thick sheet of wood. With a pull handle.

Curious, I reached to pull it up, finding there was a lever attached to the wall to pin the door up so you could descend.

To the basement.

There was a cautious surge of relief in seeing it, but the bigger part of me knew not to get too excited, knew there could be bad news below. Or no news at all.

My footsteps sounded thundering as I rushed down, lantern lifted, swinging it around into the dark space, not able to breathe at all.

Then I heard a scraping. Like something scratching against the cinderblock walls.

My arm swung out, thrusting the lantern in that direction, feeling my heartbeat skitter into overdrive as I saw a shadow. And then a figure.

Jules.

In my mind, I said it out loud.

But I guess I didn't.

And I guess the lantern cast me in shadow.

Because as I got close, I felt something swing and land across my center, knocking my breath right out of me.

"Jules."

That time I did say it aloud, hearing a gasp of inward breath followed by a weak voice. "Kai?"

I lowered the lantern as I closed the last step, going downward into a squat.

"It's me, honey," I confirmed, taking my first real, deep breath before using the lantern to check her out.

Her nose had a bit of dried blood under it. Not enough to worry it was broken. There were shadows under her eyes that would easily turn to black eyes in just an hour or so. Her eyes were small and pained, likely from the blow from behind, the one that had knocked her out.

She was drenched, her hair wet, her dress plastered to her.

And, what was likely bothering her most of all, she was filthy.

The dirt floor and her wetness had made a mess of every inch of skin. There were swirls in it where she had seemed to try to wipe it off. To no avail.

When my gaze when back to her face, I saw her eyes fill. Her lip quiver.

I put the lantern down beside her, reaching into my pocket, dialing without thinking.

"Kai!" Bellamy's voice called, laughing, happy, carefree. As it usually was. Until it wasn't. When people like me called with words like the ones I was about to say. "How the hell are you?"

"I need you," I told him, voice grave as I felt. Making the decision I was making. It wasn't something to take lightly.

"Shh," he said to whomever he was with, likely a harem of women, as per usual. Just another day in his life.

"I told you... I'm not working for Quin."

"Not for Quin. For me."

"For you?" he asked, voice going more serious. "Are you sure? Have you thought about this?"

"Someone kidnapped and beat Jules after pretending to be her boyfriend and fiancé, then stealing all her money, and leaving her on their wedding day."

"Your Jules, huh?" he asked, knowing the rumors, because no one could seem to shut up about them.

"Yeah," I agreed.

"Alright. Where?"

"Are you in the country?"

"In the city," he affirmed, making me relax slightly. It was a crapshoot with him. He could be in New York... or he could be in Amsterdam. You never knew from one day to the next.

"I need you in Connecticut. I left a present on the floor in an abandoned building. You only have until sunup. Maybe take him to visit Ranger."

"Got it. It's done. Consider it handled."

"Thank you."

"Don't mention it."

With that, he hung up, all the fun and light out of his voice, slipping into work mode.

"I hit you." Jules' voice sounded slight, airless.

"I'm fine. Those are some good reflexes, honey," I declared, trying to give her a smile. "Your head hurt?"

"I hit a wall. And um... something hit my head."

"Yeah, I saw that part. Cameras," I specified. "You ready to get out of here? Get some migraine medicine in you?"

"Gary..."

"Don't worry about Gary. Can you walk?"

"Yeah," she agreed, reaching outward, going to grab my hand, only to yank back on a hiss.

"What, honey?" I asked, reaching out for her wrist, trying to turn her hand to look at her palm.

"Splinters," she told me, taking a deep breath. "From..."

"Pounding on the door," I finished for her. "You little fighter, you. Okay, here," I offered, releasing her wrist to turn slightly, putting an arm around her waist, pulling until she got onto her feet, then grabbing the lantern, and helping her toward the stairs.

She said nothing as we went out the front door, me steering her that way because I didn't want her to see her ex trussed up on the kitchen floor, because - maybe - I didn't want her to look at me differently because of it.

"Alright. I couldn't stop the security guard from calling the police, so we are going to have to deal with that," I told her as we got to the car. "No, don't stiffen up. Let's keep it simple, yeah? You were hit over the head. You woke up in a in the woods. Got splinters from pushing yourself up. Got dirty from the forest floor. You don't know how you got wet."

"You want me to lie to the police?"

"You *need* to lie to the police," I clarified, turning over the engine, pulling back out with my lights off. "We can't have the truth getting out."

"Right," she agreed, taking a breath, holding it, then letting it out like a sigh.

"Can you do this? Do you want to go to another hotel for the night? Deal with it tomorrow?"

"I want it over with," she told me immediately. "I just... I want to go home," she added, voice uneven.

"Okay. We will deal with this now then."

"How did you find me? In the story for the police?"

"You were walking along the highway trying to get help."

"Right," she agreed, nodding, taking another deep breath.

"It will just be a couple minutes. If they push too much, get hysterical. Cry. Say you want to shower. Say you can't talk about it anymore. They will let it drop."

"Okay," she said, nodding, not sounding too confident. But I knew Jules. She would rally. She would hold it together enough not to fall apart.

Then I would be there for her when she lost what was left of that control.

There was - as expected - a cop car parked out front, engine cut, the officer inside talking to people at the front desk.

"Take a deep breath," I reminded her as I pulled to a stop, jumping out to open the door for her.

For the next hour, she was questioned, re-questioned, made to go over the story half a dozen times to well-meaning and invasive cops who tried time and again to get her to go to the hospital, to get a rape kit since she was unconscious for a period of time, not knowing what happened to her.

I was pulled a few feet away, questioned, re-questioned, and deemed useless. By design.

The detective talking to me was just thanking me for my time when I heard it.

Sniffles.

I whipped around, finding Jules hunched forward, the backs of her hands to her face instead of her injured palms, body quaking.

"I can't do this anymore," she cried, and it seemed that only I could tell it was fake as I rushed over to her, putting an arm around her waist, pulling her toward me.

"Do you guys have enough? She needs to rest," I told them."

"Yeah," the main detective agreed, nodding. "I think we have enough to go on. Here's my card. Please have her call us if she remembers anything else."

A few minutes later, the cops were gone, and I was leading Jules to the elevator.

"I hope he pays for this," the security guard called as we moved inside.

"He will," I promised as the doors closed. "Okay," I told her as we got in the room, feeling her take a relieved breath. "I know you want to get clean, but we need to deal with these hands. And maybe the back of your head, okay?"

She swallowed hard at that. "Okay."

"I just need to see what I can find to try to get..."

"There are tweezers in my purse," she declared. "And a small first aid kit."

"Okay. Go on and rinse with some warm water and soap. I will be right in."

"Give me something, Jules," I demanded fifteen minutes later, angling her hand around at the light to make sure I got all the gnarly, thick splinters.

"Something what?" she asked, voice hollow.

"I don't know, honey. Just something. You're full on automaton right now."

"I'm *so dirty*," she declared, voice desperate, but also a bit self-deprecating, enough so to make me let out a chuckle.

"Well, that is one thing we can fix," I told her, standing to turn on the shower. "Clean up. But don't scrub your head. The cuts won't need stitches, but you won't want to be rubbing your fingers in open wounds."

"I have nothing to wear," she told me as I moved around, getting towels and washcloths.

"I will grab you a shirt. I have a few packed. Are you hungry? Want me to try to order up? Or in if the kitchen is closed?"

"You know what I want?" she asked as I came back in the room, finding tufts of steam heavy in the air already.

"No, what?"

"Hot chocolate," she declared with a wobbly sort of smile, one I never would have imagined she could have, but did.

I smiled back, feeling my heart - already full of her - overflow a bit. "I can handle that."

"Hey, Kai," she called, making me turn back to find she had already freed her zipper most of the way down her back, her pale pink underwear slightly visible. How she managed to get that damn thing down was beyond me.

"Yeah?"

"Thank you for coming for me."

"I will always come for you, Jules," I told her, voice heavy, watching as something came over her eyes, something I didn't know well enough to recognize, but it made something heavy settle on my chest. But heavy in a good way, if that was possible. "Always," I affirmed, closing the door behind me as I went out, fetching her hot chocolate, finding her just turning off the water when I got back.

It was several long minutes later before she emerged. Wearing my white tee, her red hair dropping little watermarks on the shoulders.

Seeing her in my shirt was like a punch to the gut, everything within me screaming how *right* it was.

But one look at her face, the pain in her eyes, the bruises under her eyes, the gauze wrapped around her hands, reminded me that this was not under the circumstances that anyone could call *right*.

"Come on. Got your hot chocolate with a Excedrin Migraine chaser," I told her, waving to her side of the bed.

I watched as she moved there numbly, took the pills with her hot chocolate, then climbed under the covers, sitting upright against the headboard.

"Hey Kai?"

"Yeah?" I asked, watching her profile until she turned to face me.

"Who was on the phone? Back in the basement?"

I hesitated, taking a breath, wondering if I had made a mistake.

Calling him.

Siccing him on her ex.

I'd acted out of rage at seeing her hurt at his hands.

But, I reminded myself, he had been planning to kill her.

Slowly.

Painfully.

It had been the right move.

Even if admitting that to Jules was going to be one of the hardest things I had ever done.

Even if by admitting it, Jules would never look at me the same again.

I took a deep breath, keeping eye-contact.

"Bellamy."

There.

It was out.

Jules had never - as far as I knew - met Bellamy. But that didn't mean she didn't know who he was, what he was, what he did, why Quin wanted him on the team.

Because, well, Bellamy had a title like all of us did.

Bellamy was known as The Executioner.

-

Flashback - 30 months before -

"Stop it."

Gunner's voice was growly and threatening as it often was, making Jules' head jerk up to find him standing at the front of her desk, hands curled into fists, fists resting on the surface. Everything about him said *Be intimidated.*

Maybe a small part of her was.

It was hard, at times, not to be.

Not just with Gunner, but with almost everyone in the office. They were all just from such different worlds, acted in ways that sometimes didn't make sense to her, used language that made her feel like some eighty-year-old trying to translate the slang of their great-grandchildren. And each one of them had skills, had dark, murky pasts, had the ability to make actual people completely disappear, make crime scenes impossible to pin on someone, make scary men with guns agree to deals they didn't want.

They were a scary bunch.

They were a constant reminder of her very normal upbringing, of her lack of street smarts, of her naivety about some of the uglier parts of life.

She was a fast learner, luckily, and had picked up so much so quickly.

She found out that while Quin sometimes got snippy, he was never ill-intentioned. Just demanding. Just someone with high expectations.

Lincoln was a sweetheart who genuinely loved women. *All* women.

Smith was quiet in a severe way, but never so much as raised his voice at her. Not even when she tripped up a few times in the first weeks after she'd started in the office.

Finn was also quiet and compulsive, but shy, even if he sometimes gave her the creeps given that he was usually called in to make bodies disappear.

She hadn't met Ranger yet, but accounts of him seemed to suggest he was more standoffish than aggressive.

Miller had been quick to help her around the office, never with a mean word.

And Kai, well, Kai was just a sweetheart.

But Gunner, Gunner still managed to intimidate her. She tried her best to hide it, never to shock back if he growled, never cringe when he went off on some curse-filled rant.

Maybe a part of it had to do with how he looked. He was tall and burly, covered in tattoos. He carried himself like he would beat the hell out of you if you so much as stepped in his path.

But he was the one who still made her have to work not to show her fear.

And leaning over her desk like he was, glowering down at her like he was, growling at her like he was, she couldn't seem to stop the way her stomach knotted, the way her shoulders squared, preparing for whatever was to follow.

"Stop what? I'm color coding files," she told him, waving the multi-colored stickers in front of him.

"You know what," he insisted, brow raising like he found her exasperating.

And, to be fair, he probably did. Seeing as he always raised his brow at her like that. Something about her had simply rubbed him the wrong way since the first day she started. Or maybe he just didn't like anyone. Which was a definite possibility. He didn't exactly have a ton of friends.

She tried not to take it personally.

Her job was to keep his files straight, bring him coffee, not be his buddy.

She did her part.

She figured she would adjust to his abrupt way of dealing with her eventually.

"Clearly, I don't," she said, shrugging.

"What was going on with you and Kai?"

"Me and Kai? Nothing."

"Bullshit." The word cracked across the empty space, enough that she couldn't stop her head from jerking back slightly like she'd been hit.

"I'm sorry?"

"I walk out, and he is helping you file. After bringing you salad for dinner. After clearing off your desk while you were talking to Quin."

"He's a nice guy," Jules insisted.

"He is," he agreed, nodding. "And you need to stop fucking with him."

Her brows drew together at that. "Fucking with him?" she repeated, hoping the curse didn't come off as unnatural as it felt to her. Gunner was the type to respond to harsh language since he used it so freely himself. And while she wasn't a fan of cursing like some dock worker, she understood that, with him, she needed to do it to have impact.

"Yes, fucking with him. Don't play dumb, duchess. We both know you aren't."

Well, that was the closest thing to a compliment he had given her. And while it was only a scrap, her pride stole it to feast on.

As pathetic as that maybe was.

"I'm not playing dumb, Gunner. I don't know what you're talking about."

"For reasons completely fucking beyond me, that kid has a thing for you. And I'll be damned if I stand by, and watch you lead him around by his dick because you like having him do shit for you. Get a fucking boyfriend. Leave Kai alone."

Her mouth opened and closed, a fish seeking oxygen.

But it didn't matter that she couldn't find the words to say anyway.

Because Gunner had tore out of the office, slamming the door behind him.

She lowered herself down into her seat, taking a deep breath, trying to fight the frazzled feeling on her skin, the same sensation she remembered feeling all through her childhood and adolescence when an elder scolded her.

But while Gunner was surely a few years older than her, he was not her elder.

And he was not her boss.

And he had no right to speak to her that way.

She'd be damned if she let him do so again.

"Was Gunner yelling?" Kai's voice asked, moving out into the reception area with her, his hair down where it had been up when she'd seen him a few minutes before.

"Yes."

"At what?"

"Me," Jules told him, standing again, her spine set to steel, determined not to let his little outburst ruin her night. Or her love of her job.

"He was yelling at *you*?" Kai asked, voice taking on an edge she hadn't heard before. Almost, maybe, like anger.

She looked over at him, wondering if maybe Gunner was right. He was sweet on her. She'd figured he had just been sweet. It was possible she was wrong. She hadn't ever been great on the picking up on subtle signs thing.

"Yeah. We had a disagreement."

"I'll talk to him," Kai insisted, already moving toward the door, intent on catching up with him.

"What? No. It's fine."

"It's not fine," he insisted, turning back, giving her an almost hard look. "It's fine if you two disagree, but it is not fine for him to yell at you loudly enough for me to hear it in my office. Case closed, Jules."

With that, he stormed out as well.

Things with Gunner never really recovered.

And because she didn't know quite how to handle the idea of Kai being sweet on her, she chose the easiest option.

Denial.

EIGHT

Jules

Kai was having not-Gary killed.

Those words didn't seem to go together. Not even in my mind.

Kai was all love and light and goodness.

And while the stories of Bellamy could say the same, everyone else knew the truth. There was a well of darkness inside that went deep.

Maybe the truth could be said of Kai.

Even if that made my stomach feel swirly and uncomfortable.

I had no right, of course.

I worked with killers.

Quin, Smith, Lincoln, Ranger, Finn. They'd all been in the military, had all killed people. Likely many people. And while she never went as far as to say it, Miller had most likely done so as well.

I don't know why I figured Kai would be the exception to the rule in the office.

Maybe there was blood on his hands.

In this case, of course, the blood wouldn't be directly on his hands.

He was bringing in Bellamy.

He was contracting the job out to an expert.

"Kai..." I heard a mix of worry and maybe even a hint of disbelief.

"He was planning to kill you, Jules," Kai told me, closing his eyes for his exhale, like he was trying to push an image away. "He had been pulling out all the items in the kitchen when I came by. If I was so much as five minutes later..."

"You weren't," I comforted him, placing my gauze-wrapped hand on his arm, watching as his gaze went there, held for a long moment before coming back to my face. "How was he going to do it?"

"Jules... no."

"Tell me. How was he planning on killing me?"

"It doesn't..."

"It does," I cut him off. "It matters."

"He beat you over the head with a pipe. He slammed you into a wall. From the looks of your wrists and throat, he choked you and bound you. Why does this one detail matter after all of that?"

"Kai..."

He sighed at that, and I knew I had gotten what I wanted. "He was going to suffocate you with a plastic bag."

I felt those words land, sink slowly in, swirl around a bit while I mulled the implications of them, while I swallowed back the terror of them.

Five minutes.

If he had been five minutes later, I would have had a bag over my head, desperately trying to fight as my air got lower and lower.

"He must really have resented me," I mused aloud, somehow feeling the need to share the thoughts - not something I was overly prone to doing. But with Kai, I guess it was different. Because he had been on this crazy ride with me. Because he had seen me at some of my lowest lows. Because I knew I could trust him not to share this with anyone else.

"Jules, no. He's just a sick..."

"No," I cut him off again, shaking my head slowly. "He did. He really despised me, Kai. The way he talked to me," I went on, swallowing back the bitter coating on my tongue. "He wasn't cold and detached, just annoyed that I was a loose end he had to tie up. He wanted to hurt me. He wanted his words to cut me. And he knew me, so he knew exactly what to say. He threw me in the dirt-floored basement soaking wet because he knew how much I hate being dirty. On top of all that, he wanted me to suffer to death. Not just die. Death doesn't have to be slow and agonizing. But he wanted that for me. This was personal to him. He really hated me."

I wasn't sure why that bothered me.

I had always been somewhat unshakeable in my idea of my self-worth. Not because I was cocky, but because I knew what I was worth. I knew I worked hard. I knew I was smart. I knew I was loyal and dedicated and attentive.

And because I knew all that, I felt I deserved a good man. Because I thought I was a good woman.

It shouldn't have gotten to me that he hated me.

But it did.

It wiggled inside, making my heart feel low and heavy, making my stomach sink.

If someone who had shared my life with me for so long, who I had given all of myself to hated me so much... what did that have to say about what I had to bring to the table?

"Look at me," Kai's voice cut into my admittedly somber pity-party. "If he hated you, that was on him. Not you. You're amazing. Anyone who has met you knows that, thinks that. You can't be faulted for his terrible taste." He paused, watching me, reading me, and I knew what he was seeing. That I wasn't convinced. That I was about ready to use my own pride as a piñata, beat myself up, watching as little endless bits of insecurity fell out. "Don't be that girl," he demanded oddly, making my brows crease.

That girl.

Those were never good words.

I stiffened at the idea of him using them.

But this was Kai.

So he got the benefit of the doubt.

"What girl?" I asked, hearing the hesitation in my voice.

"The girl who takes some guy's damage and takes it on as her own. People have all kinds of reasons for being how they are. Maybe his mom used to beat his hands with a ruler if his bedroom wasn't clean enough, and your preference for neatness reminds him of that. Maybe his mom was a career woman who valued her work more than time with him. Maybe he sees your ambition as that cycle repeating. Or maybe he is just a heartless bastard who hates women, enjoys manipulating and hurting, and even killing them. Maybe that was a sickness he was born with. But whatever it is, it's his. It's not yours. Put it down.You weren't meant to carry it."

I felt stinging in my eyes, knew they would be swimming at any moment.

I wasn't a crier.

But Kai could do that, get to the heart of me. Why? I didn't know. I just knew it was true.

Drawing in a shaky breath, I leaned forward, my forehead pressing into his upper arm.

And I said them.

The words I felt down to my soul.

"I don't deserve to have you in my life."

"Stop," he demanded, voice soft, hand giving my shoulder a squeeze. "Don't say that. It's ridiculous. You're tired. And - whether you will admit it or not - hurt. Physically and emotionally. You need to rest. You'll be thinking - and feeling - better in the morning."

I didn't quite believe him, but pressed my lips together.

Because this wasn't some new development, this idea of Kai being too good.

It was something I had felt - known - for a long time.

Nothing I had done in life made me deserving of the kind of unwavering love he seemed to feel toward me.

It was - to be perfectly honest - intimidating. Overwhelming.

I wasn't sure I had any right claiming it.

It belonged to someone softer, sweeter, someone less rigid and ambitious, someone who knew how to relax and didn't run their entire life based off of lists and ideas of how things were *supposed* to go.

I mulled on that as Kai's breathing went deep and steady, as his body relaxed.

It wasn't for another twenty or so minutes after that that I lifted up my head, balancing on my forearm to look down at him.

My hand moved out without even being aware of it at first, reaching upward, sinking into the short strands of his hair.

I hadn't ever admitted it aloud, but it was a little secret inside my head.

I loved his hair.

Not so much like this.

But how he liked it, how he usually kept it.

Longer.

Framing his face.

Inky black and so soft looking that your fingers itched to sift between the silky strands.

I had this odd fetish of enjoying catching him tying it up. Or pulling it down.

Weird? Yes.

Because I never liked long hair.

I found it unflattering and stringy. It reminded me of dirty bikers or wannabe metal singers.

It just wasn't my cuppa.

But on Kai, I dunno, it always did it for me.

Seeing it cut had been shocking, a jolt to my system. The shorter cut showed off his rather strong jaw. It made him look older and more professional.

But that wasn't Kai.

And I missed that Kai.

The Kai before I did ugly things to him. Before I chose another man over him. Before I agreed to marry someone other than him, spend my life with someone other than him.

He'd cut it the night before the wedding.

I'd seen him on Saturday.

I had dropped into work.

He'd been there, long hair up in a loose bun.

So he had cut it because of the wedding.

It felt arrogant to even think that, but I was pretty sure it was the truth.

I had made him feel like he needed to be something different.

I wasn't sure I could ever forgive myself for that.

It wasn't done intentionally, maliciously. I didn't get my jollies off watching someone like me from afar, and get hurt when I dated someone else.

I had just been so wrapped up in my plans, my goals, my dream of how life was supposed to be.

I was, by nature, practical.

Not romantic.

That was all Gemma.

God saved all the romancey, roses and butterflies stuff for her while I got all the seriousness, the practicality.

Not even when I was a teenager, when I should have been sappy and silly about boys, all I could think of was who was going to have the better future, which boy was going to get a good job, make a good husband, provide well for his children.

I dated the boy most likely to succeed. Not because I felt my heart flip-flop over him, but because it was the most logical choice. We fit. On paper, we fit. He was most likely to succeed; I was valedictorian.

I hadn't gotten all sentimental about the dating milestones either.

The first date involved both of us explaining our plans and goals, what we wanted to do and by when.

Losing my virginity wasn't fraught with worries and demands for his happily ever after. It had just been sex. A natural progression of our relationship.

And when I had, stupidly, put all my eggs in one basket, only applying to Yale because that was where I was sure I was meant to go, where I worked so hard to get, and he got in... and I didn't... I didn't sob and rip my heart out because we broke up, both knowing it was useless to try to carry on a relationship from a distance.

So he left.

I rallied.

I worked.

Then I demanded a job at Quin's because it seemed like it would pay well, all the while telling myself that I would go back to school, would get my degree.

But then there had been no reason to. Because Quin paid me more than I could ever hope to make unless I became some big time CEO. And that would likely take a decade. Well, probably two because I was a woman.

You'll have to be twice as good. And it will still take you twice as long.

My grandmother had given me that advice, having worked up to head secretary at a large marketing firm back before she married my grandfather.

She used to regale me with stories of her male employers' inadequacies, how they couldn't use a typewriter to save their lives, how they had no idea how to brew a pot of coffee, how one genuinely did not know how to make his own phone calls.

My grandmother had been smart, skilled, deserving of much more than that company would ever give her. Simply based on her sex. And while times were better, they weren't where they should be.

She'd been right.

If I went that CEO route, I wouldn't have made the money I was making now until I was around forty. And if I wanted children - and I did - that might be out of my reach for longer still.

I had hit the jackpot with my job.

Not getting accepted to Yale and losing my high school boyfriend had been the best things that had happened to me.

According to my life plan, that is.

For my life as a whole, well, I guess I didn't really even have one of those.

It was something I chose not to think about too much, knew I would get down on myself for if I did. So I stayed busy.

It was only in very quiet moments. Like in the shower. On the way to work. right before bed. It was only then that I remembered something.

Busy did not mean happy.

Successful did not mean fulfilled.

I hadn't been to a movie in years. I hadn't gone out for drinks in just as long.

I had no idea, genuinely not a clue, what satisfied me, what brought me joy.

Not pleasure.

Because it *pleased* me to have a full bank account, to have my bills paid, to be able to go shopping if I wanted to, to have a clean home, and the respect of people at work.

But pleasure was a superficial thing.

Joy was lasting.

Joy was that thing that made you smile as you went to bed, when you got up in the morning.

Joy was a foreign concept to me.

Gemma thrived on it.

My parents found it in each other.

My grandmother found it in her kids, her husband, her garden.

But me?

I didn't know what brought it to me.

I had no free time, no hobbies.

I had no children.

And I didn't really, truly understand what love was.

Ugh.

That felt sad even to think.

But it was true nonetheless.

My partners had been chosen logically. My heart had nothing to do with it.

Sure, I *loved.*

I loved my parents, my friends who I rarely got to see, my sister, my grandparents before they passed.

But when it came to romantic love, I was clueless as a newborn baby. I was as lost as people on a road trip before Google Maps was invented.

I didn't understand it.

For myself.

So I didn't understand it in Kai.

Toward me.

I didn't mean to hurt him, and at the times the wounds happened, I guess I really didn't even see it. But I was seeing it now. I was kicking myself for it now. For every time I misinterpreted his kindness, for the way I brought Not-Gary into the office, for, Oh God, the day I showed him my ring, foolishly thinking he had just... gotten over me because he had stopped being so attentive.

He hadn't gotten over me.

He pulled away so I stopped hurting him so much.

There was a sharp, stabbing sensation in my stomach at that, something real enough to make me roll onto my back, pressing a hand there, half expecting my palm to come away bloody. That was how much it hurt.

I lay there for a long time, pressing my hand to my belly as if to staunch bleeding, wondering how many times I had made Kai feel exactly this.

"Hey, honey, what's the matter?" Kai's voice asked, soft, but rough from sleep.

"Nothing," I lied, not even remotely convincingly.

"Then what's this?" he asked, his hand reaching out, swiping across my cheek, showing me the wetness there.

I hadn't even been aware I'd been crying.

That was how out of touch I was with myself, with my feelings.

I half turned on my pillow, eyes finding his. "How don't you hate me?" I asked.

"*What*?" Kai's voice lost the sleep in an instant. "Hate you for what?"

"For being clueless," I explained. "For hurting you with my own lack of awareness or... understanding."

Kai paused, actually giving it some thought, something I appreciated more than simple assurances or denials.

"Because... while you don't understand, I do. I get you. I'm not angry or upset because I know you have never hurt me through any fault of your own. I know that you have never really... grasped this whole thing," he said, waving a hand between us. "You can't be blamed for something if you didn't know what was going on."

"But I did hurt you." I latched onto that, needing to know it. For some reason, needing to hear him say it. Just to prove that I was right. Or to punish myself with. I didn't know.

Kai hesitated, but I refused to take it back, forcing him to exhale slowly. "Yes."

My eyes squeezed shut, forcing a few more tears down my cheeks at the motion.

"Jules, don't," Kai pleaded, fingers wiping away the tears.

"I'm sorry."

"Don't be sorry. There's nothing to be sorry for. I'm responsible for my feelings, not you."

"You should like someone like Gemma."

"*What?*"

"Someone romantic and sweet and kind and good. Like you."

To that, all I heard was a low chuckle, something rolling and masculine and, well, kinda sexy, to be perfectly honest.

My eyes opened, finding him up on his elbow, looking down at me, lips quirked up, eyes dancing.

"What?" I demanded when he said nothing, just kept giving me that unreadable, but somehow amused, smile.

"You're ridiculous," he declared, shrugging as though that explained anything at all.

"No, I'm not."

"You are," he insisted, nodding almost solemnly.

"How so?"

"You are acting as though there is a choice in who you love. It doesn't really work that way. You love who you love."

"Now *you're* being ridiculous. Of course love is a choice."

"Being in a relationship with someone is a choice. Loving them isn't. There are plenty of people divorced today who still love one another. And there are a bunch of people out there who love someone with everything they have, but choose not to be with them because they're addicts or they're unreliable, or they cheated. The choosing to be with someone or not part, that is a choice. But who you end up falling for, that is completely out of your control." His hand moved out, pulling the collar of his shirt down from my neck a few inches, the brush of his fingers seeming to make the skin tingle while he did so. He ran his finger down the center of my cross. "You believe there are some things that are out of our control."

It wasn't a question, but I answered it anyway.

"Yes."

"This is just one of those things."

"Kai?"

"Yeah?" he asked, finger still tracing my cross, his gaze focused there.

"Why didn't you ever make a move? You know... way back when? Back before Gary? Back when there was no one in the way."

"*You* were in the way," he informed me, lips curing up as his eyes found mine again. "I knew how you felt about your work reputation, how you had a rule about not dating anyone at work. I heard you say it once when Gemma was going gaga over Lincoln when she first met him, asking why you didn't 'tap that.' And I knew I wasn't your type, honey. That doesn't feel great to admit. And it didn't feel great to realize, but it was true. I wasn't your type. And going for it and getting shot down might have been worse than never going for it at all." He paused then gave me a slow, almost sad smile. "I didn't - and don't - check your boxes, Jules. I get that. I've always gotten that."

My stomach lurched at the mention of my list. The first thing I was going to do when I got home was burn that damn thing in the fireplace. Along with anything left of Not-Gary's.

"What's that look for?"

I exhaled slowly, shrugging. "I want to go home, but I don't want to go home. If that makes any sense."

"It makes sense. Why don't you want to go home?"

"Everything in my apartment reminds me of him now. He's touched everything. He's been everywhere. It all seems tainted."

"So go home, but don't go home," he suggested. "Go stay with your mom. Or Gemma."

"Look at me," I said, waving a hand at my face. "I would have to tell them the whole, ugly truth. I mean, I plan to do that. Eventually. Once I sort it through. But if I went to them, I would have to explain right now. I just... I don't want to go there. Not yet."

I didn't want to say it, but I felt it went without explanation.

And I have no money to stay somewhere else.

"Come stay at my place," he suggested because, well, of course he would. Because he was just the most selfless human being on the planet. "Don't. Don't rush to say no just because you feel like you can't ask it of me. You're not asking. I'm offering. Come stay at my place for a week. Heal. Get your head on straight again. Then you can figure out what you are doing from there. We can stop on the way back, grab everything you will need, and then go to my place."

I wanted to.

I had no idea what Kai's place was even like, and I had gotten a bit picky about such things over the years. Maybe he was as sloppy at home as he was in his office at work. Maybe he put his shoes up on the coffee table or left dishes in the sink for days. Maybe he wasn't anal about soap scum in the shower like I was.

But, somehow, I found myself genuinely not caring.

I wanted to go to his place.

"Say yes," he demanded. "I will even learn how to use my coffee maker for something other than brewing hot water."

"Okay," I agreed, nodding.

"Okay?" he asked, like he was sure he had misheard me.

"Okay," I affirmed, feeling that chest tightening thing again.

-

"Is it an apartment or a house?" I asked after we had stopped to load up a few pieces of my luggage with clothes, toiletries, makeup, some books, and my own pillows. It was a weird, maybe somewhat insulting habit I had picked up from my mother who had always insisted we bring our own pillows when we went to stay over somewhere. Not because someone else's pillows were dirty, but because ours smelled like home, would make it easier to sleep in a foreign place.

Plus, well, I paid the big bucks to get the best pillows I could find - ones that wouldn't go flat in five seconds. I slept on my side. I needed a good pillow or I'd get a crick from hell in my neck.

"You'll see when we get there."

"I hate surprises."

"I know."

"I could Google it. I know your address. Get the street view."

"But you're not going to," he agreed with me.

And, well, he was right.

I wasn't going to.

I was going to metaphorically sit on my hands and wait.

Luckily, it wasn't long.

"No way," I said when he turned into an industrial part of town, nothing but old warehouses around.

"Why not?"

"I picture you with a yard."

"I'm on the road a lot. I don't have the time to maintain it. I'd like that though. Someday. A house. A backyard with a dog and some kids in it. Right now, though, this works best for me," he told me, pulling up to what had been a textile factory.

"This is your place?" I asked, not even bothering to mask the disbelief in my voice.

"Got it on a song. It had been home to some raccoons and opossums. They had their own ecosystem going. But I dropped some money into it, got it all cleaned out. Humanely," he specified as if I could ever imagine he hired someone to bludgeon the poor raccoons and opossums. "Then got to build it up the way I wanted."

"It's four floors."

"Yeah."

"What could you have possibly found to do with all of that space?"

"Two floors are the actual living space. Got three bedrooms. Sometimes Lincoln crashes if he's between girls. Bellamy and Ranger will stay if they are in town."

"What about the other two floors?"

"Well..." he said, hitting a clicker on his visor, making a giant door slowly groan open, allowing him to drive inside. To a giant garage space.

"Wait... is that Lincoln's..."

"Corvette? Yes," Kai told me, nodding toward the cherry red car in the far corner. "He ran out of room, and claimed it could never sit outside in the weather. Despite being, you know, a car and meant to sit outside. I am under strict orders not to touch it. Or breathe on it. And my car is not allowed to blow exhaust on it. Whatever that means. Come on, let's get upstairs," he said, jumping out, going around the back to load his arms down with my luggage, leaving me with nothing but my pillows to grab.

We climbed up steep cement stairs to a door, pausing to let Kai punch in a code, then moving into the dark space.

"Ready?"

"I don't know."

But then the light flicked on.

And I got to see Kai's place for the first time.

"Wow."

"Good wow? Bad wow?"

"Surprised good wow?"

It wasn't what I was expecting. Piles of stuff all over with a clean trail leading to the kitchen.

The room itself was open concept. We stepped into the living room with windows lining both sides. The living room was set up in a square of couches. They were somewhat low, black, and minimalistic. Very modern. On the center was a coffee table was a set of work files. But not strewn about, just tucked all together nicely. There was a large flatscreen across from the seating area, likely where he and the guys - or Miller - hung out and watched games or movies or... whatever people did when they hung out as adults.

Behind the living room was a simple four-chair black table set before the oversized L-shaped kitchen cut off from the rest of the space with a giant, oversized island. The counters were cement. The appliances were stainless steel. The cabinets were a deep gray.

The whole area was cool, but not cold. Streamlined and clean. There were no curtains or throw pillows, no decor accents.

It was the ultimate bachelor's pad.

Because Kai was single.

Kai was single, and not a monk.

He was good-looking, sweet, interesting.

Women had to be drawn to him.

Irrationally, I felt a sour taste flood my mouth, recognizing it for what it was. Jealousy.

Even though I had no right at all to feel that way.

"Do you have a housekeeper?"

Kai's neck went a little red, a surefire sign of guilt. "Yeah."

"But you won't let me clean your office."

"It's not your job."

"I straighten up for some of the others."

"It's not your job," he insisted before moving away from me. "As you can see, this is the main living area. Help yourself to what's in the fridge. I'll pick up some healthy stuff later for you. The main floor bathroom is... here," he declared when I caught up with him, finding a door behind the kitchen. "And back here is just the gaming room," he told me, waving before taking up another flight of wide cement stairs. I hung back, sneaking a look to see what a game room could be. It was exactly what it sounded like. A room full of old school arcade games. And a little section with a giant TV and collection of gaming consoles.

Kai liked games.

How did I never know that about him?

"I'd wipe the floor with you," he declared, having come back down to stand beside me. "At skeeball," he told me, jerking his chin toward where I was looking.

"I don't know. I used to be pretty good."

"We'll play later. Winner gets to pick dinner."

"Sounds like fun."

And it did.

Fun.

What a novel concept.

"You get to choose your room," he told me as we got to the second floor. "This is me," he told me, waving a hand toward a room with a king-sized bed with steel blue comforter. And another TV. One guy. Three TVs. So far.

"This is the first one. It's the one the guys usually pick," he informed me, flicking on the light.

"I can see why."

It was bare walls and a simple bed with a slate comforter. And, you guessed it, another TV.

"This one no one has ever picked," he told me, leading me into the last room where the walls were a soft sage green. The queen-sized bed had a lush white comforter. There was a white headboard, white nightstands, and a white and sage carpet so thick I was sure my feet would simply sink into it.

"I like that look. I guess we have a winner?"

"Oh, yes. And no TV. You know you have four TVs?"

"I do know that. I like TV. you should try it sometime."

"Maybe I will."

Maybe I would enjoy that too.

Who knew?

"Alright, so the guest bathroom is at the end of the hall. Everything you might need is in there. Feel free to spread your stuff out. I have my own bathroom. I will let you settle in. I'll be downstairs if you want some company."

"Kai," I called a bit desperately as he turned and was gone before I could even draw a breath.

"Yeah?"

"Thank you. Again."

"I'm happy to have you here, Jules." There was so much sincerity in his tone it was impossible to think he was just throwing out pleasantries.

And there it was again.

The chest-tightening thing.

And I was starting to maybe think I had an idea what it meant.

I moved around, settling in, showering, glad to find my hands were healed over, a bit painful to the touch if I tried to grip anything too hard, but tolerable. There was nothing to be done about my black eyes and the band of bruises around my neck, but I took the time to dry and style my hair, being careful to avoid the slowly scabbing over cut on my skull.

I threw on a pair of slacks and a simple camisole, happy to feel a bit more like myself, and then headed downstairs to find Kai lounging on the couch watching some crime procedural, feet kicked up on the coffee table. But no shoes, just socks.

"Wanna join me?" he asked. "We can order in lunch in a bit."

"You don't need to check into work?"

"They'll be fine without me. Miller thinks I am with Bellamy. Getting wasted and eloped in Vegas or something."

"Everyone has wild stories about him," I observed as I sat down on the other couch.

"He's a character."

"He sounds fun and light-hearted."

"And you can't figure out why he would do what he does for a living."

"Exactly."

"Bellamy was in the military with the guys. Took some personality tests. Turned out he had, I dunno, something in him that the big guys thought they could bend and warp and use. So he turned special ops. Black ops. I think... when you are ordered to kill enough, you get desensitized to it. He had a hard time after he was brought home. Had these dark spells that he couldn't control. Until he learned that going back to his old ways-"

"Killing people," I specified.

"Yes. Once he started doing that, he kept that darkness at bay. Most of the time, it only comes up when he has a job."

"Quin really has the need for someone like him on the team?"

Kai was quiet for a moment, looking out the window at the blinding sun. "You meet a lot of people on this job," he started, voice odd, distant. "Some are innocents trapped in bad situations. Some aren't so innocent, but decent people. But all the clients almost inevitably got on the bad side of some truly despicable people. The kind who enjoy torture and rape, who get off on hurting others in new and inventive ways. The kind of people the world would be a better place without. In those jobs, instead of striking deals with devils, I think Quin would like to be a part of the greater good."

I mulled on that for a long moment before blurting out the first thing on my mind. "I believe in the death penalty," I declared, making Kai's face turn to me, brows together. "That is an unpopular opinion in my friend group. My sister looks hurt if I so much as suggest it. And I think it is used a little too often, but sometimes, it is necessary. Some people are warped. There is no cure for that kind of sick. They don't belong on the streets among decent people. Child molesters and serial rapists, people who get off on killing. I believe they deserve the death penalty. So I get what you're saying. And blaming Bellamy would be like blaming the doctor who inserts the lethal injection in a way."

"Just a solid piece of advice. If you ever hang out with Bellamy, don't look away from your drink."

I smiled at that. "Got it."

So we watched some police shows, mutually scoffing over missed leads, had lunch. *While sitting in front of the TV.* Kai went out for supplies, then we had our game night.

"Damnit!" I hissed, watching as Kai's score beat mine. We were doing best out of five. And he had beaten me three of those times now.

He got to pick dinner.

"Go easy on me," I pleaded, pressing a hand on my stomach.

"You had a salad for lunch. And you will eat your body weight in tacos for dinner. It's called balance."

Because this was Kai's house, Kai's life, Kai's everything, I felt like I could do things differently; I could take a break from my life, from the limitations of it.

"Don't worry. I will make you something healthy for breakfast," he assured me as I grumbled while he cleaned up the makings.

I didn't know - almost as a rule - what eating so much that your waistband felt tight felt like. The genuine 'stuffed' feeling. Not even on holidays since my mom was more about the veggies than the starches. This was unexpectedly uncomfortable. I was pretty sure my button on my slacks was piercing through my skin.

"I think I gained five pounds," I whined.

"Don't be dramatic," Kai said, turning back from putting the leftovers in the fridge. "Three tops."

I snorted at that, shaking my head.

"I am going to beat you in that shooting game thing and force an obnoxious amount of greens down your throat."

"You've never played on an Xbox before."

"So?"

"So, I'll wipe the floor with you, and then force you to eat a bucket a fried chicken."

"I am going to need a whole new wardrobe after staying here for a week."

"You eat like a bird most of the time. Your metabolism has to be set to turbo. Want some tea to take to bed?" he asked, waving a hand to the coffee pot that he hadn't used for coffee yet. I would remedy that situation. In the morning. While watching him make me breakfast.

I'd watched him make dinner.

That felt awkward even to admit to myself, but it was true nonetheless.

I had sat at the island and watched him while I made myself useful by grating cheese and chopping tomatoes.

But I did all that while watching him move around his kitchen with a sort of masculine grace.

There was something primally sexual about a man cooking for you, nourishing you, taking care of you.

Sexual.

Jesus.

Okay.

"Do you have chamomile?" I asked, figuring something calming was certainly in order if I was suddenly thinking cooking was sexual.

"Sure do," he agreed, flicking on the kettle as he reached up for - I kid you not - a tea caddy. "Go on and get ready for bed. I'll bring it in when it's done."

With that, I did, getting into my usual sleeping attire of short silky sleep shorts and a matching camisole, climbing into bed, and waiting.

I heard him moving down the hall, whistling one of the songs that had been on while he cooked - a song from one of my playlists.

And, incredibly, I felt a rush of anticipation coursing through my system, making my pulse quicken, my skin feel tingly.

As crazy as that was.

"Hey," he said, moving into the doorway, my steaming mug in his hand. His voice was odd. Almost a little rough.

"Hey." Okay. And my voice was a bit airy.

My breathing went a bit deeper, and Kai's gaze seemed to dip. No, it didn't seem to. It *did.* It followed the line of my throat, over the exposed skin of my chest. As I took another breath, I could feel my nipples tightening, brushing up against the cool material of my camisole.

Across from me, Kai's eyes closed as he drew in a deep breath, forcing his gaze to lift, to hold mine as he approached, setting the mug down on my nightstand. "Sleep tight, Jules," he said, voice soft, running his finger down the top of my nose before disappearing out of my room, closing the door on his way out.

I barely slept, my mind and body keeping me tossing and turning all night.

I woke up around seven after catching a few short hours, shooting out of the bed in a panic.

Seven.

I never slept until seven.

I grabbed my blush pink silk robe, making a quick stop to brush my teeth and flatten my hair before moving down the hallway toward the kitchen.

I shocked back at the sound of Kai's phone ringing, finding myself pausing as there was a second then Kai's voice.

"What's up?"

"You lied to me," Quin's voice broke into the apartment, making it clear Kai had put the call on speaker.

Kai paused. "About?"

"About where you've been. See, I can't quite buy that you were out having fun with Bellamy when I got an envelope today by courier filled with a couple *hundred* grand and a note saying it was Jules', minus his fee. You lied to me."

"Technically, I lied to Miller," Kai qualified.

"What the fuck is going on, Kai? Why was Jules missing what had to be her whole savings?"

There was silence from Kai, forcing me to fight back the surge of discomfort as I moved out of the hall and into the kitchen.

"It's okay, Kai," I said, voice sounding much more sure than I actually felt in the moment.

"Is that Jules?" Quin's voice asked, sounding surprised.

"Yeah," I affirmed, taking a deep breath, having to remind myself to stay calm as Kai came up beside me, pressing a mug of coffee into my hands.

"You're supposed to be on vacation. Jules, talk," he demanded when I said nothing, just took a sip of my coffee, not even caring that it burned my tongue.

"It's a long story."

"If it ends with you hiring Bellamy for something, babe, I have the time to hear it."

So I launched into it, giving a somewhat condensed version of events, ending with coming back to Kai's for a few days without explaining about my apartment.

"Stay there," Quin barked.

"What? No. Quin, you don't need to come here."

"Stay there," he demanded again, hanging up on my objections.

"You might want to get dressed," Kai suggested. "We are about to be invaded."

Not half an hour later, we were.

Not just by Quin.

Oh, no.

Following behind him into Kai's place was Miller, Smith, Lincoln, Finn, and - believe this or not - Gunner.

And, even more amazingly, it was Gunner who broke away from the pack, charging at me, hand raising, grabbing my chin, yanking it up a little roughly.

"Mother fucker," he growled, eyes on my neck.

"It's fine," I insisted, shaking my head.

"Fine. Some bastard puts his hands around your neck, it's not fucking fine, Jules."

There was a warm, blooming sensation in my belly. At Gunner's reaction. At everyone else's. These people who dropped everything to come see me after a traumatic event.

I took a deep breath, meeting Gunner's hard gaze. "Well, the way I hear it, he won't be a problem anymore."

To that, the tightening in his jaw loosened, his lips curved up slightly. "Got that straight. If Bellamy didn't handle it, I'd have done it myself."

"We'd have all needed to get in line," Smith affirmed, coming up to angle my head down, reaching to part my hair. "Not too bad."

Quin moved in next, shaking his head at me. "You should have come to me, Jules. This is what I do, remember? Fix things."

"It's embarrassing," I admitted.

"Embarrassing? This is what conmen do. And they're good at it. There was no reason to feel embarrassed that you got taken by a pro. And he *was* a pro. Got a hold of Bellamy before I left. He got a real name. Looked into him on the way. Got a rap sheet dating back to when he was ten years old. Violent shit at times too."

"What was it?"

"Hm?"

"His name," I clarified. "What was his name?"

"It doesn't matter."

"It matters," I told him, dropping my voice so no one else could overhear. "I lived with that man. I *slept* with him. It'd be nice to know his actual name instead of the one he gave me."

"Jameson Decker," he explained. "Bound to be a criminal when you're named after alcohol."

With that, he moved away to join the others making cups of coffees. It was such a foreign site that I stood there and watched it for a moment.

"So, you all *do* know how to make your own coffee," I told them with a sneer.

"Don't get any ideas. Soon as you're ready to come back, you're making it again." That was Quin.

"You know," Miller started, coming up toward me and Kai, but looking only at him. "On the one hand, I'm pissed that you lied to me. On the other, you were helping Jules, so I don't know if I have a right to be mad."

"If it's any consolation, I felt guilty about it," Kai offered.

"That helps. You," she declared, pointing then crooking her finger at me. "We need to talk."

With that, she headed down the hall like she'd done so many times before. Maybe she had. Maybe she knew this place better than I did.

With nothing else to do, I followed, watching as Finn caught my eye on his way out the door.

"He's on his way to clean your apartment," Miller informed me with the kind of authority that said she was speaking from knowledge, not conjecture.

"What?"

"He's not so great with the words thing, but he wants to show his care. So he cleans your place. I woke up after that trip to Turkey, remember that one? I got my ass handed to me. Could barely get around. But yeah, I woke up to find he had broken into my place, and scrubbed it spotless. He was in the process of separating my laundry to do the wash when I caught him."

"What'd you do?"

"Let him finish, of course. I hate doing fucking laundry. And he loves it. So it was a win/win for us. I did get a lecture about my mediocre cleaning supply options. I woke up the *next* day to a giant delivery of gallon jugs of cleaning shit and rags and scrub brushes. I have gone through exactly a third of one of those jugs. I have seven more stashed in my basement. So, yeah, your place is going to be clean. It will be like Jameson never touched anything in there."

"That's why I'm here," I admitted as we ended up upstairs, heading toward my bedroom. Like she somehow knew that was where I was staying, despite there being another guest room.

"Hm?"

"Because I feel like everything in my apartment is tainted. I didn't feel ready to go back."

"Kai's place is like a vacation anyway. With the game room and the fourth floor." I had learned the fourth floor actually boasted an above-ground pool and hot tub. "And he cooks for you. It's a win/win/win to stay here." She paused inside the doorway to my room, looking around. "He did this himself, you know."

"The decorating?"

"Yeah. I mean he did the whole place, but this room is so different from all the others. It's not his style. It's..."

"Mine," I supplied when she wouldn't.

"Exactly. He went through catalogs and websites and paint swatches looking for the things that he knew would suit you. Because he wanted you to come stay here. I mean, I'm sure the ultimate hope was to have you in his room, in his bed. And he certainly didn't want you here because you were hurt. But he always saw you here."

"I don't..." I paused, searching for the right words. "Understand that, I guess."

"Because you're not like him. You're more practical. I get it. I am too. I wouldn't know how to handle his feelings either, if I were in your place. When you genuinely just didn't seem into it, I told him to back off. But... now I'm not so sure."

"Not so sure what?"

"That you're genuinely not into it. Into him. I was just out there, you know," she added, leaning back against the wall. "When you looked over at him, you had that moon-eyed thing he always has when he looks at you. So... what's going on? See,

I figure that you haven't filled in your family yet, or they'd all be setting up camp here. So you have no one to talk to about it. Granted, I am about as good as you seem to be at handling this shit. But that's cool. We can try to suss it out together."

"That, ah, sounds good," I admitted, sitting off the side of the bed, taking a deep breath. "I have to admit. I thought you were calling me in here to yell at me."

"For being bad with guys? Girl, I am the last person who can lecture about that. Remember Renzo?" She asked, and I nodded. I'd met him a time or two. He'd been rough and tough, dark-haired, dark-eyed, with a thick New York accent. "He ended up being some mafia enforcer. Whoops. I mean, it was good while it lasted. He could fuck like a porn star. Like with the intensity of James Deen and... you have no idea who I am talking about, do you?" she asked, watching as I shook my head. "Oh, girl. Up your porn game. Anywho, yeah, I have an enforcer, a Russian spy, and a Colombian drug dealer under my belt. Literally. So I am not going to judge you."

"That almost makes my conman story seem tame."

"Totally. So spill. What's going on? About Jameson? About Kai? Unload on me while Kai gives the boys details."

"He was just... there for me."

"Kai."

"Yeah, Kai. I mean, he came over after the wedding. He helped me stitch my sanity back together. He hatched a plan to find Gar... Jameson. He let me unload all the feelings on him. And he.. came for me."

"Yeah... he's Kai," she said in a way that clearly said *Duh*.

"He kissed me."

"Whaaaat?" Miller asked, mouth opening yet somehow managing to smile at the same time. "I'm going to need more details than that."

"I had asked him why he liked me. Even though I didn't seem to return the feelings. And he explained how he didn't like me because I wanted him, he just liked me. And I asked if he didn't want me to like him... and yeah. We kissed."

"And you're not like behind locked doors getting fucked seven ways to Sunday because..."

"Because he stopped it."

"What? Why?"

"Because he thought I was too vulnerable, that I would regret it."

"Oh, that idiot. I mean he's well-intentioned, but he's such an idiot."

"That was when I went downstairs for some air... and when Gar... Jameson found me."

"He didn't..." she trailed off, but the implication was there.

"No. He just hit me and said some awful stuff. Then Kai came and got me."

"He totally did the white horse thing on you. That is some serious cheesy romantic shit."

"It kind of was."

"And yet he still didn't make a move."

"Well, I had like a hundred splinters in my hands that he took out. My head had a still fresh cut on the back. I had a wicked migraine. We just talked. And went to sleep."

"So, what I am hearing here is... you have changed your mind about Kai."

Had I?

I guess I had.

Maybe that wasn't even accurate.

Maybe I had just changed my opinion on his potential as a partner.

Now that I was ready to burn my list.

Because there had been hints over the years that there was something there. Like when he'd rubbed my shoulders, and my body had set fire. Like how that kiss had made it feel like I never wanted to stop.

"Yeah, I guess so."

"You seem different here," Miller said, changing tactics.

"Different?"

"I don't know. You're still dressed like you, but you seem calmer, less frazzled. You don't have your shoulders jacked up and your spine all tense."

"I played games and watched TV. And ate tacos."

She smiled at that, seeming to understand that while for most people, those were not groundbreaking declarations, but for me, it was huge.

"Tacos beat the hell out of garden salads, don't they?"

"Yeah, kinda."

"Alright, look," she said, pursing her lips for a second. "I don't think it's gonna happen."

"What?"

"Kai making a move. I don't think it is gonna happen." Those words made a sinking feeling move through my center. "He's just too good, y'know? He will be treating you with kid gloves for a while, thinking you're too hurt - physically and emotionally - to think straight. Which is sweet. Sexist as fuck, but sweet. Then, enough time is going to pass that he is going to feel like he missed his shot. Then he will be insecure. And it will never happen. So.... I think you need to ovary-up, Jules."

"Ovary-up?" I asked, brows drawing together.

"If you want him - and that is an if. Because I don't mean 'I am heartbroken over my ex being a fuckhead, and I want someone to make me feel better' kind of want. I mean want. Him. The whole package. In a serious way. But if that is what you decide after some soul searching, then you are going to be the one to need to make the first move."

"I... I don't really make first moves."

"Well, get over that. If you want to see how Kai's devotion translates in the sheets. Okay," she said, clapping suddenly, pushing away from the wall. "So, that was some successful girl talk, right?"

"Right," I agreed with a smile.

"And look... not a bottle of nail polish or a face mask in sight. Go us."

With that, she was gone, leaving me sitting there, thinking.

"Hey you," Lincoln said from the doorway a moment later, taking up the space, watching me with knowing eyes. "I've always wanted to come into *Jules' Room*. I mean, he never called it that, but it is pretty obvious. How you holding up, sweetheart?" he asked, moving to sit beside me off the bed. "How you doing? And don't feed me assurances. How are you really?"

"I'm... digesting still," I admitted. "Now that more people know, I think I will feel a bit better."

"Shrouding it in shame was silly in the first place," he informed me, giving my knee a squeeze. "I get it, but I hope you are seeing now that it is better to share it, to bring us in. We will always be here for you, Jules. We don't just care about you because you make great coffee and keep the office running smoothly. We care about *you*."

"I get that now," I agreed, nodding.

I wasn't sure how long I had placed my worth in my usefulness, in my productivity, but I was finally starting to understand that there was more to me that people might feel drawn to, that I was more than what I brought to the table.

"No more going off on your own chasing down scumbags. Agreed?"

"Agreed," I promised.

"Come on out. Kai is making breakfast," he told me.

So I did.

And I shared a meal and a few hours with these people who I had only ever known as coworkers before, not so much as human beings.

And, well, it was one of the best mornings in my recent memory.

They headed out a while later, Quin demanding I take all the time I need - but hopefully not too long. Smith and Lincoln gave me a smile. Miller, well, Miller made a circle with one fist and thrust a finger in and out of it when Kai wasn't looking, shooting me a wink before heading out.

"Told you that you could trust them, Jules. They all care about you. Even Gunner."

"I see that now," I agreed, feeling my heart swell up.

"Here," he said, holding out an envelope.

"Wow. That's everything, huh? I felt like it should be so much bigger."

"Bellamy got you large bills."

I nodded at that, opening the envelope, seeing my future restored to me. I was still on track. If not with the marriage and kids part, then at least with the home part. I could plant a garden - something I used to love doing with my grandmother when I would visit as a kid. I could decorate, make a life for myself. And then worry about the wife and mom part later.

The schedule didn't seem to matter to me as much as it used to.

"Do I want to know how much Bellamy's fee was?"

"He gave the friends and family discount. Twenty-five grand."

"And if I wasn't a friend?"

"Fifty to seventy-five for someone normal. Up to one-fifty for someone high profile or extremely dangerous. And I called Bellamy. He is sending you the twenty-five k back."

"What? No, that's..."

"It wasn't your request. It was mine. I pay."

"It was my case. I pay."

"Unfortunately, the client doesn't get to choose how much or what they pay."

His lips were turned up at that, knowing that logic was impossible to argue with.

"Well, you got me there." I tucked the money into my purse, planning to go to the bank as soon as my face looked less frightening. It would be another three days at most, I imagined, before makeup could cover up the bruises well enough.

"So, can I interest you in a small *Criminal Intent* binge?"

"Yes!" I perked up, practically throwing myself down on the couch.

And so went the next several days.

Kai went into work for a few hours here and there, but spent most of his time with me, cooking, watching TV, playing games. As it would turn out, I was pretty good at the games on the Xbox, had gotten Kai to get salads or wraps three times in as many days. He'd wiped the floor with me on the arcade games though. I'd been plied with a bucket of fried chicken with a side of potato wedges and then a huge pile of pancakes and, as if those weren't bad enough, huge, greasy Philly cheesesteaks.

But then it happened.

My bruises faded.

I woke up one morning looking just like myself.

There were no more excuses.

It was time to get back to my life.

I stood there in the mirror after that realization with a sinking feeling in my stomach.

It didn't feel like enough time.

I wanted to stay.

I knew he would let me, wouldn't even make a comment if I simply kept staying for another week or two... or even months.

But I couldn't do that.

Keep playing house in a place that wasn't my own.

I needed to settle back in my own place.

I needed to get back to work.

I felt the weight of all my untaken chances.

To make a move.

Like Miller had suggested.

Each night, he brought me tea.

I should have reached out, grabbed his wrist, pulled him down in the bed with me.

Each morning, he stood there making my coffee.

I should have walked up and just kissed him.

At some point each day, we would sit in the living room and watch TV.

I should have got up from my couch, and sat with him, cuddled up next to him.

Should have should have should have.

Should - as far as I was concerned - was the worst word in the English language. It represented so much potential, so much self-denial, so many chances that may have led to wonderful things.

But I could never muster that confidence to do it. Partly because I simply never had to do so before. But also partly because I wasn't sure I could handle the rejection if it showed again.

"I feel like you're about to tell me you are heading home," Kai guessed accurately as I walked into the kitchen after getting ready for the day, carefully packing my things away as I pretended to ignore the distinct sensation of *wrongness* inside me.

"I think it is time to get back to things. Work. My life." I cringed as soon as the words were out, interpreting them the way Kai might. The way that said this was fun while it lasted, but I had no interest in this life long-term. And, judging by the almost guarded look - something wholly unnatural to him - I was right in thinking he would take it the wrong way. "Don't get me wrong," I rushed to add. "I have had such a great time here. But I will never get used to being in my apartment again if I don't at least try."

He nodded at that, understanding, even if his eyes seemed a little less happy than they had been when I had seen him before bed the night before.

"I get that. I know you feel weird about going back. But, hey, if you get there and decide it's not going to work after all, I'm here. The room is here. You don't even need to call," he told me, reaching into his junk drawer - something I cringed at existing at all given that it was really just a catch-all for every odd thing from paper clips to screwdrivers and birthday candles and tape with absolutely no organization of said contents at all - for a pad and pen, jotting something down before handing it to me.

"What's this?" I asked, looking down at numbers.

"The code to get in."

I looked down at the numbers again, feeling a twinge of recognition, but unable to have the memory surface, so I took the code and tucked it into my wallet.

And just like that, it was over.

-

Flashback - 35 months before -

He had thought it was a simple case of attraction.

That made the most sense, didn't it?

She was beautiful after all.

Any man would feel a pull toward her right away.

But it had been a month.

A month of the strange sinking feeling in his chest when he saw her. The only way he could even think to describe it was like when you were driving a little too fast on some backroad - the kind that was hilly and bumpy. And you shot up over a hill, feeling the whole car go airborne for a second. And your stomach dropped. And your heart dropped. Then you flew down the hill feeling exhilarated, alive, tingly, and happy.

That was how he felt.

Absolutely *every* single time she came into the room.

After a month.

Maybe he had been trying to call it simple attraction, seeing as the other option was, well, ridiculous.

But as much as he tried to lie to himself, he knew the truth.

Attraction was like a punch to the gut, it was a shock to the groin.

And while he felt that too, it was more.

So it had to be more than just wanting to get her into bed. As much as he delighted at that idea.

It was more.

And it was getting harder and harder to even lie to himself about it.

The fact of the matter was, he felt it the second he laid eyes on her.

Instantaneous.

That was what it was.

Uncontrollable.

Nonsensical.

Sure, he had always been perhaps more romantic than a lot of guys, more prone to putting women on pedestals.

But this was different than that.

This was something akin to something within him recognizing something within her.

Like fate.

Soulmates.

All that insane, over-the-top, cheesy stuff.

That was what it was.

There was no way to look at it through any other lens anymore.

He knew it the moment he saw her.

Something in his soul said *Mine*.

Every interaction since then had only reinforced the idea.

There wasn't a thing he had seen so far that he didn't like.

Her ambition.

Her perfectionism.

Her cleaning and organization compulsion.

He even had a thing for the parts of her that maybe others would consider flaws - her detachedness, her desire to keep everyone at a distance, her stone-cold rationality.

They weren't flaws.

Just parts of the whole.

And the whole, yeah, he dug it.

He spent too many idle moments thinking about it. About her. About him. About possibilities.

Fanciful, sure.

But he couldn't seem to help it.

Even though he knew how things stood.

He knew that she didn't feel it too.

He knew that she didn't look at him and see a future, see a house and kids and a dog and family game night.

She didn't see that.

Not with him.

Jules was someone who would likely approach relationships with the same mindset she approached everything else. With thought. With careful consideration.

Not hearts and flowers.

But boxes of the right traits checked off.

He wouldn't be surprised to learn she had an actual list for men. Along with a timeline for when she should meet him, date him, marry him, move into a home with him, have babies with him, give up her career for it all.

That was how she was.

And he didn't fit into that picture.

There was no denying that bothered him, maybe even hurt him - even though he really had no right to hurt given that she hadn't led him on, he'd been alone in his feelings.

And he hadn't made a move.

He hadn't even suggested his interest.

He hadn't opened that door.

But he figured he had time.

After he knew her better.

After she knew him better.

There would always be time.

Until, of course, there wasn't.

But he wasn't thinking of that.

He was thinking of how well her navy blue slacks and white camisole brought out her eyes and hair and figure. About how she had four different smiles that he knew of.

Her customer service smile, the one that got tense at the ends, that made her eyes squint a bit. The fake one.

Her 'you're an idiot' smile. She gave that one to Kai a lot when he was being silly. And Lincoln when he was having more girl trouble.

Her 'everything is as it should be' smile. She got that one when the finished her files, her transcription, the cleaning and organizing. When everything was perfect. That was her smile of relief.

And then the big one.

The best one.

The one that made lines etch in her cheeks and her eyes dance. Her genuine happy smile. He liked that one best, of course, and saw the least. She seemed to save it for her little sister when she stopped in, or her mother when she sent her lunch without asking. That was her least prominent smile. But it was the one he loved the most, the one he secretly hoped she would flash in his direction at some point.

But he was starting to think maybe she never would.

Maybe he would never get up the nerve to tell her, to make a move, to make things happen.

And that thought was enough to make his heart feel deflated in his chest.

NINE

Kai

"Chickenshit," Lincoln's voice broke into my office, making me snap out of my own swirling thoughts, finding he had already opened my door without me noticing.

"Sorry?"

"You heard me," he said, moving in a foot to kick his door closed. "You're a chickenshit. And I'd forgive it if I thought you were just some poor sucker without any game. But I've been on jobs with you, man. I've seen you charm life back into old, dusty panties. You can turn it on and use it to your advantage. It's not that you don't know how to get what you want. You can sweet talk anyone into anything. So I can't forgive it that you are sitting your ass in here being a fucking pussy. What? Daydreaming about her. When she is fifteen feet away. And you could finally stop daydreaming about her. Because you could have the real thing. So, in conclusion, you're a chickenshit." He finished as he dropped down in the seat across from me, propping his legs up on my desk, interlocking his fingers and using them to hold onto the back of his neck, making his chest broaden.

Lincoln didn't get the Jules thing.

Not my feelings for her per se, but my lack of action regarding them.

Lincoln was an action person. Especially when it came to women. You would never find him nervously peeling the label off his beer while he tried to get up his nerve to talk to some girl at the bar.

And, sure, maybe it helped that he looked like he could star as the leading man in some primetime dramatic romance.

But Lincoln was a firm believer that it had nothing to do with looks on our part, that it had everything to do with how we presented ourselves, how we approached the women we were attracted to. I'd seen him give lessons to some sad little milksop we had been on a job for a while back, taking him to the bar, telling him what to wear, what to say, how to approach women.

And it worked.

If he ever needed to give up his job as Quin's negotiator, he could charge good money to host pick-up artist courses for men who had no game.

And Lincoln used his own personal game constantly, picking up women in bars, in supermarkets, in the line at the coffee shop. Sometimes just for fun, just because he could. Other times, because he wanted to hook up. And, oddly, just as often, because he wanted to start something up. Something more serious. Well, as serious as he ever got with women. They almost always petered out around the three-month point. Whether that had to do with the women he chose or his own lack of commitment to long term was anybody's guess.

But as such, he didn't get it.

My interest in Jules.

And my acceptance of there never being anything more than what there already was.

"She just got her heart broken, Lincoln," I insisted, already knowing how lame an excuse that was.

Even if it was true.

Which, to be perfectly honest, I wasn't sure about.

She'd cried, sure, right at first. On my chest Through my shirt.

But since then - aside from getting teary about hurting me - she hadn't seemed to be mourning.

Maybe it was hard to mourn someone who had been ready to kill you. Or maybe her feelings for him weren't as you might have expected them to be.

Maybe she hadn't loved him.

Maybe she had been in love with the *idea* of him.

Or maybe if there had been love, it had been the kind that grew from shared experiences in life, in learning to live with one another. The way people with arranged marriages learned to love one another. Maybe it hadn't been a mad love affair like it had looked like from the outside with how quickly things had progressed.

"Don't give me that," Lincoln insisted, shaking his head. "That girl has a good head on her shoulders. So good, in fact, she let herself think she loved that bastard when it was clear she just thought she should love him. She's not heartbroken. Maybe her pride took a bit of a battering, but all the more reason for you to get your head out of your ass, and help her build it back up again. And not as her friend, Kai. She's got enough of friends. She needs a man who sees her for who she is, who digs everything she has to offer. That is what she needs after all this. And you and I both know you are the man for the job."

"She doesn't..."

"Then show her. Convince her. You know Jules. She sometimes can't see things that fall outside her tunnel vision."

"She's been distant since we came back to work."

"'Cause you seduced her with your game room and mad cooking skills and TV marathons, then let her go ahead and act like nothing at all had transpired between you."

"I didn't let..."

"You let," he cut me off. "You say she's been distant, but Kai... you've been skirting around her. I haven't seen you at her desk, fiddling around with her organizer. You don't massage her shoulders anymore. How can you accuse her of the same thing you are clearly guilty of?"

Maybe I had been giving her space.

I had convinced myself that she needed it. To get back into the swing of things. To focus on getting her life on track.

I didn't want to pressure her when she had enough on her plate.

Hell, telling her family about Jameson alone likely took a huge toll on her. I could tell when she had done it. She had come into work on Monday looking weighted, moving a bit slower than usual. She'd likely had brunch with her mom and sister, spilling it all. Then, I imagined, she had needed to go home and tell her father as well. Her friends. It was a big deal.

"She needed to focus on telling everyone about this whole thing."

"Sure," he agreed, nodding. "But don't you think that maybe the whole experience of doing so might have been a lot easier had she someone to come home to, to lean on, someone to help lift the weight off her shoulders?" he asked, raising a brow when I could find nothing to say. "Exactly. You should be ashamed of yourself, man. Letting her go home to that empty apartment full of ghosts. And, sure, Finn had cleaned the place, changed the locks, put in some better security, but you know she doesn't feel good there. You could have been there with her."

From what I overheard Jules telling Miller, Finn had cleaned everything from top to bottom, going so far as to shampoo all the furniture, and then removed and replace her old mattress. Because Finn was one to understand that there was no cleaning some things, there was no way to get the ick out. You had to rip it out and start again.

"What's going on in here?" another voice joined the room, making us both look to see Gunner moving in, closing the door.

"Oh, nothing. Just telling Kai that he's a chickenshit. Care to pile on?"

"Sounds good. I don't have dick going on," Gunner agreed, moving to lean back against my door, crossing his arms. "So why the fuck haven't you made a move yet?" he asked, casually, but in that gruff way he was so well known for.

I wanted to tell them to back off, to get lost. But the thing about this particular group of guys was, if you tried to push them away, they charged closer. I was surrounded by uber alphas. I barely stood a chance.

"Nah," Lincoln said, looking over at Gunner. "You know his M.O. He's gonna mope and moon and then when he can't take anymore, he's gonna scurry on down to the woods to visit Ranger where he can daydream about Jules instead of making a move and getting that dream to be a reality."

"I mean aren't you sick of fucking your hand all these years?" Gunner asked, blunt as ever. "Don't try to deny that isn't the case. You never spend time with any women. Sure, you let everyone believe you did, but you can't fucking fool us all for long, you know... easy, woman," he growled when Miller shoved at the door, nearly knocking him away from it.

"Oh, is this an intervention?" she asked when Gunner moved aside to let her in. "Why wasn't I invited? I am good with the ass-kicking. I mean who was it who got the balls to tell Kai he missed his shot when Jules got serious with Jameson? Hm? Oh, right, that was me. The one without actual balls. So how far have we gotten?"

"So far," Lincoln went on, making me close my eyes as I took a deep breath, steadying myself for another round. Words, to be fair, were often worse than an actual ass-kicking. Especially from people close to you who knew exactly what to say. "We have covered... he's a chickenshit and... isn't he sick of yanking the crank when he could be getting the real thing."

"Hmmm. What does that leave me?" Miller mused, moving to sit on the other end of my desk opposite Lincoln's kicked-up feet. "How about... not only are you a shitty love interest, but you are a crappy friend right now too?"

"Got that," Lincoln said, raising a finger in the air.

"Damn. You guys got all the good stuff."

"Maybe if you weren't so busy mooning over Quin's new client, you would have gotten here sooner," Gunner suggested.

"Hey, did you see him? Can you blame me? The man looks like he would win a fight against a stone wall. And that voice..."

"The man is a drug dealer, Miller," Gunner insisted, rolling his eyes.

"Hey, we all have our flaws!" Miller said giving him a self-deprecating smile. "Speaking of flaws. Yours is you are too fucking nice, Kai. Jesus Christ. You had her in your house. You brought her tea to her bed every night. And I know what Jules wears to bed, Kai. Hell, I'd be half-tempted to do her, and I don't swing that way. But no, you had to be the shoulder to lean on, the sexless best friend."

"You're acting like being nice is a bad thing."

"It is when it makes you choke when you really want something," Miller explained. "Look, Jules has been opening up since she came back. Hell, I even caught Gunner bullshitting with her about various self-defense options."

"Self-defense?" I asked, straightening up.

"Yeah. I mean, of course. She had someone beat the shit out of her, Kai. I know you aren't a woman, but it does something to you. The possibilities of what *could have happened* does something to you. It doesn't matter that Jameson is dead. She wants to ensure that no one gets the better of her like that again. And, I mean, she's living all alone. Working in a job where some of the scumbags hit on her, show too much interest in her. Of course she is looking into ways to defend herself."

"I helped her fill out her gun permit," Lincoln added.

Jesus.

So much was going on under my nose.

While I sat in my office, refusing to be part of that world, to help her pick what kind of self-defense to do, to help her with her gun permit.

"This is pointless," Gunner said, moving to stand up again, shaking his head. "If he hasn't been able to make a move in all these years, he never will. Who wants to go get a drink?" he asked. "Sloane is having dinner with her editor."

"I'm always in," Miller declared, jumping up to follow him out.

"I'll be right there," Lincoln called, slowly unfolding, putting his feet back on the floor, leaning forward toward me."Learned a lot of shit in my life, Kai. But maybe the most important is this - taking chances and getting shot down sucks. But nothing is worse than never taking them at all. Don't be leaving this Earth with 'what-ifs' on your mind."

With that, he jumped up, walked out, went to join our friends.

Quin was still in the office with his drug-dealing client. But he would file out sooner rather than later, wanting to get home to his woman.

And that would leave us.

Me and Jules.

Like so many nights in the past.

I wouldn't leave before her.

Because I always walked her to her car if no one else was left to do it.

I took a deep breath, wondering if I could find it.

The nerve to do something.

To take a chance.

A chance to ruin everything, sure, to kill the possibility of a future with her once and for all.

But a chance to get everything I ever wanted too.

I guess we would see.

-

Flashback - 36 months before -

She got the job.

She got the job, and she was going to be paid a borderline ridiculous sum of money to file, answer phones, and fetch coffee.

It was hard to wrap her head around it.

Because, sure, she had been looking for secretarial work after a string of hospitality jobs, had even been on a few interviews at doctors' offices, lawyers' offices, and even a tanning salon. But she had expected the usual.

A nine-to-five job making between ten and twelve dollars an hour.

Not great money, but decent. Enough. To hold her over until she could go through yet another round of college applications.

She'd learned her lesson, too.

Sure, she would re-apply to Yale, where she had envisioned herself since she was a little girl.

But she had smartened up; she would never again put all her eggs in one basket.

It had been incredibly short-sighted of her.

And as someone who had prided herself on being rational, it didn't sit well to be so foolish.

So she would also re-apply to Yale, Harvard, and Princeton. But this time, her third time, she would also apply to Montana State, Oklahoma State, and Montana State - places with nearly one-hundred percent acceptance rates.

She was getting too old not to get accepted somewhere.

But a job between ten and twelve dollars an hour would give her more than enough to pay her few bills. And then she could save up a lot to use to buy books, or pay for food, transportation, whatever she might need while on campus.

It was temporary.

She didn't need to make a fortune.

And because of that mindset, she had traipsed herself into the offices of Quinton Baird like she owned the place. Because, in her mind, it was a stepping stone. Not exactly beneath her, but certainly not a job that would require all of her potential.

Even after meeting the somewhat intimidating Quinton Baird who was a *Fixer*, whatever that might mean, she had all but demanded the job, had practically told him he would be a fool not to hire her.

And, unbelievably, he had just... agreed. On the spot. With a waiting room full of other older, more seasoned applicants.

This professional, confident, worldly, somewhat scary man had agreed to hire her.

That was surreal enough.

But then he had given her the employment binder.

In it she found the usual things.

Her employment forms that looked almost alarmingly official.

There was her paperwork for the company health plan, something that made her immediately feel like an adult more so than anything else. She'd get off her parents' plan. Even before she legally had to. It even had dental.

Then, of course, there was the fine print.

She would be expected to be in the office when she was needed, whether that meant from nine-to-five or seven-to-eleven, she would be there.

She would handle the normal tasks of office-keeping as well as run errands and, oddly, deposit files in some lockbox off premises.

She would also have to sign a confidentiality agreement.

But in return for all of that, she would get paid just shy of six figures.

Six figures!

With the potential for a yearly bonus.

As if six-figures wasn't already more than enough money.

She couldn't help but take to a bit of a fanciful - and therefore uncharacteristic - moment to daydream about what that kind of money could do for her.

Get her an apartment.

Fill it with all the things she saw in magazines that she loved, but thought she couldn't even hope to own until after she got her MBA and a lush corner office.

She'd even given serious thought to stopping. Applying. The colleges would be there if she should ever need them in the future. But why go, racking up debt, if she had such a stable job already?

It wasn't that she devalued the importance of an education, but she was also a bit too practical to choose a potential over a reality.

So she took the job.

Within three days, she had decided to stick it out, put college out of her mind.

She met the major players in the office.

Quin, of course, was the boss, The Fixer.

Smith seemed to be his second-in-command, The General.

There was Finn, The Cleaner.

There was Lincoln, The Middle Man.

There was Miller, the only girl in an all-boys club - The Negotiator.

There was the guy who lived in, oddly, the Pine Barrens. Ranger. Named, for reasons she had yet to suss out, The Babysitter.

And last, but not least, there was Kai. He was The Messenger.

What that meant, she had no clue. But she was sure it was important. They all seemed to be important for some reason. They got paid ridiculous sums of money to 'fix' things for people. She'd seen the invoices. She'd nearly spat out her coffee at a few of them, unable to fathom what problem there could possible be that could cost upward of one-hundred-fifty-thousand dollars.

Whatever it was, they paid it.

So these men - and Miller - did crazy jobs.

They were all in possession of something she could only begin to understand in the way of skills.

"Heya honey," A voice called, making her head shoot up, finding Kai standing there holding out a coffee to her.

She was picky about her coffee.

Her own mother never seemed to get it right even though she had drank it the same way for over a year.

But she appreciated the gesture anyway, reaching out for it, feeling her fingers brush over his. A sizzle seemed to meet at the contact, only to spread up her arm, over her chest, down her belly. Lower. Her breath sucked in, surprised, unsure.

"You really brighten up this place," he declared, giving her a brilliant smile, pulling his hand away, and moving down the hall, leaving her standing there with her system starting to catch fire.

What the hell was up with that?

TEN

Jules

New normal.

That was the phrase.

Everything felt different, but this was just how it was now.

My new normal.

I had heard Quin give this speech to clients over and over through the years. It had sounded somewhat trite back then. But now that it was my reality, I got it. I got why he needed to say it to everyone. Because it was true.

No matter what had happened, you learned to adjust.

Humans were adaptive creatures that way.

People could - and did so every single day - come back from terrible things. Not curl up in a ball and half-live forever. They came back. Stronger. More determined than ever.

That was what I planned to do.

It started with moving back into my own place, finding it spotless, making a mental note to send something nice to Finn. I mean, the man had gotten me a new mattress. I didn't know exactly what he was into - cleaning supplies aside - but I had to get him something.

And I did what many others who had to go home had to do. For some, that meant trashing old photographs, for others it meant hosing down the blood of loved ones off the driveway.

For me, it meant making what changes I could to make my space feel like mine again.

I rearranged my living room, donating all my old throw blankets and pillows, replacing them with new. I got rid of every item in my cupboards that had belonged to Jameson. I cleaned the box he'd left out of my closet. I got a new computer. I got my wedding dress cleaned to remove the mascara, then donated that as well. Out, too, went the dresses that Jameson had made comments on. They were the ones least like my wardrobe anyway, the too short or too low cut ones, the ones that clung like a second skin in thin material that meant nothing was left up to the imagination, that meant I had to invest in panties that were laser cut to avoid any kind of lines.

Once all that was done, the air in my apartment felt lighter, easier to breathe.

Then, finally, I did the unthinkable.

I got a TV in my living room. Sure, I attached it to the wall then hid it behind an oversized canvas print so it wasn't an eyesore all the time, but it was there. It was part of my new normal. Where I planned to continue watching the crime shows I had suddenly found myself hooked on.

I also signed up to take lessons from Janie and Lo at the local self-defense gym. I'd settled on Krav Maga because that was what Gunner had suggested. And I had plans to go visit the local shooting range over the next weekend. Instead of cleaning my already clean oven.

Maybe those things sounded fear motivated, and maybe that was a part of it, but it was more about excitement. When the idea of self-defense came to me, I was exhilarated. It was something I hadn't felt in so long that I almost didn't recognize it. So when I finally did see it for what it was, I knew it was something I had to pursue.

I needed to start having a life again.

Not plans, not goals to reach, a life.

I had agreed to go out for drinks with Miller after work the following Friday too.

Actually, things with my coworkers had changed entirely.

And, what's more, I knew it wasn't because of what had happened to me, per se, that it wasn't pity attention from them. It was because I was suddenly just *open* to connections with them. They sensed it. They pounced on it.

They had all always been a close-knit group. And I had been keeping myself as the outsider. For reasons that didn't truly make sense to me even as I tried to analyze it. It really came down to the fear that if they got to know me, they would think less of me because I wasn't from the same world that they were. Which was ridiculous. Quin and Gunner were with women who were not from this world. Lincoln dated a never-ending line of women who weren't familiar with the darker areas of life.

It all came down to useless insecurity.

For someone who had always thought of herself as self-assured, everything kept coming up as pure, undiluted insecurity.

It was why I had my life mapped out so perfectly, why I wanted this flawless little picture of a life. Not because that was truly what I wanted, but because it looked right. From the outside. It was why I settled for Jameson who I didn't love, who didn't even manage to please me in bed. He looked right from the outside.

Because I was worried what others thought about my life, my choices, my likes and dislikes.

What a ridiculous, unfulfilling way to live.

Once I saw it clearly, I became determined to make changes, to make my choices based on want and desire and a pinch of prudence - because I was still me.

I had never really realized how tense I was about, well, life until I decided to make changes, to open up, to live more honestly, more joyfully.

I had to let in my family and friends on the insanity that was the reality of mine and Jameson's relationship.

My mother and father had gone red with rage. My sister had wept, being a soft soul that way. My friends had regaled me with stories of how they thought he was a creep, how he had a wandering eye.

Instead of coldly taking that all in, stewing on it, internalizing the outrage and embarrassment, I had demanded that in the future, they tell me if I was dating a scumbag, no matter how infatuated I seemed to be with them. Surprised, they had agreed. And just like that, my relationships with them went deeper as well, became more honest.

After them, it was work.

Miller was easy. She simply burst her way into my life. Lincoln, too, just forced his way in. Quin was still my boss, still kept a professional distance, but talked to me more, asked about my day, my new schedule with taking an hour off each afternoon to go out to lunch instead of working at my desk like I had every day since I started. Finn had kept his awkward distance, but had thanked me when he had opened his gift, doing so with feeling. Hell, even Gunner had stopped being so gruff with me. Things weren't exactly touchy-feely, but this was me and Gunner we were talking about here; no one could ever accuse us of being touchy-feely. We'd skewer them if they did.

The lone stranger in the office to me, incredibly, was Kai.

The one who had always been the closest thing to a friend I had there.

But since I left his place, all I had gotten from Kai was careful pleasantries.

He didn't order me lunch, instead going out by himself. He didn't come out to hang at my desk, bugging me while I tried to get work done, something I didn't know I could miss until I was missing it.

It was a situation that constantly stole my focus away from work. I found myself obsessively thinking about it while I was typing, making me have to go back and delete, then retype it all, something I never had to do before.

But I couldn't help it.

It was such a one-eighty from the Kai I had left just a few days before, smiling, telling me I could come back should I ever feel the need to, giving me the code to his place so I could let myself in at any time.

Now, well, he could barely look me in the eye.

It hurt.

Maybe I didn't have the right to feel hurt after how much he had already done for me, but I felt it nonetheless.

It was a stabbing sensation to the gut.

I would sit there trying to figure out what had caused such a drastic change.

But all I could ever come back to was that he was over me.

It was the only thing that made sense, right?

He had - for all these years - built up some idea of me, put me up on this pedestal. And then he had gotten a chance to spend some time with me, real time with the actual woman, not the idea he had of me, and he simply... changed his mind.

That idea had been crippling.

Prior to it, I was planning to do it.

What Miller said.

I was going to make a move.

It made my heartbeat speed up just to think about it.

But I would swallow back that anxiety and I would do it. Make a move.

But there was no way I could ever get up the nerve to do it now that he had gotten so cool toward me.

There was no way to describe the sensation of disappointment I had felt.

All these years when I had been clueless or in denial or actively reminding myself why he was a bad idea even when my body and that constant chest-tightening thing said otherwise. And now that I was ready, that I saw things clearly, that I was done trying to lie to myself, that I was fully aware of my feelings toward him, he was no longer into me.

What a cruel, fickle bitch fate could be.

"Ugh, stop looking like a wounded puppy," Miller demanded, having left, but run back in claiming she forgot her house keys, and that she didn't want to have to crash at Lincoln's because the chick he was currently seeing was an aspiring - and terrible - singer and *Can you imagine dealing with that and a hangover at the same time?*

"I don't know what you're talking about," I lied, tamping down the guilt at doing so.

"Oh, please. You can't lie to me," she declared, moving down the hall toward her office, coming back waving her keys around her pointer finger. "Where was I? Oh, yeah. I thought you were over the whole denial thing. You know you want to jump him. Go jump him. Or, if you don't like that vernacular, go and rub your bits over his bits until you reach very dignified orgasms."

"I'm not denying I finally realize how I feel about him. But you've seen how he's been with me since I got back. I think he got a little too much reality with me, and has changed his mind."

"Oh, for the love of God," she declared, looking up at the ceiling for patience. "Finding out you pick your nose and *eat* it wouldn't make that man change his mind about you."

"Then why can he barely look me in the eye lately?"

"He's being Kai, dumbass," she declared affectionately. Miller, as it turned out, often showed her love by calling you names. "He thinks you need space, need to figure things out, don't need him complicating things for you. Yada freaking yada. He's no less in love with you than he was when he drank himself to freaking oblivion in my living room the night that he found out about your engagement."

I didn't know that.

I couldn't imagine that.

Kai wasn't a big drinker as a whole. I had never seen him so much as tipsy.

"Stop being such a pussy... and march on in there and show him yours," she suggested on her way out, beaming at me from the other side of the door as she reset the lock.

Could she be right?

It made sense.

Kai was that kind of person.

Selfless to the point of complete and utter self-denial.

I could definitely see him doing that, giving me space even if it hurt him. And if he was hurting, it made sense why he avoided seeing me too much.

Taking a deep breath, I grabbed my purse, going into the bathroom to refresh my makeup, spritz on a little perfume, work some of the tension out of my muscles, then dropped off my purse, squared my shoulders, and made my way down that hall.

My pulse throbbed in my ears, a whooshing sound that even managed to block out the click of my heels on the hard floor.

My skin was flushed, overheated, my body flooded with nervous energy, anticipation, and a healthy dose of fear.

I took a second outside his door, schooling my breath to something that didn't make it seem like I had just run a half-marathon instead of just walking the fifteen feet from my desk to his office.

When I was relatively sure I wouldn't absolutely pass out from panic, I raised my hand to knock, thinking better of it at the last possible second, then reaching to throw open the door.

Kai's head shot up from where he was leaning off the front of his desk, a stress ball in his hand.

Seeing me, his brows creased, but there was no denying what I saw in his eyes.

Miller had been right.

He was just trying to be the good guy.

Because those were moon-eyes if I ever saw them.

"Jules, is everyth..."

I briskly moved across the floor, grabbing him by the front of his tee, my fingers balling in the material as I pulled him closer just as my lips claimed his.

Claimed.

That was right.

Mine.

He was mine.

I guess he had always been. I had just been too blind to see it.

And for the first time, I was his.

Completely.

"Jules..." he tried, breaking away, trying to be rational, tell me I was hurting, or rebounding, or whatever he was going to come up with.

"Shut up," I demanded, taking his lips again, pressing harder, demanding more.

When my tongue moved to trace the seam of his lips, any thought of being the good guy seemed to disappear as his hands lifted, framing my face, parting his lips, and mating his tongue with mine.

The tremble that moved through me was almost violent, something I knew he felt as well as one of his hands left my face, tracking down my spine, landing on my ass, squeezing hard for a second before using it to drag me closer, until there was no such thing as space between us, until I could feel his hardness pressing against my belly, something that made a low moan escape me.

My restless hands moved over his body, up the sides of his stomach, feeling little etches of muscles beneath, a hint of rib cage, then over to his arms, moving upward, finding his biceps tense, corded in his desire, something that made mine burn all the hotter as my fingers slid under his arms, moving down his back, getting close to their destination before Kai suddenly pulled away in an action that felt all-too familiar.

I knew what would follow next.

The rejection he tried to soften with excuses. Excuses I didn't want to hear. Excuses that were not relevant anymore.

I reached up, pressing my fingers against his lips for a second before dropping them, moving back a few feet, summoning every bit of self-confidence I had ever possessed in my life, and reaching to slowly start to lift my shirt, exposing my belly inch by inch before discarding it to the floor at my side, standing there in my slacks and a simple strapless nude bra.

Taking a deep breath that made his eyes lower from my face, I reached behind my back, unfastening the clasps before I could lose my courage, and pulling the bra free to fall with my shirt on the floor.

The cold air made my nipples twist tight, making my already desire-heavy breasts feel all the more sensitive to the way the air was washing over them from the fan overhead.

My hands went to my slacks, seeing his eyes almost begrudgingly follow, like he hadn't gotten enough of an eye-full of what I had shown him already.

I unfastened them, pushing them down, stepping out of the feet.

I wanted to go all-in.

I wanted to be brave enough to stand there completely naked.

But at the last second, I couldn't seem to force my hands to hook my panties and yank them down.

Kai's breath shuddered out of him, his gaze slowly moving down my legs, then back up, over my belly, up to my breasts, then finally finding my face again.

All I found there was a need so strong it made my sex tighten painfully, made me sure I had done the right thing, made it possible to muster just a bit more confidence to take the few feet back I had put between us, pressing my front to his, taking a second to soak in the sensation of his scratching t-shirt on my hardened nipples before I leaned in, my hand going to the back of his neck, my lips going to his ear.

I hadn't been sure what I was going to say. I had hoped on something R-rated, something sexy enough to break any last threads holding together his control.

But all that could come out was the truth.

"I'm yours, Kai."

The words sounded soft, choked, but there was no denying the sincerity behind them. Not even Kai could find a reason to discredit them.

He didn't grab me and ravish me like I might have hoped, but his arms went around me, squeezing tight enough to make it hard to draw in a breath. His head pressed down on my shoulder, taking a deep breath like he was trying to draw my scent in, or find strength, or maybe a combination of the two.

"Don't just say that," he demanded, lips pressing into my shoulder as if to soothe over the words. "Don't say you're mine just because you want me right now."

My eyes closed for a second, taking a breath, everything in me responding to the raw vulnerability in his tone.

I pulled back, waiting for his gaze to find mine, seeing nothing but openness there.

"I wouldn't do that to you," I told him, voice a little fierce. "Ever since we met, I have gotten this... thing," I said, pressing a hand into my chest.

"Thing?"

"Right here," I explained, sliding my fingers to where they met the center of my chest, fingers brushing my clavicles. "I never understood it. Or I just refused to try," I allowed, knowing that was the more likely story.

"What kind of thing?" he asked, brows drawn together.

"It gets tight. My chest gets tight. And... I just never understood it until recently." I paused, looking down for a second, shaking my head. "It has only ever happened with you. I didn't know what to think of it."

"It's only ever happened for me?" he asked, pressing his forehead down to mine.

I nodded a bit, reaching down to grab his hand, pressing the palm against my chest under mine.

"Only you," I confirmed, feeling my belly go a bit swirly at the admission.

Under mine, his fingers tensed for a second before relaxing.

"But Kai?" I started, feeling emboldened, feeling the absolute *rightness* of this moment, knowing that nothing I could do when we were like this could lead to rejection, that there was no place safer to act on my impulses than with him.

"Yeah, honey?" he asked, voice deeper than usual.

I reached to close my hand around his wrist, slowly pulling his hand down, between my breasts, over my belly, past my navel, then finally, quickly pressing it into the piece of material between my thighs, feeling his breath catch at finding it damp with desire. "I want you too," I added, smiling a bit when he let out this choked sound that seemed almost like a chuckle, but was drowned in too much need.

His forehead lifted from mine, eyes heavy as he met my gaze.

As soon as he did, his finger shifted upward. Perfectly. Expertly. As though he had known my body for years. His finger brushed over my clit, making a tremble rack through me as my air exhaled hard on a choked moan.

At the sound, his eyes closed for the barest of seconds before they opened again, his free hand moving to my lower back, using it to guide me as he turned, lowering down into the chair, pulling me down on top of him, knees straddling both his legs, leaving me completely open to him, a fact he was all-too-happy to exploit as his finger did another swipe, making the swollen bud pulse with the need for release.

Feeling so open, so utterly laid bare, my mouth moved to find words again, to find admissions, to tell him something I had never told anyone before.

"You made me feel like this before," I told him, feeling his fingers still as he gave me his full attention.

"At the hotel," he concluded.

"Then, too, yes. But before that. A long time ago."

"When?" he demanded to know, his hand sinking into my ass, the only sign that he was just barely holding onto his control.

"The first night you rubbed my shoulders," I admitted, watching as his lips curved up slowly, sweetly, like it had been a fond memory for him. "It was overwhelming," I added, it feeling so good to share it. My secret little truth. "I had to go to the restroom and... ah..."

Okay , so maybe I wasn't *that* bold yet.

"Do this?" he asked, letting his finger swipe once again. But just once. A little harder than before.

"*Yes*." The word came out more like a moan than an affirmation. Maybe it was both.

"I barely ever let myself hope that could happen," he admitted. "I wish you had told me," he added, swiping my clit once more. "But this was worth the wait," he concluded, fingers moving away to slip into the side of my panties, his finger raking up my slick cleft with nothing between us, the realization of that alone enough to make me shudder.

"Kai, please," I pleaded, fingers gripping his shoulders, holding on as though I was afraid I would fall without doing so. My thighs were shaking with the intensity of my need for release.

A muscle ticked in his jaw as his finger pressed down into my clit, making the orgasm crash unexpectedly through my system, pulling me under wave after wave as I buried my head in his neck, crying out through it all.

I stayed planted there even after the orgasm finally released its grip on my body - made ravenous after so long without - as aftershocks made my body tremble slightly, making Kai's free hand leave my ass, stroking gently, soothingly up and down my spine, giving me time to come back down.

As soon as I pressed back to look down at him though, his fingers moved suddenly, one thrusting unexpectedly inside me, making my walls tighten around him, beg for more of the invasion.

"Oh, my God," I whimpered, trying to take in a deep breath, finding it impossible as the need slowly build back up inside me.

"Can't tell you how many times I thought of this," He told me as his finger got faster, more demanding. "Dreamed of this a million times, but even my imagination couldn't let me imagine you as wet as you are for me right now." The declaration made my walls tighten harder still, something that made a sexy little smirk pull at his lips.

All these years.

All of them.

Thinking Kai was a sweet little puppy dog.

And he was.

But it had blinded me to the possibility that he might also be sexy as hell, that he could make me wanton with desire just from his words.

"Kai, please," I demanded again, hips grinding down onto his hand, feeling his palm press my overly sensitive clit again. "No?" I asked, a crushing hopelessness moving through my chest as he shook his head at me.

"No," he confirmed. "The next time you come, I want it to be on my lips," he declared, closing an arm around my lower back as he surged to his feet, taking me with him, moving until my back hit a wall.

I lost his finger as he urged my feet to touch the ground.

The second they did, he yanked up one by the knee, pinning it to the wall, moving in close, and grinding his hard cock against my heat. My head slammed back into the wall, making pain shoot across my skull, but it was overwhelmed by the way his cock pressed into my clit, then slid down, teasing at the entrance to my body, promising an end to the primal, overpowering need within.

"Not yet," he reminded me as he ground against me, as my whimpers became moans that turned into choked gasps for air.

"I can't sto..." I started to object when suddenly his cock was gone, and my foot hit the ground with a slam as he released it.

He had lowered himself to the ground in front of me, eyes looking up at me almost reverently for a long moment before his hand reached out, snagging my panties at the front, slowly lowering them down my legs, helping me keep my balance as I stepped out of them.

I thought he would go slow, kiss up my thighs, drag it out impossibly long, make me beg for it.

But his hand grabbed the underside of my knee, lifting up, pinning it to the wall again, exposing me to him fully. And before I could even register the change in position again, his mouth was on me, lips closing around my clit as his tongue explored it, found the rhythm that made my hands go into his short hair, curling, holding him to me in case he got any ideas of trying to pull away, to deny me what was promised just moments before.

But if there was anything you could know about Kai, it was that he was a man of his word.

He didn't even try to drag it out.

He found what I liked and did it relentlessly, almost savagely, not even caring that my thighs were shaking so hard that I wasn't sure they could hold me much longer, not trying to slowly drive me to the cliff.

No he tossed me there, then grabbed a hold, and shoved me over.

It felt like that this time.

Like free-falling.

Like a moment of soaring nothingness until I slammed down into it, the impact ripping everything from me - my thoughts, my insecurities, my usual quietness.

All I knew as the pleasure started to ease was that my throat hurt like I had been screaming, my body felt slick, trembly, overwrought.

It was then that Kai kissed over my thighs, up my belly, slowly getting up, running his cheek over my breast before taking my nipple into his mouth, sucking it, working it with his tongue. Then moving across my chest to continue the beautiful torment.

Then, just as slowly, up between my breasts, tongue tracing my clavicle, then lips whispering up the side of my neck, teeth gently snagging my earlobe before his lips found mine again, softer, teasingly sweet, so gentle and unassuming that it took me by surprise when I felt the weight in my breasts again, the heaviness in my belly, the tightening in my core.

So caught up in the sensations, I hadn't realized he was driving me up to the edge again in the most unassuming way possible.

My breath quickening, my hands moved down his back, grabbing the hem of his tee, slowly pulling it, watching as his arms lifted, allowing me to free him of it. My palms flattened on his shoulders, gaze holding his for as long as I could, wanting to see the pleasure in him like he had seen in me, but soon I couldn't keep my eyes on his, and watched as my hands moved over his chest, tracing the gentle indentations of muscles beneath his smooth skin, delighting in the way they tensed under my touch. My fingers met the waistband of his jeans, anticipation making my skin electric as I worked the button and zipper free.

I took a deep breath as the backs of my knuckles grazed his boxer briefs, forcing my fingers to stay trained on their task as I pushed my hands toward the back, holding onto the waistbands with hooked thumbs so my other fingers were free to graze over his ass on the way down, my gaze rising to see heat in his eyes and the smallest of sexy smirks on his lips.

He didn't get a chance to step out of the legs.

I couldn't seem to contain my urge to give back, to show him even a hint of what he had shown to me twice already. So I lowered down to my knees in front of him, looking up to see him looking down at me, pure hunger overtaking his face. My hands went out, grabbing the material of his boxer briefs, pulling it wide as I pulled it down, watching as his cock came into view, thick, demanding, promising fulfillment.

But not yet.

Even if my sex was pulsing almost painfully at the idea of having him inside me.

Right now was all for him.

As soon as the material fell away, my gaze went back up, wanting to watch his reaction as my hand closed around the base of his cock, and my tongue moved out to trace over the head, lapping up the bead of precum there.

His air hissed out as his hand slammed into the wall, bracing himself as he watched me as my lips went around him, drawing him in inch by inch, feeling him grow thicker still as I started to work him, feeling the way his body tensed, his hand curled into my hair, his breath shuddered out of him.

Just when I was sure I was going to taste his release - an idea that sent a thrill through my body, suddenly the grip in my hair increased, yanking, pulling until I had no choice but to lose him, to rise to my feet to ease the sting.

He moved so fast that I could hardly catch it as he slammed me back against the wall, bent to retrieve his wallet, pulled out a condom, and protected us. I swear it happened at warp speed, before I could even register the ease of the sting at my scalp, he had finished those tasks, reached down to yank up my knee, slamming it back against the wall, then thrusting inside me, deep, hard, claiming every inch of me in the span of a blink, making a choked whimper escape me at the invasion, at the perfect way he filled me.

"*Jules*." My name seemed to claw its way out of him, deep, needy, primal, and something within me called back to the sound.

He had stilled within me, buried deep, and my hand rose, moving to frame his jaw, waiting for his eyes to open as he took a steadying breath.

"All yours," I reminded him, my leg breaking free, moving to curl around his back, holding him to me as I ground down on him, needing the motion more than I had needed anything else in my life.

His eyes went soft for a short second, full of everything that had happened over the years, all the hopes, fears, disappointments, and finally... triumphs.

His lips claimed mine again, hard, hungry, demanding. Mine, in turn, became the same as my walls tightened around him, begged for release.

His cock withdrew, and his lips broke from mine as he slammed back inside me, eyes so intense it was almost unsettling. "All yours," he told me, starting to thrust - hard, fast, needy, proof of how long he had waited for this, how much he needed it.

His hand went down, snagging my other knee, dragging it around his waist, his hands going to my ass, using it to make me take him deeper each time, slamming me down on him as he thrust inside, the near violence of it all driving me up faster than ever before.

I felt my walls close around him like a vice grip, that suspended nothingness overtaking me, promising oblivion once it floated away.

"Come for me, Jules," he demanded, eyes watching me as he kept thrusting, refusing to let the orgasm ebb. "There," he growled as my walls started spasming, as my voice caught on a moan. "That feels good," he added, voice rough trying to come out of his clenched jaw.

"Kai," I whimpered as another wave came on the tail-end of the first.

And that was his undoing as well.

Her thrust harder for a couple seconds, slamming deep, jerking hard upward as a shudder racked his body.

"*Jules*," he hissed out as he buried his head in my neck, his body pressing mine into the wall as he fought for control of himself.

His breathing had barely leveled out before his hands cupped my ass harder, as he walked back toward the chair, dropping down with me on top of him, both of us too overwhelmed to do anything but be there, hold each other, come to grips with what had just happened.

I seemed to be the one to recover first, feeling my heart rate return to normal, my breathing settle back into is usual rhythm.

My lips pressed a kiss into his neck before I pushed back a few inches, watching as his eyes opened slowly, something in their depths I didn't know how to interpret.

"Are you alright?" I asked, feeling my heart sink a bit, hearing old ugly words spoken from a mean-hearted man fill my head, sucking up the pool of confidence I had felt with Kai.

He sucked in a deep breath as his hand moved up, tucking my hair behind my ear gently. "Ever have a dream come true, Jules? A big one. The one that has been on your mind almost obsessively for a long time?"

I swallowed hard, realizing the truth.

"No."

"Me either. Until tonight," he told me just as my heart was ready to shrink to nothing at the idea of his dream being crushed by reality. He shook his head for a second, like he wasn't quite sure it had happened after all. "It was better than I could have imagined. *You're* better than I could have ever imagined. The reality surpasses the dream. I didn't know that was possible."

I felt the telltale sting in my eyes, blinking hard, not sure why I was feeling so emotional. I never felt emotional.

"Stop," I whispered, shaking my head.

"Never," he told me as one of the tears snuck out, sliding down my cheek. His thumb moved out, catching it, before pulling me forward, taking my lips again, slow, deep, full of the emotion thick in the air around us. And I didn't even bother trying to stop the other tears as they fell.

Happy tears.

They were a new concept for me.

But there was no denying their existence.

He kissed me until my lips felt swollen and sensitive, letting me finally rest my head against his shoulder as his hands moved up to sift through my hair.

It was a long time before he spoke. When he did, he was Kai. The Kai I had known every day for years. Sweet. Light.

"Alright, the silence is killing me," he declared. "What's going on in there?" He didn't miss the way I snorted a little, feeling caught. "What?" he demanded, giving a bit of my hair a playful tug.

"It's just..."

"What?" he demanded when I trailed off.

"Miller was telling me about this really amazing eggplant parm that you make and..."

His laugh cut me off, happy, carefree, so *Kai* that I felt it again. My chest tightening. But this time, it was accompanied by something else, something new. A swelling feeling in my heart.

"You want to come back to my place so I can cook for you?" he asked as I pushed back, finding him smiling easily, eyes bright.

"And watch *Criminal Intent*," I added.

"And watch *Criminal Intent*," he agreed.

"Then maybe..."

"Maybe what?"

"You can show me your bedroom," I suggested.

His eyes went gooey at that, making my belly do the same. "I think I can manage that."

With that, we both hopped up, getting back into our clothes, mine feeling oddly scratchy, maybe because my skin was more sensitive, begging for more contact.

I moved back out into the reception area, powering down my computer, realizing this was the first time since, well, ever, that I was leaving with work on my desk that still needed to be done, with a mini kitchen that still needed to be stocked.

And, quite honestly, I couldn't have cared less.

Because I was going home with Kai.

I grabbed a note Quin had left me for supplies he needed picked up on my way into work the next day, opening my wallet to tuck it in.

And another note caught my attention.

Kai's note.

The one with his alarm code on it.

The code that sounded so familiar, but I hadn't been able to remember why before.

It wasn't a code.

It was a date.

Exactly thirty-six months and twenty-one days ago.

And I finally knew what that date was...

-

Flashback - 36 months and 21 days before -

He hadn't known why Quin had called him in. His office wasn't even fully finished yet, even if business was up and running. He'd been a bit of a late addition, had been hard to track down as he bounced around Europe, staying in hostels with people on pilgrimages to find themselves.

But he must have needed him if he was having him come in.

So he reached for the handle of the door, pulling it open, walking into the reception area - all dark and streamlined everything. Quin had never seemed to shake that military minimalistic thing. He liked things neat and predictable.

Kai wasn't sure how they were going to get along. No one would ever really accuse him of being something such as *neat*. He worked better with messes around, seemed to think more clearly when he was rummaging around for a missing file. It was when his best ideas came to him.

But Quin wanted him, so he must have been ready to put up with that. Kai figured he would be fine with it so long as his mess stayed within the confines of his office.

He would make sure it did.

He knew better than to mess up an offer like this, to let down a man like Quin.

Because Quinton Baird was, well, a particular kind of person - severe, very rational, and he expected perfection.

It *said* something that he wanted him on his team.

The lineup was impressive.

Smith, Finn, Lincoln, and Ranger had all served around the same time, had brushed shoulders, knew each other by skills and reputation.

Miller hadn't served, but had been in the hard life for a lot longer than any of the rest of the team, had needed to claw her way out of her past, fingernails bloodied and body bruised. It should have made her bitter and mean, but while she was sometimes a bit aloof and blunt, she was relatively stable, funny, easy going.

He had a feeling they would get along well given some time.

So the fact that Quin wanted *him* to join his team of all of *them*, it was an honor, a privilege. One that came with a great health plan and a 401k. Which he really didn't need thanks to the almost laughably large salary he was promised.

After bouncing around for so long, never making any really tight connections with anyone, he thought it would be good to put down some roots, to create some lasting friendships, to do what he did - not just because he was good at it - but because it secured him a safe future.

He was getting a little old for hostels.

Or at least that was how it felt when he was surrounded by kids taking gap years from college to go *find themselves*.

Besides, he would be around people who were *in* the lifestyle, who wouldn't look at him weird when he told them that he, essentially, was a sweet-talking adrenaline junkie for a living.

That wouldn't be weird to this team of cleaners and middle men and negotiators and babysitters and generals and fixers and ghosts.

The office was silent save for the blowing of the air and the quiet tones of voices toward the end of the hall.

He would know Quin's voice anywhere.

It sounded like the other voice was a woman.

Not sure if he was supposed to join or not, he hung back at the reception desk, hauling himself up on it, waiting.

The door to Quin's office opened, bringing the voices out in the main space.

Definitely Quin.

And definitely a woman.

As if to further prove that point, he could hear the steady click of heels on the hard floor as they approached.

The smile he had been ready to give them froze and fell from his face as they emerged from the hall, moved into his line of sight.

And he realized that he would always remember this day, this date.

It would be burned in his memory forever.

Because it was the day he met *her*.

EPILOGUE

Jules - 1 day

"What are you doing?" Kai's voice asked, still slow and rough from sleep, a sound I never could have known would be so sexy, but now did. "Did you go to the store already?" he asked, taking in the plastic bags littering the counter.

He moved around to face me, shirt off, pants slung low, eyes only halfway functioning.

And my chest did it again.

Tightened.

And, what's more, something else.

Something within me growled out *Mine.*

Mine.

He was mine.

Entirely.

I had never felt possessiveness before, never had a need to possess something - some*one* - so entirely.

"Are any stores even open this early?" he asked, glancing at the clock readout on the stove.

Six-fifteen.

"Walmart is twenty-four hours," I reminded him. "I just needed a few things to tackle... this," I declared, waving an arm at his junk drawer.

"Tackle it," he repeated, brain clearly a little slow in the morning. How he got going without coffee was beyond me.

"Organize it," I clarified.

"It's a junk drawer."

"Yeah?"

"Junk drawers aren't supposed to be organized," he informed me like this was somehow common knowledge. And if it was, then the human collective was crazy. If you needed to find birthday candles, wouldn't it be better to have them right there in a designated spot instead of having to rifle through fifteen other things before you found them? Likely half-crushed?

"Well... be that as it may, yours is going to be. It woke me up in the middle of the night, Kai. It was calling to me, taunting me with its clutter."

To that, he seemed to lose his sleep, face cracking into a grin as he let out a small chuckle.

"Then an organized junk drawer we shall have. But you get to explain it to everyone if they ask."

"Ask. About a junk drawer? Your friends really struggle to find topics of conversation, huh? What... oh," I let off on a small moan as he came to me, dragging my body to his, sealing his lips to mine.

I felt myself melting into him, my lips becoming demanding, needy, even though we had had each other three times the night before until our bodies just refused to do anything other than sleep.

Insatiable.

That was how to describe me now.

With Kai.

"Only you would lose sleep over a cluttered drawer," he declared after breaking the kiss, pressing his forehead to mine.

"What if I needed a wrench in an emergency?" I asked, digging in the drawer to find the item in question.

"A wrench emergency, huh?" he asked, lips twitching, trying not to laugh at me. "Have you had coffee yet?"

"No," I said, shaking my head. I'd been in too big a rush to get to the store. I knew I wanted to get organizers, get the mess contained properly, then get to work at least a little early, knowing I had left things unfinished the night before.

"Don't worry," he said, brushing my hip as he moved past. He did that a lot. Even just in the eight-ish hours we had technically been together. He always touched me. Like he needed confirmation that I was there. He had no idea how stuck with me he was now. Now that I understood the feeling in my chest, could call it what it was, even just to myself for now. Something I had never experienced with anyone else, something that was his alone. "I will jump in the shower while you organize," he added as I heard water running to fill the coffee maker. "Then we can both head in to finish what you didn't get to last night."

The man got me.

That was such a new sensation as well. Someone getting you, understanding your concerns without you having to spell them out all the time, someone who cared enough to get to know you to root level.

It was a little one-sided still.

I had a lot to learn about Kai.

Luckily, I decided as I pulled the stickers off the little plastic drawer organizers, I had nothing but time to figure out his story.

"You had sex," Miller declared about five hours later.

My head jerked up, eyes going wide, frantically looking around to make sure we were alone.

"What?"

"Oh, don't give me that innocent look. You finally got the balls to jump him, didn't you?" She moved closer, smile wicked. "Was it amazing? All those years of pent-up frustration, it had to be amazing. I mean... unless he didn't last. Which would be a huge bummer. But I get the feeling that Kai would be the sort who would compensate otherwise if he blew too fast and... no," she said, nodding. "Homeboy wanted this too much. No way did he shoot it off early. It was amazing, right?"

"It's my turn to talk now?" I asked, lips twitching. "You seemed to be carrying that conversation just fine all by yourself."

"Oh, it was *good*," she concluded, pulling herself up on my desk. "You are in too good a mood for unsatisfying dick. I feel like a proud mama when her little girl got her first big and stiff one."

"I'm pretty sure moms don't feel *pride* in that situation, Miller," I told her, snorting. Mine had handled the situation with a sort of resigned understanding that I couldn't stay little forever.

"Oh, what do I know? I never had a mother. Anyway, fuck yes. This is great news. Are you doing it like rabbits? Ew, is this desk tainted?" she asked, lifting her butt a little and eyeing the top of said desk like it might give her a disease of some sort.

"There are *cameras* in here, Miller," I reminded her.

"I know. You kinky bitch."

"We didn't do it out here," I clarified.

"Ooh, but you *did* do it here. Kai's office, right? Desk? Chair? Wall? Shut up," she said, slapping my arm with the back of her hand when I must have looked a little guilty. "All three?"

"Well, not the desk."

"No worries. There is time for that. He wasn't sappy, right?" she asked, wrinkling her nose at the very idea. "Like... he didn't get cheesy and cry..."

"No, he didn't cry," I told her, leaving off the part about how I had gotten a bit emotional.

"What'd he do this morning? Bring you breakfast in bed? He seems like a breakfast in bed sort of guy. I need to find me one of those."

"Well, stop dating drug dealers then," I suggested with a smile.

"But where's the fun in that? Come on. Did he?"

"He made me coffee while I organized his junk drawer."

"Oh... hot?" she said, brows drawing together. "I mean... whatever turns your gears, you freak."

"It's not like that," I said as she jumped off my desk. "It's..."

"Remind me never to get you office supplies. It might turn you on too much. And, no offense, Jules, but you're not my type." She moved down into the hall, popping back out with a big smile. "Congrats on the fucking though. I am going to go tease your man now."

And, yeah, that was how the office learned that Kai and I were together.

And how everyone suddenly had jokes about office supplies and organization tools.

Kai - 2 weeks

I couldn't get used to it.

I probably should have already.

Gotten used to seeing her in my place, around my things, with her hair down, with her bare feet.

But I hadn't.

Every time I walked into a room and found her there was like a jolt to my system that brought with it this almost overwhelming warmth, this sensation of rightness.

Even if she was down on her knees meticulously scrubbing my oven like a lunatic. At least there actually *was* some grease in there for her to clean up since I did cook whenever I was home to do so.

"I have a housekeeper."

"I don't mind," she declared, voice muffled a bit since her head was inside the oven.

Moving closer toward her, I found a row of cleaning products lined up. Yes, a *line* of them.

"This an all day project?" I asked, enjoying the view of her jean-clad ass sticking out at me, the way her tank top had ridden up a bit, showing off a sliver of her back.

"Just an hour or so," she declared like that was a totally acceptable amount of time to devote to one appliance.

"Want company?" I asked, moving to sit down on the floor near her, not caring if it made me seem clingy to want to be close to her as much as possible.

"Sure," she said, turning her head over her shoulder to smile at me a bit. "Tell me about your childhood," she suggested. At my blank look, she shrugged. "You know everything about me. I want to know more about you."

"Not too much to tell. Lived with my parents as a kid. Technically, but not really. They worked in a factory. If I saw them two or three hours a week, that was a lot. And that time was usually full of them scolding me about doing better in school, so I could get a better life. I did get to spend some weekends with my grandfather who taught me martial arts. But other than that, I kinda raised myself most of the time."

"You were always alone?" she asked, climbing out of the oven, sitting back on her heels, sad eyes meeting mine.

"Don't feel sorry for me, honey. I turned out just fine."

She hesitated at that, knowing it was true. I might not have had bedtime stories and hugs and bottomless love, but I managed to get through the system relatively well-adjusted.

"Well... you can share mine now," she declared, giving me a somewhat wobbly, insecure smile, like she was worried about rejection.

As if there was any going back for me.

I was so far gone I didn't even consider a future without her.

I'd prove that to her eventually.

Given time.

She was still learning how to trust again.

We'd get there.

"I would love to be part of your family, Jules."

Jules - 2 months

"Stop fidgeting," I told him, swatting his hand away from the button he had been messing with at his wrist.

He was nervous.

It was so bizarre, for him at least, that it was hard to wrap my head around it.

I understood, of course, this was always supposed to be a somewhat nerve-racking experience.

Meeting the family.

But he had met my family!

He knew my mom and sister and father.

He had even met my grandmother before she passed on.

And, what's more, my family liked him.

But he was nervous. He had spent longer in front of the mirror than I had, screwing around with his hair that was slowly growing back in, but not quickly enough for my liking. I missed his long hair. I had fantasized so often about running my fingers through it. I wanted to be able to experience that finally.

"I promise they will love the surprise."

Maybe that was unfair of me.

I was sort of... springing him on them.

I hadn't even told Gemma about us being a thing.

I had wanted to have just a little time with just us, before I got them all involved, had to handle all their questions.

But it was time.

Mom was getting suspicious.

I think she thought I was developing a drinking problem or something because whenever she asked where I was, I fibbed and said I was out on the town with Miller. And since she knew Miller liked to have a good time that included Jägerbombs and tequila shots, she had sort of come to her own conclusions.

Hell, even if she hated Kai, she would be relieved I was just with him instead.

We walked up the driveway that my mother had lined with bales of hay because she was one of those moms who was heavy into decorating for each holiday or season. Scarecrows flanked either side of the front steps. Fake pumpkins lined the path leading to it. And she was only halfway into her decorating.

"I love this house," I declared as we made our way up to the colonial - white with black shutters, as it had always been. There was a tire swing in an old oak in the front yard even though Gemma and I hadn't used it in almost a decade.

"It's the kind of house you want," he informed me. Not guessed or questioned. Informed. "It's all over your Pinterest vision board," he told me. "Colonials and golden retrievers."

"And natural home cleaners. Even though Finn would flay me if he heard that."

As we talked, his body seemed to relax.

That was until I opened the door without knocking because, well, this wasn't my house anymore, but it would always be home, and dragged him down the hall toward the kitchen where the voices were coming from. Voices that stopped abruptly at the sight of us standing there. Holding hands. Leaning into each other.

Gemma's mouth fell open. Comically open. Eyes huge.

My father's brows rose.

It was only my mother who spoke, shocking the both of us.

"Well freaking finally," she declared, waving the wooden spoon around in the air. "I was sure I would have to hire a damn skywriter to inform you two that you were both into each other, and needed to get your heads out of your rears and act on it."

"Honey, I don't think a skywriter could do all that," my father informed her, always a bit too logical to understand sarcasm.

"The sky is endless, Mitch. He could fit it," she told him, eyes smiling as much as her lips were. "Kai, I am so happy to finally have you in the family," she told him, moving across the room to throw her arms around him.

I moved back a step, looking at them, finding a second later that I was so glad I did. Or I might have missed it. The longing in Kai's eyes. The joy at their acceptance.

"Now," Mom said, pulling away to put her hands on his shoulders. "Let's talk about grandbabies!"

"*Mom!*" I hissed.

"We're not talking to you," she informed me as she led Kai away.

Gemma took the opportunity to bounce over to me, hands grabbing mine, squeezing hard.

"He's the one, Julie-Bean," she told me with some authority. Like she had known it all along. Maybe she had.

I felt my lips curl up, looking over at Kai who seemed to sense it, casting a smile over his shoulder at me.

"Yeah, he is."

Kai - 1 year

Now this, this was what she had always dreamed her wedding would look like.

Indoors.

In the winter.

Snow falling lazily, big, fat flakes outside the floor-to-ceiling windows lining the reception hall she had mooned over.

The tables were draped in champagne finery. The chairs all matched. And there wasn't a damn thing in sight that could be called 'rustic.'

Except for maybe Ranger.

You could dress the man up, but you couldn't make him look like he fit in with the city folk. Even as Miller tried to drag him out of his shell a little. After the ceremony, she was all but guaranteed to try to ply him with alcohol until he loosened up a bit. It wouldn't work, of course, but she would try her damnedest.

We were T-minus twenty minutes until show time, until the woman I knew was supposed to marry me the moment we met finally agreed to it.

'Finally' sounded dramatic seeing as we had only been dating a year, had only been together six months when I'd gotten on a knee and asked her.

But it felt like a long time coming.

It felt like I had waited a whole lifetime.

I wasn't nervous.

There was nothing to be nervous about.

This was right.

In every way possible.

"You ready?" Miller asked, giving me a smile as she approached in a three-piece suit.

See, we didn't want a big bridal party.

Gemma would be maid-of-honor.

And I was debating my choices for best man, Miller had barged in, informing me that since she was the only one in the office with the balls to push us together finally, she deserved the honor.

So, yeah, Miller was my best man.

"Been ready," I agreed, taking her arm, walking down the hall to the ceremony room.

It was nothing short of a fairytale, everything white and gold and gleaming magically.

Jules would have normally wanted to be married in a church, but since we chose one of the snowiest months of the year to get married, we decided a one-stop location would be our best bet. There was a hotel upstairs too with rooms for our guests should the weather not hold out, or the open bar prove too tempting.

From their location in the front row, Jules' family all beamed at me. There hadn't been any kind of adjustment period with them. They had welcomed me with open arms, pulling me into their family unit like I had always belonged there. It meant more to me than I could say. And now we were all becoming family in an official way.

Across from them were what was, essentially, my family.

Gunner, Lincoln, Smith, Finn, Ranger, and the man who brought us all together in the first place - Quin.

There were two more people to the team than there had been this time the previous year, and one more woman on the arm of one of the men.

But those were stories for another day.

This was the story for today.

The music turned on, bringing Gemma down the aisle in a dress Jules had clearly let her choose for herself since it wasn't Jules' style, but it was completely Gemma's - a gold and white skater dress with a pair of golden ballet flats on her feet. Her hair was down. Wildflowers were in her hands.

She beamed at me as she took her place.

I beamed right back.

But only for a second.

Because there was no way I would miss what came next.

Jules stepping into the doorway on the arm of her father.

In my chest, my heart felt like it would break the confines of my rib cage it was so full.

They paused there for a second, Jules giving me a slow, sure smile, the lights catching on her red hair that she had left down to flow around her shoulders, like she knew I liked.

This dress was different than the previous one. The prep dress, if you will. Sleeveless, tight around the chest and down the center and thighs, only flaring out around her knees in layers of light fabric.

Beautiful.

More beautiful than I had ever seen her before.

They moved toward me in what felt like slow motion.

I barely remembered to shake my father-in-law's hand and thank him in my rush to get Jules' hands in mine.

One ring already gleamed on her finger.

Real.

Pear-shaped.

In just a moment, there would be another one there.

Mine.

She was finally, finally mine.

"Alright you two," Miller declared, walking up after most of the others at the reception had already filed out to find rooms or head home. She'd loosened her tie. Her suit jacket was open. And her eyes were heavy with exhaustion and liquor. "We wanted to give you your wedding present before we head out."

"You all chipped in?" I asked, brows drawing low. What could they have gotten us that they all needed to chip in on?

"Yep," Lincoln agreed as Quin moved forward to hand Jules a small white box wrapped in a golden bow.

"Open it," Gunner demanded when Jules didn't immediately go to do so, it not being proper etiquette to open wedding gifts in front of guests.

But with permission, her fingers tore at the bow, ripped open the top box, eager for our first gift as a married couple.

Inside was a small white notecard.

With an address.

Under that, a key.

"Go build a life there," Quin told us, kissing Jules' cheek, clamping a hand on my shoulder, then leading Aven out with him.

We both sat there in stunned silence as the rest of them congratulated us, told us to have a fun honeymoon, demanded we bring back souvenirs.

"They bought us a house," Jules whispered, voice uncomprehending.

"Did you check the address?" Jules' mother's voice asked, making us both look up to see her and her husband standing there, eyes dancing.

Both our eyes moved down at the same time, finally taking it in.

The house across from theirs.

A colonial.

With black shutters.

And a big yard.

"This house wasn't for sale," Jules insisted, shaking her head, not believing it.

"Well," her mom said, smiling warmly. "Edgar and Louise are up there. It's a big house to try to maintain. When your friends told me about their plan, I asked if they would be interested in an offer. They were. It's all yours. You can move in when you get back from your honeymoon."

"I'll hang a tire swing up while you two are away," her father added, giving us a smile as he led his wife away.

Jules turned to me, eyes glistening, not quite overflowing, but getting there.

I guess I had one little surprise left that might push them over the edge.

See, I let Jules handle the wedding plans, knowing she was dying to get her hands on it, having absolutely no preferences when it came to it. But I demanded she let me handle the honeymoon. With no input at all for her.

I reached into my suit pocket, pulling out the plane tickets.

"You ready?" I asked, holding them out to her.

She took them with shaking hands, turning them to read.

And then the tears fell over.

"Ireland? You're taking me to Ireland?"

"I'll show you where I got you that snow globe. Maybe we will pick up another one."

On a sweet little sniffle, her head pressed into my shoulder. "I love you," she declared, the words steeped with feeling.

It didn't matter how many times I'd heard it, it always landed with the wonder of that first time she'd said it.

"I love you too, Jules. Always."

Jules - 8 years

"What is the point of a shoe rack if no one uses it?" I asked, letting out a sigh as I put them all back in their rightful places.

Kai's shoes.

And our son's.

Our daughter, bless her heart, always picked up after herself. She arranged her toys in her room every night before bed. There was so much of me in her.

Our son, well, he was all Kai. Warmth and light and this unstoppable need for new and inventive ways to get his adrenaline pumping.

After having walked in on him using a cardboard box to *surf* down our hardwood stairs, I pretty much decided that sons were the sole reason wine was invented.

"Where are you guys?" I called, dropping two overflowing canvas bags down on the counter from the farmer's market Gemma and I went to every weekend, picking up all the healthy stuff I'd been raised on, having always wanted to give that to my children as well. With a smattering of junk in there every now and again. I reached for an empty sippy box on the counter, tossing it as I moved through our kitchen, huge, white, a place we spent so much time cooking, baking, creating memories.

We even had a junk drawer with birthday candles and wrenches and sticky notes.

All in their rightful drawer organizer compartments.

"Kai?" I called, moving through the living room, the one with huge windows that allowed me to have sills full of houseplants.

On a sigh, I saw the door open leading from the back porch. They'd leave the door open, then have fits when they found a fly or grasshopper in the house.

I moved in that direction, fanning the aforementioned fly until he found his way back outside, closing the door from the other side, standing on the back deck, looking out at our yard.

It always made me sigh in relief.

I had my gardens.

Kai had his manly grilling station.

The kids had space to run and play.

It was everything, everything I had ever wanted.

As if I had called their names, our children flew in and out of my gated vegetable garden, a place they knew they weren't supposed to be unless they were helping me tend or harvest it.

I moved in that direction, wondering where Kai was that he hadn't shooed them out, only to feel my hands grabbed on each side by the little ones of my son and daughter.

"Come on Mommy. We have a surprise."

Oh, God.

Surprises, coming from kids, almost inevitably meant something was muddy, markered permanently, or broken onto to be reassembled. Badly.

Taking a breath to resign myself to one of those fates, I let them lead me down the rows of green beans, rounding at the end.

And there was Kai.

"Surprise, Mama," he declared, beaming.

Beaming because he was clutching something small and golden to his chest.

We'd always talked about it.

But the time had never seemed right.

Kai was on the road a lot.

I worked a lot.

Then we'd had kids that stole all our energy.

It just never felt like the right time to do it.

To get the final thing on my vision board.

"One-hundred thirty-two months and twenty-one days," he added as I closed in on him. On them.

One-hundred thirty-two months and twenty-one days since we met for the first time.

And he had given me his heart, his hand, a home, a future, our children. And now my golden retriever puppy.

He'd given me everything.

Everything.

There had been no more lists, no timelines, no plans.

We had let everything play out as it seemed meant to. And everything had fallen into place perfectly. Beautifully.

My chest tightened as the puppy lapped wet-tongued kisses over my chest.

I looked up at Kai, sliding his long hair behind his ear, leaning in to kiss him.

Hard and long to a chorus of heckling noises from our children, my heart overflowing with a love I had never known could exist.

Until he had shown it to me.

Until I had finally allowed him to.

And look what could happen with a love like that.

X

#KaiAndJulesForever

DON'T FORGET

Dear Reader,

Thank you for taking time out of your life to read this book. If you loved this book, I would really appreciate it if you could hop onto Goodreads or Amazon and tell me your favorite parts. You can also spread the word by recommending the book to friends or sending digital copies that can be received via kindle or kindle app on any device.

ALSO BY JESSICA GADZIALA

If you liked this book, check out these other series and titles in the NAVESINK BANK UNIVERSE:

The Henchmen MC
Reign
Cash
Wolf
Repo
Duke
Renny
Lazarus
Pagan
Cyrus
Edison
Reeve
Sugar
The Fall of V
Adler

The Savages
Monster
Killer

Savior

Mallick Brothers
For A Good Time, Call
Shane
Ryan
Mark
Eli
Charlie & Helen: Back to the Beginning

Investigators
367 Days
14 Weeks

Dark
Dark Mysteries
Dark Secrets
Dark Horse

Professionals
The Fixer
The Ghost

STANDALONES **WITHIN NAVESINK BANK:**
Vigilante
Grudge Match

<u>OTHER SERIES AND STANDALONES:</u>

Stars Landing
What The Heart Needs
What The Heart Wants

THE MESSENGER
What The Heart Finds
What The Heart Knows
The Stars Landing Deviant

Surrogate
The Sex Surrogate
Dr. Chase Hudson

DEBT
Dissent
Into The Green
Stuffed: A Thanksgiving Romance
Unwrapped
Peace, Love, & Macarons
A Navesink Bank Christmas
Don't Come
Fix It Up

ABOUT THE AUTHOR

Jessica Gadziala is a full-time writer, parrot enthusiast, and coffee drinker from New Jersey. She enjoys short rides to the book store, sad songs, and cold weather.

She is very active on Goodreads, Facebook, as well as her personal groups on those sites. Join in. She's friendly.

STALK HER!

Connect with Jessica:

Facebook: https://www.facebook.com/JessicaGadziala/
Facebook Group: https://www.facebook.com/groups/314540025563403/

Goodreads: https://www.goodreads.com/author/show/13800950.Jessica_Gadziala
Goodreads Group: https://www.goodreads.com/group/show/177944-jessica-gadziala-books-and-bullsh

Twitter: @JessicaGadziala

JessicaGadziala.com

<3/ Jessica

<<<>>>

Made in the USA
Las Vegas, NV
03 August 2022

52617157R00154